T0007742

Falling Toward Redemption

FALLING TOWARD REDEMPTION

A NOVEL

B.D. VANNOY

NEW YORK

LONDON • NASHVILLE • MELBOURNE • VANCOUVER

FALLING TOWARD REDEMPTION
A Novel

© 2022 B. D. Vannoy

All rights reserved. No portion of this book may be reproduced, stored in a retrieval system, or transmitted in any form or by any means—electronic, mechanical, photocopy, recording, scanning, or other—except for brief quotations in critical reviews or articles, without the prior written permission of the publisher.

Published in New York, New York, by Morgan James Publishing. Morgan James is a trademark of Morgan James, LLC. www.MorganJamesPublishing.com

Publisher's Note: This novel is a work of fiction. Names, characters, places, and incidents are either products of the author's imagination or used fictitiously. All characters are fictional, and any similarity to people living or dead is purely coincidental.

Unless otherwise noted, all referenced scripture contained within, is taken wholly from The Life Application Study Bible, King James Version, The Holy Bible.

Proudly distributed by Ingram Publisher Services.

A FREE ebook edition is available for you or a friend with the purchase of this print book.

_____

CLEARLY SIGN YOUR NAME ABOVE

Instructions to claim your free ebook edition:
1. Visit MorganJamesBOGO.com
2. Sign your name CLEARLY in the space above
3. Complete the form and submit a photo of this entire page
4. You or your friend can download the ebook to your preferred device

ISBN 9781631953248 paperback
ISBN 9781631953255 ebook
Library of Congress Control Number: 2020945963

Cover and Interior Design by:
Chris Treccani
www.3dogcreative.net

Morgan James is a proud partner of Habitat for Humanity Peninsula and Greater Williamsburg. Partners in building since 2006.

Get involved today! Visit MorganJamesPublishing.com/giving-back

Acknowledgments

To Kimiko:
You were chosen by *Father* to put my feet firmly on the path of the spiritual revelation that *Elohim* assigned me this message to deliver to the world. Without your trust in our *Creator* and allowing yourself to be used like this, *Falling Toward Redemption* might not be here. Thank you for believing in me when I didn't believe in myself and never allowing me to give up for almost thirteen years.

To my daughter Stephanie, my "little Buddha:"
You will always be my crowning achievement. I am so very proud of you.

To Jennifer:
Father brought you to me at a critical moment in the survival of this project and this mission. You will be blessed for being sensitive to the urging of *Shekinah Mother, The Holy Spirit*, your open heart, and your unhesitant response to supporting the book's survival.

To Ms. Loretta Leslie:
Thank you for your final editing diligence, divinely-inspired creativity, and uncompromising dedication to making *Falling Toward Redemption* the very best it could be.

To the entire production team at Morgan James Publishing:
Thank you for having the courage to step out in faith and take a chance on my premier Christian fiction novel, *Falling Toward Redemption*, when hundreds of others passed on an unknown author.

To Ms. Ilana Diallo at Simply Inspired Words Publishing in Reynolds, Georgia:
Thank you for your belief in me and your tireless editing efforts on my very rough original drafts as I was just beginning this long journey.

To Mr. Paul Wilbur at Wilbur Ministries in Jacksonville, Florida:
Thank you for your anointed praise and worship music, which is known around the world. Your gift and ministry was, and continues to be, my "nitro" on days I am not feeling the power to write.

To Mr. Mark Malatesta, author, coach/former literary agent, and former AAR member in New York and Beverly Hills.
I learned so much from you in a very short period of time. Your query format was a game-changer for me. You convinced me to believe in myself.

Foreword

Hope revealed.

A spiritual, supernatural novel, *Falling Toward Redemption* delivers on the author's covenant with the reader. That is: "the eternal message of hope we all have in the power of the redemption in Christ Jesus."

It is an honor to contribute to the foreword for Mr. Brian Vannoy's Christian work. His story is one of depth and climax, in a unique and enthralling redemption sequence. Circumstances are vivid, engaging, and emotionally gripping.

The narrative never strays from the primary message of hope and securing guidance from the Scriptures.

Keep love alive in your life.

"Tell them my message is contained within the words of my Son's apostle." (Proverbs 7:1)

Enter God's Grace in a blanket of redemption, a transformative act of saving ourselves from depravity, inaccuracy, and wickedness.

Woven throughout Mr. Vannoy's meaning are colorful threads, releasing us from bondage, whether physical or spiritual.

Falling Toward Redemption has the reader ascend toward courage, optimism, and the infinite potential possibilities in the Universe.

"Fix your hope not on the uncertainty of riches but on God." (1 Timothy 6:17)

—Dr. Diana Rangaves, PharmD, RPh, University of California San Francisco, author of *Escape into Excellence*, *Embrace Your Excellence*, and the *Rosy Posy Papillion* children's Christian value series

[Dr. Diana Rangaves is a pharmacist, philanthropist, and ethics professor-turned-writer. An accomplished educator, award-winning teacher, and business professional, she uses her powers for good.]

Author's Note

The Enochian script used herein is based on the work of the sixteenth century mage, Dr. John Dee (1527–1608), and his associate, Sir Edward Kelly (1555–1597). Both men collaborated, claiming the alphabet and the Enochian language was transmitted directly to them by angels.

(English, the human tongue)

Father, this is for you.

You and *You* alone are worthy of all praise, honor, and glory. Thank you for the guidance of *Shekinah Mother,* your *Holy Spirit* throughout the process of this endeavor. At every attack of self-doubt and my lack of writing prowess, *You* encouraged me, nourished me, scolded me, and above all, loved me enough to not allow me to give up or fail.

May it be in *Your* perfect timing and will that I am allowed to return home to spend eternity worshipping *Your* majesty.

It is my profound supplication that this modest effort accomplishes *Your* will in helping to bring the message of *Your* priceless gift of redemption and salvation to mankind.

Amen.

ChamuEL

𐤁𐤀𐤔 𐤀𐤉𐤊

Archangel of the *Most High*.

Chapter 1

Triumph of Evil

One thousand years ago in the world of the Nephilim of Illumination.
For Chamuel, it was merely yesterday.

he needle filled with the experimental serum that pierced the captive human's skin also pierced my angelic sensibilities. My mind rebelled against the *Father's* edict of noninterference where the Nephilim of Illumination was concerned as images of the writhing body filtered through the portal between the heavenly and earthly planes. The close-up view turned my stomach, and bile rose in my throat as the human's skin erupted in boils, which oozed puss as they split. I refused to turn away from the being's suffering even though instinct wanted me to, especially given I could do nothing to alleviate it. I persevered as its veins blackened and swelled while the human thrashed and screamed. I forced myself to stay focused as the skin ruptured and peeled back, revealing muscles the color and texture of charred meat. The eyes devoid of lids stared at me as if pleading with me to do something. The teeth in his lipless mouth moved, but the sounds emanating from it did not register as human.

The head scientist of the Alanterian Pharmetequia clapped his hands. "We are making progress. This one lived. We just need to tweak the formula to produce something that looks human but obeys us."

My soul cried out against the injustice. If only I could smite the Alanterian scientists for their quest to create a species from human stock to use against their kind in a bid to subjugate the human world.

I'd lost count of the number who had suffered similar fates—enough for today. My strength failed me to face another.

As I moved from the viewing portal, the creature broke free of its restraints and lunged at the scientist. I cheered mentally, but an arrow plunging into the tortured being's eye cut short my celebration.

I sighed and consoled myself that the poor creature's spirit was at peace and home with *Father*. Ultimately, I lay the blame at the demon Lilith's feet, but that did not absolve Queen Alequora from her rejection of the *One True God*.

I'd file my report, just another in the long line since I'd first pointed to Lilith's interference. In that first report, I'd expressed my opinion that Lilith had to be stopped, in the strongest terms possible without being disciplined. But the *Father* replied:

Chamuel, I have given mortals free will to choose between me and all others. Alequora must either find strength through me to withstand Lilith or succumb to her wiles.

To Lilith's credit, her disguise as Alequora's childhood friend had fooled me for some time, by which point she had Alequora's ear; she'd subtly poisoned Alequora's mind with dissatisfaction over her limited rule and convinced her that she should rule all humans . . . hence the experiments.

After some searching, I'd found the friend, but the enchantment imposed on her had left her mind vacant, and I feared that by the time it healed and the friend returned to her rightful place, it would be too late.

An uproar broke out in the senate when Alequora appointed Lilith as chancellor. Soon after, the disappearances began. I reported my suspicions of Lilith's involvement, but I could not confirm the fate of those missing. I had no proof.

I had sat at the portal for weeks now, and my eyes bled at the atrocities committed in that once honorable hall of science. This afternoon, I had a reprieve. I had been charged to observe the Alanterian Senate.

The energy coming from my intuition crawled on my skin like a poisonous caterpillar when Alequora advised the senators that the meeting had been called; she had an important announcement. Whatever the announcement was, it didn't bode well for Atlantis.

Fanfare announced the arrival of Queen Alequora to the hall. The velvet train of her cloak, fringed with ermine, trailed behind her, as did her entourage. Shafts of light from the candles in the chandeliers fired upon the flawless diamonds embedded within the Royal Scepter, which the queen held in her left hand, and the Royal Orb in her right, which could be attached to the scepter.

The notes of the trumpets echoed in the vaulted ceiling, with its beams made of whalebone, and bounced off the polished coral walls inlaid with gold and silver. The senators and former king stood as one around the glass table filled with seawater and fish—cunningly crafted so the swell of the ocean moved within it—as the queen progressed to the dais.

The queen flicked her train to the side as she lowered herself onto the jewel-encrusted throne. To her right, Lilith fussed in the submissive disguise of a friend over the queen's comfort. To her left, the scribe took his position at the shell-inlaid desk.

Queen Alequora gave leave for those assembled to sit, her imperious tone lacking any respect for the time-honored positions of the senators.

Lilith's influence in changing Alequora from an open-hearted, loving person who ruled her people with compassion into this, this arrogant brat irked me. I wanted to shake Alequora until she snapped out of this delusion of her own self-importance and return her to being the faithful servant of the *One True God* she had been not twelve months ago.

Alequora banged the narwhale tusk scepter on the polished, pink, coral dais. It echoed in the silence of the hall as every face focused on her.

"It is time for the people of Atlantis to take their rightful place as supreme rulers over all of the humans in this world. It is clear those insects, those dirt-eaters, cannot govern themselves."

At last, Alequora's true motives had been revealed. My hope lay in the power of the senate and mages to stop her.

"We are the chosen race. We are the glorious progeny of the *Lights of the Sky,* or what those bugs call "angels." We are the Nephilim of Illumination. It is long overdue that we rule supremely over this world. It is our birthright."

Chief Senator Alcon Kenesius rose to speak. "Your Majesty, the *One True God* has given us dominion over Atlantis. Yes, it is true, we are a superior race to the humans, but the *One True God* commands us to be compassionate in our dealings with them and to treat them as equals."

The members of the senate murmured among themselves. Agreement with the senator prevailed, but, to my consternation, voices supporting the queen numbered more than a handful.

Lilith leaned down and whispered in Alequora's ear. I didn't hear what she said, but from the sly look on Alequora's face, the outcome was not going to be to my taste.

"Senator Kenesius, do you question my ultimate right to rule?"

Her voice was too sweet and calm for my liking.

"No, Your Majesty, but—"

"Did not my father, the king, abdicate in my favor?"

"Yes, Your Majesty, but—"

"And do I not hold the instruments of power?"

"Yes, Your Majesty, but—"

"But what?" Alequora's manner was as dark as her flashing black eyes.

The senator's head bowed and his shoulders hunched, but he persisted. "But for time immemorial, the royal household has taken into consideration the advice of the senate and the mages and submitted to the will of the *One True God.*"

"Silence!" Her bellow cut through the applause. "There will be no more talk of the *One True God.* From this day forth, the mention of *His* name will result in the offender being expelled from their home, their wealth confiscated, and they, along with their contaminated offspring, will be cast into the trench. All reference to *Him* will be struck from the records. *His* name will be removed from the sacred temples, public buildings, statues, and monuments. In its place, my name, as the Supreme Being, Queen of all Creation, will take its place. You will bow before me and worship me as your god!"

I barely heard my own thoughts over the ruckus in the hall, but there it was: Lilith's real intent. She, after all, was the power behind the throne. This declaration gave her ultimate control. I seethed at the stupidity of mortals in being taken in by the promise of power. Why could they not see it came at the price of their very souls? The trench, with its host of flesh-eating denizens of the deep, was preferable to serving the devil.

Alequora slammed the scepter onto the coral hard enough to crack it.

As a hush fell over the hall, I studied the faces of the senators. Many registered disbelief, others mutiny. Those I could count on, but the extent of support for defiance of the *Father*, as shown by the grins on many faces, troubled me.

Chief Senator Kenesius's arch rival, Senator Keuron bin Alexius, cleared her throat and stood smiling longingly at her queen, suggesting more than just professional or political acquaintance. "I must commend you darl . . . Your—forgive me—Supreme Being, for your foresightedness. For too long, we have been ruled by the antiquated dictates of a faceless

God. What has *He* done for us of recent times? Men continuing to attempt to subjugate women; they're afraid of our power over them!"

Several voices shouted, "*He* has given us our abundance, our rich resources, our very sustenance and existence!"

The senator waved a dismissive hand. "Trivialities. I mean real action. I mean expanding our territory, bringing glory to the name of the Nephilim of Illumination! Nothing but our queen, the true Supreme Being, has a vision that will elevate us to our rightful place—with women in ultimate control, not you weak-minded men!"

Several impotent senators thumped the table and cheered. The others cast furtive glances among themselves.

Senator Keuron bin Alexius was about to continue her oratory when the hall doors slammed open as the head scientist burst in.

"Supreme One, it worked! The experiment was a total success! We have found the answer to the complete control and subjugation of those insects, those dirt-eaters! Your Majesty—"

Queen Alequora's Grand Royal Pharmae, or lead scientist, Chief Pharmae Zax Liporien, rushed into the heart of the Alanterian Senate, disrupting the entire prophetic scene of the destruction of Atlantis and making it irrelevant.

Once more the Eye of the Mages went black as it lowered itself onto the steady hands of the Chief Mage.

"Guards, chief of the Royal Protectorate, do your jobs! Protect the Supreme One!" Several senators shouted in unison, but the queen held up her hand against their advance on her Grand Pharmae.

"No, stand down my faithful Protectorate. Stand down. It is of no alarm. I called him here to bring me any news of success immediately!"

He got no farther than a few steps as the senators shouted for the guards. The circle of lances pointed at the scientist's chest brought him to a halt.

Alequora held up her hand. "No, I commanded you to stand down! I instructed Chief Pharmae Zax Liporien of the Grand Royal Pharmae to bring me news of success no matter where I was. Report, Zax."

The jubilance of Chief Pharmae Zax Liporien infected the queen, who leaned forward in her chair with an air of anticipation.

"We finally have success." The chief scientist held out his hands. "We have created a creature, which, given any scrutiny, looks like a human but is under our complete control. With it and others we will create, we can begin the subjugation of the dirt-eaters."

Alequora's eyes sparkled, and beside her, Lilith fairly purred. "Have you brought it?" the queen asked.

"Yes . . . Your Majesty;" the scientist returned to the open doors and signaled for the creature to be brought in.

As it shambled through the doors, guided by two assistant scientists, the clamor that rose from the assembly drowned out horrified questions of the former king.

"My daughter, child, what have you done? This is an abomination against the *One True God*. I may no longer be king, but as your father, I won't stand for it. What is this about . . . what is going on here? What experiment? Why was I not told about this? I may not be your king now, but I am still your father!"

King Ilsofur looked at his daughter with instinctive remorse and impending dread. He knew full well of his daughter's immovable will, but he had been blind to her evil intentions toward the humans and her complete contrition to the dark malevolence of Lilith within her.

Alequora and her father gazed upon one another silently for what seemed an eternity. For all who witnessed it, there would be no questioning the significance later. It was that moment found in every royal passing of authority. The king was dead; long live the queen!

Queen Alequora continued to hold up her hand for complete silence within the Alanterian Senate, even against her own father, King Ilsofur. She commanded her grand pharmae to give a full report right then and there on the very floor of the once noble Alanterian Senate. Under threat of exile and certain death, the entire senate sat—powerless—and witnessed the foundation of their imminent demise, of the ultimate destruction being laid.

They were wrestling against forced entrenchment of absolute power while trying to hold on to some reasonable vestige of their ancient civilization, the Nephilim of Illumination. Now they wept as the horrors of Queen Alequora's experiment were laid bare before them, revealing the queen's true intentions. The noble Alanterian Senate had honored the millennia-long traditions of not interacting with the humans that lived on land.

This was handed down to them from the time of the immortals—the Lights of the Sky, their angelic fathers. In return, they reaped the countless benefits from that lineage. From a long life to supreme intellect, secrets of the universe in language, music, art, mathematics, science, medicine, physics, farming, and aquaculture that produced a society and civilization, unparalleled in history, and one, they now understood, would never be seen again.

Grand Pharmae Liporien slowly reported to his Supreme One—and by default, the entire Alanterian Senate—the painstaking plans that had been secretly designed, laid out, and then coldly implemented over many years. They had been totally out of view of all but a few hand-picked pharmae and senators who were sworn enemies of King Ilsofur.

They had jumped at the opportunity to be part of his daughter's unholy quest for ultimate power. What they were ignorant of, however, were the depths of depravity and demonic influence the young queen was under.

The grand pharmae reveled in the gruesome details of how the resources of the Alanterian Pharmetequia, which was the governing body having complete control over all the health and welfare of the entire Alanterian civilization from birth to passing, was re-directed to develop ways to gain control over the human population . . . by any means necessary.

Experiments using a modified and concentrated sonar frequency of certain marine mammals had been discovered to induce permanent damage to the cortical function of the human brain. This would push the human subject into a perpetual vegetative state.

Pharmae Liporien cackled as he said that the same focused sonar frequencies also neutralized the function of the human pineal gland. He held up a dried and shriveled example that had been removed from yet another human subject who didn't survive.

⌒⟨❈⟩⌒

Revolted, Camie forced himself to observe the Nephilim of the Illumination's scientist crack open the skull of the latest human they had captured to insert the probes into her brain, which they believed would make humans compliant to the Nephilim of Illumination's will. Camie's heart skipped a beat at the screams of the live victim, and his stomach turned with the bitter, metallic smell of blood oozing from the wound. His glimpse of the human brain became the proverbial cherry on top. Camie retreated to the heavenly plane, his aura pulsating rose quartz and now, it was becoming dark with crimson rage as his angelic senses tore at the injustice. The compulsion to tell someone propelled him toward Atlantis where he was sure to find Raphael or Rochel. He needed the calm guidance of the archangels.

⌒⟨❈⟩⌒

"Supreme One, we can now completely control the dirt-eaters through our developed and targeted sonar procedure. By killing this odd little pinecone-shaped organ from their pathetic insect brains, we can remove their need for much sleep at all. This means we can work them without losing time from their weak rest periods."

"This will substantially reduce their life spans, but that doesn't matter, as we will have millions more available to use up and discard."

"Their usefulness will be maximized, and when they are used up, we will discard and recycle them back into the deep."

The horrors of the Alanterian Pharmae sonar procedures were conducted on a massive scale. They performed it on kidnapped humans across a broad spectrum of races, cultures, genders, and ages, painstakingly conducted over hundreds of human years.

They included both mind control, physical and psychological torture, and chemically-induced attempts at isolating parts of the human brain that could be controlled, or even altered, to produce a malleable population of millions of indentured humans.

"We would use this army of controlled humans for further experimentation and the development of weapons, medicines, and many products that would further enrich and fortify the position of the Alanterian people, our civilization, as the preeminent species on the planet for millennia to come. We would also use them as agricultural slaves to produce food for an ever-increasing, global Alanterian population and to establish newly envisioned capital cities in each of the world's oceans and seas."

⊂⊰⊰⊰⊱⊃

Atlantis was the capital city and positioned in the turquoise waters of the sea, now known as the Caribbean.

King Ilsofur and his now adolescent daughter, newly enthroned Queen Alequora, were the Supreme Ones of this oceanographic region. More importantly, the queen was now also the head of the ruling council known as The Twelve; who were over all five oceans and the seven seas of the world.

There was one Supreme One for each of the world's oceans and seas, and all answered to the enthroned sovereignty of Atlantis. This was ultimately the overarching plan, hatched by Queen Alequora even before her father relinquished his throne.

Her demonic-induced vision was that of the bondage and eternal servitude of the human race through the establishment of eleven more capital cities in each of the earth's five oceans and the six other seas. The plan would be ambitious, relentless, and efficiently cruel in its design and ultimate implementation.

It would not matter if there were any indigenous human populations on the newly targeted island capital cities. They were to be eliminated from their island homes to make way for the construction of a new Alanterian regional capital city.

The targeted islands of the globe's five oceans had been methodically identified for their strategic positions and access to human shipping lanes, which would make furthering of Alanterian culture and concentration of power that much easier.

These included New Guinea in the Pacific Ocean, Greenland in the Atlantic Ocean, Madagascar in the Indian Ocean, the Svalbard archipelago in the Arctic Ocean, and King George Island in the Sothern Ocean near Antarctica.

Those that would be established within the world's largest seas, including the modern Arabian, South China, Weddell, Mediterranean, Tasman, Bering, the Bay of Bengal, and the Gulf of Mexico, had yet to be chosen; they would be determined later along with the actual capital cities to be established on continents and various landmasses around the globe. This network of control would be tightened with vastly superior Alanterian weapons and fortified with even more superior technology, all against a largely hunter-gatherer human population. One that had not even formed its own settlements, developed basic farming, or created any kind of rudimentary societal or organizational structure. This assured the Alanterian conquest and complete subjugation of mankind. It would have given birth to a very different—and for humankind, a much more inhospitable—world, indeed.

I guessed many of the senators' reactions resembled my own. I struggled to comprehend the vacancy I found in the creature's eyes, its seeming lack of purpose, the disjointedness of its movements, and the absence of a soul. I doubted the senators picked up on the latter.

Lilith's salivating eclipsed Alequora's glee.

Alequora banged the scepter again to regain control of the senate. "We have before us the prototype of our attack force."

Senator Keuron bin Alexius asked, "What is it supposed to do? It doesn't look functional."

The head scientist stepped forward to explain. "It only functions when it is commanded. I'll demonstrate. Kugel, disarm the guards."

Life sprang into the creature's face, and its body became a cohesive and lethal weapon. The speed at which it launched itself at the first guard caught me by surprise. It attacked with such force that it had him disarmed in a few seconds. By the way the guard held his arm, the creature must have broken it. The other guards charged it, but it ducked and wove around the lance thrusts, sword swings, and punches, each time finding a way under the defense of its opponent. It landed a punch of its own onto one guard's jaw. The splintering of bone drew a groan from some of the senators. It kicked the feet out from another, dropping onto his chest and quickly pummeling the guard's face beyond recognition. It twisted the arm of yet another, and the pop that followed indicated a dislocated shoulder. The few cuts it did sustain didn't impede it in the slightest. Neither did they bleed. It rendered the guards ineffective within a matter of minutes and while barely breaking a sweat.

Alequora cheered each takedown, showing no concern for the injuries of her men. Lilith's face held unbridled lust.

Once it completed the task, it reverted to the lackluster lump of flesh from before.

Alequora's voice came in breathless gasps. "Our plan is to build an army and send them forth carrying the message that the humans must submit to the Supreme Being, Queen of all Creation, Queen Alequora. If they encounter resistance, they are to kill the dissenters. By the time I send governors and troops, the populous will be willing to bend their knees to me."

Senator Kenesius placed his hands on the table to lever himself out of the chair. He did not address Alequora by either title, a sure sign of his disgust. "You have gone too far. You push us to the brink of ruin with this latest insanity. You have been warned by the mages numerous times that there are two destinies for Atlantis and its people: one the path of righteousness and the other, annihilation. My Liege Ilsofur, have you no control left over your daughter?"

Tears streamed down the former king's face. "I do not know her anymore. My once kindhearted princess, the joy of my life, no longer listens to me . . . only to that sniveling friend of hers. It is as if my daughter has been replaced by a darkness that rules her better judgment. I am at a loss."

Senator Kenesius turned back to Alequora. "I implore you Aleqi"—reverting to the name he called her when she was a child—"turn back from this course before you bring the wrath of the *One True God* down on the heads of your people."

Alequora's barely concealed fury foamed from her lips. "I told you not to say *His* name. I am your god. I am the Supreme Being."

She shoved herself from the throne and stomped off the dais, yelling over her shoulder, "Enough of impotent old men for today."

Chapter 2
Raise the Stakes

⟨⟨⟨⟨⟨⟨   ⟨⟨⟨   ⟨⟨⟨⟨

The scribe handled the thousand-year-old parchment he'd retrieved from the vault of the Alanterian library with reverence. A tear formed as he struck through the name of the One True God. He wiped it away with his finger, leaving a black smudge on his cheek.

Next to him, a second scribe erased the name with unbridled delight, making great slashes across the page.

I compared their attitudes with the others I'd monitored over the last month.

In the beginning, a few true-hearted souls had taken a stand and refused to deface the name of the *One True God*, but after they and their families were thrown into the trench, active defiance faded to nothing. Some secreted sacred manuscripts in their robes to prevent vandalization. Others let the odd reference slip by. But they still went about their work, hearts heavy and eyes red.

To my mind, theirs were the actions of cowards. They did not have enough faith in the *Father* to make a stand. What matter if they died? Heaven rewarded the faithful. No, I found their tears about as insufferable as the joy, with which those beguiled by Alequora, or more precisely, Lilith, displayed.

The ones I liked even less were the ambivalent. Those who chose to sit on the fence to see to whom the victory fell.

The defacement happened everywhere. Stonemasons disfigured ancient statues and magnificent buildings. Artists desecrated images of the *Father* in the sacred temples. Even those involved in handcraft unpicked embroideries, scorched the name off woodwork, and smashed casts of the *Father's* image.

But today, I occupied the seat before the portal because the prayers of one of the faithful alerted Heaven to an imminent atrocity. Again, I begged the *Father* to allow me to intercede to prevent it, but *He* said, if *He* breached *His* word, *He* was no better than the lowest demon.

A small crowd in a coastal village on the mainland near the island of Atlantis had gathered to be entertained by a group of traveling minstrels. A man in a jester's costume stepped up onto the open wagon and held out his hands to the gathering. The air buzzed with excitement.

But he didn't juggle or sing. He began, "I am here today to tell you of a new power that has arisen. She will protect you and provide you with opportunities for wealth and glory, health and longevity. She is merciful and gracious. All she asks is that you submit to her will and worship her as god."

The hypnotic quality of the voice held the small crowd in its thrall, while the other members of the minstrel band infiltrated the crowd or positioned themselves on the gathering's periphery.

"Who is this new power?"

"Ah, I'm glad you asked. The Supreme Being, queen of all creation, Queen Alequora asks you to be her loyal subjects."

A man called out, "The queen used to be fair when we traded with the Alanterians, but now she cheats us. Why would we trust anything she has to say? Why would we—"

Blood spouting from where the blade had severed the artery cut his question short. It showered those nearest to the man. They crashed into those behind them as fear drove them to get away. Shrieks and curses flooded the air.

The deviants slashed and stabbed at the fleeing mob. They appeared to attack at random, but then the yell of a woman reached me. "Demons sent by the devil herself."

The deviant drove his sword into her belly and ripped up. The woman screamed as she clutched her intestines and crumpled to the ground.

My heart seized at the sight of a boy of about six, frozen in front of a mutant. I strained to hear the exchange over the shouting and crying.

The mutant asked the boy, "Is the Supreme Being your god?"

In his innocence, the boy replied, "My mummy says Zeus is the head of the gods."

I bit my finger when the golden-haired head of the boy tumbled to the ground.

My muscles ached and my head throbbed when I eventually turned from the portal. Would this report be enough for my *Father* to act?

◦◦◦◦◦◦

A few days later, I perched on the chair again. Word of the attack had reached Senator Kenesius, and he demanded the senate meet to have Alequora explain her actions.

Kenesius addressed the senate. "It has come to my attention that the deviants and mutants attacked a coastal village on the mainland a few days past." He waited until the hubbub quieted. "I have been informed that the carnage was extensive, including women and children."

Alequora yawned and studied her nails. "What of it? They refused to bow to me."

Kenesius's stillness contrasted with the warring emotions crossing his face. "Need I remind you of the mages' warning: you cannot . . . you must not ignore their predictions. We are the most-blessed children of the Lights of the Sky. Our place in the Eternal Kingdom is assured, but we also have a responsibility to those of less noble lineage, the humans and the animals, both on land and in the oceans that we have been given dominion over. Your actions jeopardize our place in the Eternal Realm."

I applauded how he skirted the use of titles. Had he spoke of the *One True God*, I am sure Alequora would have had him run through.

Alequora's knuckles whitened as she clutched the arms of her throne. She snarled the words through clenched teeth. "I am the Supreme Being. My will is the rule of the land. I will conquer the human world and reign supreme."

Kenesius sighed. "Then, as chief senator, I have no choice but to call for the Eye of the Mages to judge Alequora's fitness to rule."

Alequora vaulted out of her chair and brandished the scepter at Kenesius. "How dare you? I will not be subjected to some hocus pocus by a bunch of withered old men. I repeat; I am the Supreme Being."

One of many of Alequora's senatorial ally's began, "I concur with the Supreme—"

"Sit down, you old windbag. Chief Senator Kenesius is within his rights. The Eye must be brought," the senator to Chief Kenesius's left said.

Kenesius signaled for the senate runner to call the mages to bring the Eye.

In the ensuing confusion and partisan bickering, the senate dissolved into warring factions. My hope of stopping Lilith dissolved with it. One of my brother Lucifer's ultimate weapons against humans: division!

The four ancient spirits, whose gifts of control of the natural element elevated them to seniority, tottered into the great hall. In the chief mage's hand rested the Eye of the Mages, which pulsated with the Holy Fire of *Elohim*.

I had been present when the Eye was gifted to the Nephilim to serve as a guide and direct link to the Heavenly Realm. I had witnessed its use in discerning many a course of action in the Nephilim of Illumination's responsibility in their stewardship of lesser beings.

Alequora waved them to approach. "If I must listen to the pontificating diatribes of dried-up old fish, be quick about it."

I grinned at the defiance of the mages who continued their solemn pace.

Once before the throne, the chief mage lifted the Eye to shoulder height and whispered to it. It levitated to about two-thirds of the height of the hall. In a voice whose strength defied the age of the mage, the chief mage cried, "Behold the outcome of the path your actions have forced your subjects onto!"

With that, the Eye let forth a burst of Holy Fire of *Elohim*, projecting the fall of Atlantis.

The senate erupted. Calls for Alequora's abdication were jumbled with accusations of forgery. Arguments raged between those for Alequora and those opposed.

The chief mage's voice boomed, "Silence!"

Once the senators resumed their places, he turned to Alequora. "Will you desist from this course of action and return to the *One True God*?"

Alequora screeched, "How many times do I have to say it? I am the Supreme Being."

The mages maintained their calm as their chief pronounced, "Given your refusal to turn from your present course and given the undeniable outcome of the destruction of Atlantis, we, the mages, judge you unfit to rule. By the laws of our fathers, we order you to step down immediately. You are unfit to rule this great race!"

Alequora's skin turned puce. Her eyes blazed black. An otherworldly shriek accompanied the pitch of the Royal Orb at the Eye. The giant pearl collided with the holy stone, but that was not what shattered it. I felt the power of Lucifer. A shower of pearl crystals and gold particles rained down on the senators.

Alequora's voice cut through the senators' clamor. Her voice rumbled with darkness. "Hear me and hear me well. I am the Supreme Being. My will is all. I do not recognize the authority of the mages, and I abolish the senate."

With rehearsed precision, the Royal Protectorate took their place of protection in front of their queen and benefactor. Their loyalty paid for even before the old king was abdicated.

Like the senators, I sat back in the chair mute. A thousand years of tradition abolished. What would she do next?

Lilith whispered in her ear.

Her heartless voice commanded, "Guards seize the mages and Kenesius and throw them into the trench."

That.

Two days later, Alequora announced her anointment as Supreme Being to take place in the sacred temple. That she chose to desecrate the Holy Sanctuary with her vile plans appalled me, but whether Lilith managed to cross the temple's threshold denoted the real test of how far the Nephilim had fallen.

Alequora's proclamation decreed that all citizens line the main thoroughfare between the royal palace and the sacred temple.

From my seat at the portal, I zoomed in on the crowd. Alequora's supporters waved banners at the front. The farther back I scanned, the more subdued the well-wishers appeared.

Trumpets blared from the palace walls signifying the beginning of the procession, so I switched my focus to the palace.

The four matching horses pulled the royal carriage, the plumage in their halters dancing in the breeze and the silver bells adorning their harness tinkling with every step. The blackness of the glossy exterior contrasted with the white satin-lined seats, but two things struck me. The insignia inscribed on its doors read, "Supreme Being, Queen of all Creation, Queen Alequora." The other, more startling, was Alequora's dress.

The color of the clinging silk left me grasping at reason—gold, the color of divinity, the eternal deity. It was *God's* color. Her audacity knew no bounds.

A cheer went up from her supporters, who threw brightly-colored shells before the carriage. Those behind clapped half-heartedly.

A disturbance at the barricade interested me. I changed views. A man forced his way through, brandishing a sacred text and shouting, "Repent of this evil and throw yourself on the mercy of the *One True God*."

As Alequora's eyes hardened, I knew the man was as good as dead. I almost missed the flick of her wrist as an arrow streaked from a guardsman. Her supporters whooped in delight when the arrow exploded the rebel's eye and lodged in his brain, while those at the back bowed their heads.

The royal carriage simply rolled over him, jostling Alequora as it went.

I'd lost count of how many she had executed. The Keeper of Records kept the tally, but the numbness that took hold of me when I read it made it difficult to comprehend. Understanding also eluded me when I referenced memories of Alequora's devotion to the *Father* and her people against what she'd become—the devil's handiwork indeed.

Speaking of the devil, Lilith sat opposite her, demurely clothed in the body and garments of Alequora's friend. Tendrils of her dark power coiled around Alequora's waist and hands, wove through her hair, and circled her neck.

The carriage halted before the grand steps of the temple, whose polished white coral façade, with its intricate gold patterns, shone in the sun. The liveried footman handed Alequora and Lilith out. As Alequora ascended the steps, her fifteen-foot train trailed behind her, dazzling the onlookers.

I drew a breath. Real gold thread, the whole thing.

Alequora swept into the temple. Lilith, on the other hand, paused at the threshold. She raised a hand and extended a finger toward the opening. The finger froze millimeters from the space.

I yelled, "Go on. Fry yourself to a crisp!"

Bitter disappointment gripped me when nothing happened. I had my answer. The evidence of the Nephilim of Illumination's choice stared me in the face. The sacred temple no longer housed the power of the *Father*. I shuddered when I looked inside. All the glories of the *Father* had been replaced by images of Alequora.

Alequora proceeded up the aisle, failing to acknowledge the court's lords and ladies, the former senators, or other dignitaries. After she mounted the steps of the specially-built dais, she ensconced herself on the throne, her train snaking around her feet.

A cleric entered, a hood over his head shrouding his face. Not knowing who it was, I feared one of my favorite clerics might have succumbed to Lilith's wiles. He pushed the hood back. My eyes ballooned. My tongue stuck to the roof of my mouth. *Lucifer.*

His incantation as he placed the crown on her head tunneled under my skin like so many hot needles. It made sense only if one knew the Angelic tongue. Alequora had no idea that it bound her to the darkness.

Black root-like structures sprouted from the crown and burrowed into Alequora's skull and mind.

I knew only the *Father's* will had the power to remove it.

Chapter 3
Embrace of Darkness

⟨ᛝᛂᛩ⟩ᛟᛤᛩᛞᛯ ᛚᛑ ᛟᛤᛯᛞᛩᛯᛚᛚ

I bumped into other angels, knocking a couple over as I streaked through the marble halls on my way to the Father's Holy Inner Sanctum, my mind distracted by the unholy alliance Alequora had just made.

While the *Father's* door remained open to all residents in Heaven, the angels chose to disturb *Him* as little as possible. Today's situation, however, warranted it, given the seriousness of Alequora's situation and what it meant for her people.

As I raised my hand to knock on the door with its ever-changing intricate carvings of the past, present, and future, it opened, and *God's* messenger collided with me.

In his odd, apologetic manner, he stared at his feet and mumbled, "Please forgive me, but I have an urgent message for Chamuel." Then he raised his eyes, which brightened perceptibly. "Oh, it's you; saves me a trip." He fumbled in the pouch to retrieve the message and shoved it into my hand, turned, and disappeared back through the door.

The *Father's* soft spot for the inept puzzled me. So many capable angels would kill for the opportunity, figuratively speaking, to serve *The One True God* in that way. Apart from the fact that angels can't be killed, except by the *Father's* hand, killing is not something that happens in Heaven. If I could actually cry, I'd most likely cry while laughing over the number of gaffs this messenger had made, but angels can't cry in the heavenly form. Interestingly, in corporeal form, we can.

I broke the holy seal. The *Father's* elegant handwriting blazed on the page.

Chamuel, if you would be so kind as to attend the Sanctum. I have something I need to impart to you. Your loving Father.

The humility with which *Father* requested my presence rather than command it humbled me.

I knocked on the door, and at *His* invite, entered the Sanctum. Here, in *His* presence, I folded one pair of my auras over my face out of respect. A second pair covered my feet. The third pair kept me aloft.

Then I prostrated myself before *Him*.

The chiming of bells touched my soul.

Arise, Chamuel.

My auras lifted me from the inlaid floor, but I remained lower than the *Father*, head bowed.

The rippling of the bells washed over me.

Chamuel, given the intensity of your emotions regarding the Nephilim of Illumination, I charge you with the mission to correct the behavior of the queen. First, I will provide her with one last opportunity to repent. You and Raphael will attend the queen to implore her to relinquish her claim as a deity and return to me. If she does not, you will warn her that I will unleash signs of my power upon her.

I give you permission to command the Alanterian volcano to spew forth molten lava over the outskirts of the city and a tsunami to crash onto the shores of the island.

The Father's message contained the weight of His grief that the situation necessitated such actions. *This, and no more, do you understand . . . warnings only. No one is to die. Are my instructions clear?*

My heart rejoiced at the *Father's* decision to take action. "Yes, *Heavenly Father*. I am honored to be chosen. I will fulfill your command to the letter."

Take my blessing with you, my son. Go now and find Raphael.

A wave of holy power swept over me as I left *His* presence, bowing and treading backward.

A guard ushered Raphael and me into the audience chamber in time to hear a snippet of the conversation between Alequora and the Royal Protectorate.

Alequora's strident voice carried across the chamber. "Have you taken care of that insufferable Kenesius and his family as I ordered?"

"Yes, Supreme One." The pained expression on the protectorate's face indicated that he had not relished the task.

"What is that look for? Don't tell me they prayed?" Alequora snorted. "Did they plead with that useless creature in the sky for their salvation?"

"No, Supreme One, Senator Kenesius prayed to the *One True God* for the release of your soul from the darkness that infests it."

The conviction in his words must have impacted Alequora because her voice grew shrewd. "And where do you stand on this matter?"

The protectorate's Adam's apple bobbed. "I . . . my duty is to serve the throne."

Alequora harrumphed. "You're treading a thin line with that answer."

She took a sip of her drink. "I suppose I must see these Lights of the Sky; most inconvenient."

On registering our presence, she showed no contrition for her remarks, nor when she spoke, did her manner convey the deference due to us. "Gentlemen, welcome to our majestic city. We are honored and blessed to be standing in your presence."

The fact she called us gentlemen rather than Lights of the Sky spoke volumes about her welcome, as did her forced smile and the fact that she did not get up from her chair or stop consuming her drink.

I lamented the loss of her once vibrant violet eyes. Eyes that once had held a unique power, intelligence, and spirit inherited from her angelic father, my brethren. Those that scanned me with distaste lacked the vitality of life, and their blackness revealed how far Lilith's influence stretched.

I did not foresee a positive outcome to this meeting.

⋘⋙

Even though the *Father* had given me a mission, my mind leaped to the easiest solution to the problem. I communicated with Raphael in my mind.

"Can I please just incinerate her? We've only been here for five human minutes, and she has disrespect us twice and, by implication, the *Father*. You can see how influenced she is by Lilith."

I was already calling for my Holy Fire of *Elohim* when my less impulsive brother put his finger to his lips.

"Shh, Camie, at least give her a chance . . . the *Father* wills it so."

"But if we take her out, the problem is solved."

"Camie, your answer to everything that opposes *Father* is fire and brimstone. You know that blind rage will be your undoing, brother . . . almost like—"

"Don't say our names together. I am nothing like Lucifer."

"Brother, I love you; you know that, but everybody—your entire angelic family—knows the only difference between you two is that you accepted it when *Father* elevated the humans; Lucifer could not. You and Lucifer were graced by *Father* with the same power, majesty, and passion. *Father* created you and our brother to be the opposite sides of the same . . . um . . . coin."

Raphael was correct, of course. I just hated to admit it. I fought a constant battle within my angelic spirit not to want to just, as he so eloquently put it, rain down fire and brimstone.

"Your sudden arrival here, while most welcome, did not offer us the opportunity to prepare a much grander reception worthy of your stature and majesty, oh mighty Lights of the Sky." The subtle implication that Alequora did not welcome our visit replaced the warmth that should have accompanied her words.

Raphael was not moved. He raised his right index finger and muted her before her impudence became too much.

Her guards hastened toward her.

I had my brother's left flank and immobilized them.

I reminded everyone that while we meant no harm, we needed them all to listen.

"Alequora, I am the Archangel Raphael, and this is my brother, Archangel Chamuel. We have been sent by the *One True God* to provide you the last opportunity to repent and return to *His* grace."

While Raphael spoke, I examined her heart for signs of contrition or even remorse. Finding none, I prepared to implement the *Father's* instructions to me, but as Raphael had pointed out, the *Father's* will bound me to allow her one last chance. I waited for him.

Raphael laid Alequora's sins before her.

"You have committed the egregious act of blasphemous pride by removing all references to and mention of *His* mighty name throughout Atlantis and by replacing it with your own.

"You have foolishly placed yourself as equal to the very *One* who gave you life. You dare to have yourself proclaimed Supreme Being and worshipped as a deity when every one of your capabilities and accomplishments is a gift from the *One True God.*

"You have murdered innocent men, women, and even children who refused to capitulate to your childish attempts at self-deification.

"You have levied horror upon horror against your own kind, Alequora."

He concluded with a quote from the story of Cane and Able as a parable of her story.

If you do what is right, will you not be accepted? But if you do not do what is right, sin is crouching at your door; it desires to have you, but you must rule over it . . . from Genesis 4:7.

Raphael flicked his finger to allow her to respond.

For the briefest of seconds, Alequora's eyes flashed their former vibrant violet, but Lilith clamped her hand on Alequora's shoulder and hissed, "You cannot have her. She is mine."

"Silence in the name of *El Gibor*," I commanded and with a wave of my hand, I restrained her, but Alequora's eyes returned to their blackened, lifeless state.

Although I could stop her voice, I could not counter Lilith's malevolent gloating.

Alequora's dismissive hand gesture preceded her contemptuous remark. "What care I for the ranting of a *God* who is supposedly so concerned, yet who does not put in an appearance *Himself.*"

I bridled at the remark and opened my mouth to give her a tongue lashing, but Raphael cut me off.

"In your current state, Alequora, as consumed by the powers of darkness as you are, you could not stand in the presence of the *Father*. You'd be burnt to a crisp by *His* holy radiance."

I chimed in, "The *Father* wishes it known that since you, Alequora, have not repented and returned to *His* fold, *He* will unleash signs of *His* power upon your city so that you may know *He* is the *One True God*, in the hope you will amend your ways and prevent its annihilation."

Alequora rose from the chair, her body shaking. She clenched the cup so hard it shattered. Where her eyes had been black, the fires of Hell raged in them now. Undertones of Lucifer flowed through the menace in her voice. "I am the Supreme Being! Your threats are meaningless as I have the power to stop any attack leveled at me. Get out of my sight before I destroy you."

Black whips of dark power lashed from her hands only to fizzle to smoke on contact with our auras.

Raphael hung his head. In the millennia I had known him, he had never failed an assignment. I felt his pain at having disappointed the *Father*, but my heart knew the *Father* had foreseen this. I wanted so badly to tell him that he did not fail our *Father*. It was not his mission to win. *Father* had already given me the assignment before we left home. I searched for words of encouragement for my brother, but any I offered fell woefully short of the mark. I resigned myself to stand silently in support as I watched Raphael agonize about what he could have said or done differently to affect the outcome.

"Go home, angels. Fly away and never return. Atlantis is mine . . . forever," Lucifer ridiculed us.

The power of Lucifer's deception slammed into me. He taunted us over our failure. And to prove his abilities, he released Lilith from my invocation of silence.

We took flight and left the human, corporeal plane through the portal toward home.

I paused, as the demonic taunts of not only Lucifer and Lilith but many of the Alanterian Nephilim of Illumination, whom Raphael had pleaded for, sounded in my skull. I had a duty to the *Father* to fulfill. At the speed of thought and the authority of *Jehovah*, I found myself back once more, above Atlantis.

Lucifer and Lilith sensed my presence and flashed into view.

My righteous Holy Fire of *Elohim* smashed into Lilith's pathetic countenance as I dispatched her in a single burst. She screamed as I hurled her through time and space back into the abyss. "Where are all your pontificating diatribes now?" I roared.

Lucifer dodged my first blast and cast a cloak of darkness around himself for a second. He preempted my next volley with a fireball of his own. I flicked up an aura, which sizzled a little where the ball hit. His yin to my yang, but the power of the *Father* wore him down after a few more hits.

Rather than admitting that the *Father* had bested him once more, he left on his own accord, shouting over his shoulder, "Today is yours and *Father's*, Chamuel, but this world is mine to abuse and torment until the last second my time is up, and I am going to thoroughly enjoy everyone."

Lucifer opened a door between the planes of existence. He strode through it with all of the posturing he could muster and then turned toward me. His eyes, now fiery embers but which once burned Cerulean blue with the Holy Fire of *Elohim*, faded against the absolute blackness of *God's* void.

I slammed open the queen's audience room door. She bolted upright and said, "I told, you be gone. I have nothing further to say to you or your imbecilic *God*."

"Alequora, hear me and hear me well. I have been charged by the *One True God* to exact *His* justice that you might know *His* power and seek *His* mercy. Only *His* love can remove that cursed crown."

"Remove my crown?"

Alequora's merciless laugh chilled me.

"Why would I do that? It is the source of my power, and I am powerful." She pointed at a statue, and a fireball shot across the room, disintegrating the sculpture. "Let your puny *God* wreak his worst. My power is greater. I am greater. He should bow before me."

The insolence of her statement struck me dumb. Then my corporeal form shook. My muscles tensed, and my fists clenched. My auras flashed like the birth of a new star. *His* own creation would not mock *Him*, not on my watch.

I flipped that coin and embraced the darkness. I knew then what I had to do.

The fate of the Alanterian civilization, fueled by evil arrogance and blasphemous pride, would now be sealed with their own blood.

Chapter 4

Judgment of Blasphemies

ᎭᏍᎧᎦᏴᏞᎮ ᏟᏝ ᏔᎾᏍᎤᎦᎦᏔ

Righteous fury welled from deep within me, and the Holy Fire of Elohim leaped from my hands.

I sent a blast at Alequora, which streaked across the room, smashing furniture as it went. I gauged her reaction as she muttered, concentrating on her hands to ready a fireball, her face a mix of consternation and defiance. When the two balls met and hers fizzled to smoke, I watched the kaleidoscope of expressions dance on her face, finally settling on terror as the Holy Fire of *Elohim* continued on its trajectory. It all gratified me.

She screamed, "No!" as it consumed her. The crown clattered on the floor, a symbol of her defeat, but Lucifer's claiming of her soul replaced the release she might have had with the *Father*.

Before Lucifer could claim the crown, I blasted it to dust.

That should have been enough, but when my mind recalled the senate, the very battleground where repentance and return to the *Father* might have been won if only they had resorted to the power of the *Father*, my anger swelled. Yes, some of the senators had held fast, but only Kenesius had the conviction to die for what he believed. Others had leaped at the opportunity to seize power from the humans, giving their support and blessing to Alequora, and worshipping the ground she walked on. I elevated myself above the city and charged another blast of Holy Fire of *Elohim,* driving it into the beautiful hall that housed the senate, reducing it to rubble. I mourned more for the building than for the souls within it.

As my eyes swept the city, ignoring the screaming citizens who were running like ants, they came to rest on the Alanterian Pharmetequia complex. At the thought of the vile experiments and excruciating suffering that had been inflicted on the innocent in what had once been a beacon of learning, my outrage exploded to the extent that I left nothing but a hole.

The beloved temple shone in the sun, but at the memory of the anointment where Lucifer had defiled the sanctuary, I vented my ire. The Holy Fire of *Elohim* I expelled ignited the structure on fire instantly. It burnt like a sacrificial lamb.

With each demolition came death, and I watched as the souls departed the earthly plane, rejoicing at those scant few who went heavenward. The number who descended to the nether realm justified my actions. Lights of children passed me, and I regretted their deaths, but what would be left if I spared them—no city, no adults, no food. They'd die a far worse death.

I hesitated when I gazed down at the Central Alanterian Pharmetequia Hospital and Sanatorium. Here, the truly vulnerable existed—the elderly and maimed, the orphaned and mentally unstable, Surely, I could spare the truly innocent.

A massive explosion at the city's main energy refining complex brought me out of my temporary fog of uncertainty and remorse. My attention returned to the stark reality of what I had commenced.

My chosen course demanded that I proceed. If I succumbed to sparing these less-than-perfect Nephilim of Illumination, they'd be alone and abandoned with no resources. As with the children, I would sentence them to a languishing death.

I focused my concentration, building the Holy Fire of *Elohim*'s intensity past anything I had achieved so far to ensure I dispatched the inhabitants as quickly as possible, I struggled to control the ball. It seemed to have a mind of its own, and when I threw it, it split into a myriad of arcs I assumed represented each soul.

Fires raged through the city. One front encroached on the school. The heavy chains that encircled my heart as I blasted the children were going to take a long time to remove, but better a quick death by Holy Fire of *Elohim* than burning alive. As their bright sparks shot to Heaven, tears formed.

Even yet, I still had more to do. The memory of Atlantis must be buried forever.

I summoned the power the *Father* had given me to wake the Alanterian volcano, but I embellished it. The volcano rumbled and shook the island. Plumes of volcanic ash jettisoned into the sky. Streams of lava coursed down its sides, fusing everything in their paths. But I craved more. Instead of merely spewing a few streams of lava and a little hot ash, I caused it to implode. In that instant, thousands upon thousands died. The air swirled with departing spirits, which mixed with the poisonous gases. I wish I could say the sky filled with innumerable stars as their lights transcended to Heaven, but alas, they numbered less than a third of those whose darkness the underworld sucked away.

My instinct warned me of the potential for future generations to discover the secrets of Atlantis. I raised my arms, and like Moses of old, commanded the seas. I fashioned a tsunami whose towering face ascended to the heavens. I released it, and the waters crashed and thundered over the place where once a fair city, filled with light and joy, had existed.

And yet, it required another safeguard, so I called upon one of the greatest of all the fallen angels, a prince of Hell, Leviathan the Unspeakable One, who had been transformed into a great dragon of the sea. The *Father* had given me the authority to order him to whatever duty I deemed fit because he betrayed me at the time Lucifer fell. I demanded he rise from the depths of the Mariana Trench and stand guard.

I thought it a perfect fit perfect and prayed he would find peace through this act.

As I surveyed the result of my wrath, my mind said there ought to be some feeling, but with my energies spent, a void stood in place of emotion. I made to return to the heavenly plane, but as I did so, a voice cried, "Chamuel, what have you done?"

I spun toward the speaker. Nemamaih's stricken eyes stared at me, her bottom lip trembled, and her auras drooped. "The children . . . they were innocent."

Nemamaih's tormented countenance and the despair in her question hit my conscience like a blast of my own rage. It shattered the numbness, and the magnitude of my actions exploded like the volcano itself. My emotions churned like the ocean over the ruins of Atlantis, and as it sank deeper and deeper into the abyss, I sank into depression. My stomach heaved, my head pounded, and my hands shook.

I spread my hands. "I . . . the *Father* . . ."

Nemamaih's sorrow flared into anger. She swooped at me, yelling, "And don't tell me *Father* ordered all of those children to be murdered. *He* knows how many angels have family in Atlantis."

The impact of my actions on my brethren had been so far from my mind that it hadn't occurred to me. A pariah . . . I'd be a pariah. Why had the *Father* done this to me? My conscience pinged. *He* hadn't. I had.

Raphael appeared. "Why, Camie? We could have saved the righteous," motioning to the other angels in our small cadre sent by the *Father*.

Nemamaih spat, "He gave me some crap about the *Father*."

Raphael cocked his head to the side.

"Were you on a mission from the *Father*?"

I nodded.

He folded his arms across his chest.

"And you didn't think to tell me before we spoke to Alequora?"

"I swore to *Father* I wouldn't."

"How convenient;" Nemamaih's contempt twisted her lips. "Hide behind the 'I can't say' excuse."

"In fairness, Nem' . . . the *Father* often swears us to secrecy over our missions." Raphael studied the muddy water below. Pain etched his perfect features. "I can't believe they are gone." He turned back to me. "We were to attempt to reason with Alequora. I had children here. We all did . . . except you."

As he wept rivulets of gold and mercury for his lost children, I cringed like some caged predator who had given up its will to live. His aura pulsated in rich violet and golden yellow bursts of blinding energy and deafening frequency. He was the healer of worlds and men, but now he seemed almost broken. He looked at me, or should I say, through me. I can only describe it as a warped combination of horror, rage, deep sadness, utter disbelief, and shock. At that moment, I feared, for the first time in my life.

"He is guilty of this atrocity. He annihilated the Nephilim of Illumination, and he must pay for that."

Nemamaih's auras flashed orange and red.

She lunged at me, aiming to tear at my face. If she had the power to call on the Holy Fire of *Elohim*, I was convinced she'd have used it.

"Be still, Nem." Raphael's command brought her to a stop. His brilliant aura pulsated, a clear, emerald light that would have blinded us had we not covered our faces. "You know the *Father* forbids retribution between angels. Believe me, when I say, it is the only thing stopping my hand."

I shivered. Raphael's ability, given his power, to inflict grievous harm even though he could not kill me left me questioning my safety. But I put my trust in his unwavering adherence to the *Father's* word.

Raphael asked us to join him in prayer.

"*Heavenly Father*, this is a day of sorrow, the end of a great civilization, perhaps the greatest ever in the brief history of this planet. We ask *You* to accept the souls of the children and the righteous into *Your* grace. We pray for the souls of the lost and ask that in *Your* mercy, they might find redemption."

He raised his hand to his heart in tribute to the fallen city and its people.

"Come, Camie, the *Father* will judge your heart and your actions. I suggest you make your peace."

Chapter 5

Reckoning

had been summoned. I balked at the reality. How could my *Father* call me before the Angelic Hierarchy Tribunal when I had done *His* bidding? OK, I disobeyed the specifics, but *His* will commanded it. And when I think of Alequora's blasphemies and how she executed Senator Kenesius and his family, I would do it again. I do regret the death of the children and those who held fast to the *One True God*, but the corruption of the society as a whole precipitated their fate.

Now, on the appointed day, at the appointed hour, I stood before magnificent guilt doors to the Arc of the Covenant as it exists in the heavenly plane. It is where *He* meets *His* servants to deliver judgment on whether they have fulfilled *His* holy word.

Today, my turn had come.

I laid my hand on the surface, which crackled with the Holy Fire of *Elohim* and sent my signature vibration. The doors swung open, and the *Breath of God* washed over me. For the first time in weeks, my spirit rejoiced, as the overwhelming depression shifted somewhat. Hope glimmered, believing that my *Father's* faithfulness to those who serve would deliver justice to me against those who falsely accused me as only the

Father knew the circumstances of my mission. A prayed of gratitude flowed from my lips.

The leather sandals I wore slapped against the polished marble floor, whose design reflected the story of the creation of Earth. As I proceeded to the dock, the cold of the marble floor penetrated the thin soles, and a cold fear penetrated my soul. Gone was the belief that this day held absolution for me as the heavy silence of the chamber conveyed the seriousness of the situation. I imagined leaving muddy footprints of guilt in my wake.

The filled gallery rustled with murmurs as I passed. Prosecutions of Archangels of the Seraphim rarely occurred so curiosity ran rampant. Rumors of my destruction of Atlantis and my motives had taken on a life of their own and my gut knotted at the condemnation I sensed from the glares I received.

Before me, *God's* blinding light and that of *Jesus Christ* seated at *His* right hand, which glittered off the chandeliers, dazzled me to the point I could barely make out my assembled brothers, who served as jurors, standing to my right. My brothers' auras vibrated in iridescent colors, each representing one of the nine Angelic Choirs, or Realms. Even as I contemplated my fate, the peculiarity of how humans perceived the auras as wings when angels manifested in the corporeal form on the earthly plane lifted me a little.

The scribe of *God*, keeper of the Akashaic record—the Book of Life— sat before *God's* dais. *God* had accorded Metatron the right to sit due to his work. Everyone else stood.

I studied the painted scenes of *God's* glories in the panels on the walls to calm my nerves as I stepped into the dock. How to defend myself without breaching the command of the *Most High* not to disclose the terms of the mission to anyone held uppermost in my mind.

Satan acted as my defense counsel. Not the red devil with horns and a pitchfork, breathing fire and brimstone. This complete fabrication of millennia, of the human's self-serving dogmatic organized religions, annoyed me.

It frustrated me that religious leaders used this image, this fear, to subjugate the devout, uneducated masses, not for the benefit of their respective flocks but to coerce financial servitude. It is Lucifer on whom they should throw this mantel. Satan and Lucifer are not the same being.

However, Lucifer has a time limit, but he intends to squeeze every last drop of human suffering while he can from a species for which he has nothing but disdain and bitter hatred.

And much to my shame, Lucifer is my true brother.

In fact, there is a third archangel involved, Samael, who was a great cherubim; predetermined by *God* to be the enemy of humanity.

Samael is the true "Satan," and he was and is not Lucifer, the fallen archangel.

Today, I put my future in Satan's hands to ensure a fair trial.

Nemamaih acted as the prosecution, I suspected because her passion over the matter exceeded even Raphael's, and he had lost children.

The enveloping nuances of frankincense, myrrh, and cedar incense swirled around me. The flickering yellow, white, orange, crimson, and cobalt blue flames of the candles suspended overhead danced in my vision as Zedkiel stepped onto the platform to read the sentence. He placed his official papers on the lectern, cleared his throat, and focused his attention on me.

"Archangel of the Seraphim, out of the House of Chamuel, you are hereby charged with the willful destruction of Atlantis, in which countless Nephilim of Illumination perished, including the young and elderly, ill and infirm, and believers in the *One True God*. Further, such act was fueled by your disdain for mortals, which is against *God's* will."

Zedkiel paused, the expression on his face one of consternation.

"How do you plead?"

My voice croaked. I made a second attempt.

"Not guilty."

I barely heard the booing and catcalling as I stared into Zedkiel's eyes. I read there a sadness that said, *you have not learned your lesson. It would have gone so much easier if you would have just accepted your fate.*

My heart sank. Zedkiel held my utmost respect. His name meant "righteousness of *God*." He belonged to the house closest to man, being amongst those sent to prevent Abraham from sacrificing Isaac. If he thinks I made the wrong call, it's not looking good.

Zedkiel turned to where Nemamaih bounced on her toes, bowed, and said, "You may begin the prosecution."

Nemamaih almost pushed Zedkiel off the platform; the zeal her body expressed not waiting for him to vacate indicated just how badly she wanted me to pay. I hoped Satan exhibited the same exuberance, and where was he anyway?

She plunked a binder filled with paper on the lectern, the thud resounding through the chamber.

"I call my first witness, Archangel of the Seraphim, out of the House of Rochel."

Rochel fluttered down from the jury stand, his auras pulsating cerulean blue and sea-foam green.

Zedkiel's solemnity quieted the gallery.

"Do you, Archangel of the Seraphim, out of the House of Rochel swear on the Word of *God* to tell the truth?"

"As I honor the *Father* in all things, I take His Word to be holy. In swearing on it, I am binding myself to *His* judgment if I tell a falsehood."

Zedkiel motioned to Nemamaih.

"You may examine the witness."

Nemamaih elicited from Rochel that he had been fourth on the scene, that I had seemed dazed and would not explain my actions, saying that I answered to the *Father*. He attested to the destruction of Atlantis, which I did not deny.

When she finished, Zedkiel's eyes scanned the chamber. He hesitated as he said, "Satan, you may cross-examine the witness."

A puff of red smoke and the smell of sulfur preceded Satan's appearance. Having said he did not wear red, there he stood dressed in a ridiculously red, cliché Halloween costume from the tips of his horns to the point of his spiky tail, complete with a pitchfork.

His appearance included a pointy beard that made his teeth to appear like shark's teeth. In the midst of the seriousness of the court, I couldn't help but smile at his impudence.

"Satan, what is the meaning of this? Why are you dressed in that idiotic costume?" Zedkiel's admonishment was clear in his tone.

"Because this scene, this trial, and with respect brothers, you nine are about as ridiculous as my costume. Chamuel has done nothing wrong. He did not disobey *Father* at Atlantis. I know that for a fact, but *Father* has sworn me to secrecy. That our strait-laced brother here disobeyed a direct order from our *Father* is also as laughable as my costume or this trial."

Satan folded his arms and glared at Zedkiel.

Zedkiel blanched, then straightened to his full height and squared his shoulders. "You are not here as a witness but as defense counsel. I suggest you confine yourself to that role."

"Fine." Satan flounced to the platform and snapped his fingers. His outfit transformed into a custom-tailored, black Brioni two-piece suit with a crisp, white Burberry shirt, fire-engine red Gucci bow tie, Balmain metal appliqué oxfords, and finished nicely, with a pair of classic Ray Bans. I admired his style. Not many angels can pull off mortal high fashion with the causal panache Satan does so effortlessly.

Satan flipped off his sunglasses and launched his attack on Rochel.

"Rochel, did you witness Chamuel commit this act?"

"No, but—"

"Answer yes or no only." Satan's eyes beaded. "Did Chamuel say he was on a mission from *Father*?"

"Yes, but—"

"Yes or no only." Satan strutted to the dock and leaned on it. "So, is it possible that Chamuel simply carried out *Father's* orders?"

"Yes, but I can't see—"

Irritation tinged Satan's reply: "Again, yes or no . . . so you have no proof that Chamuel acted alone out of disdain for mortals, do you?"

Rochel fidgeted and cast a silent glance at Nemamaih that spoke volumes.

"No further questions."

The next two witnesses went much the same way, and with this questioning, my hope rose.

Nemamaih's voice boomed, and I jumped. For such a tiny stature, she sure packed a wallop when she wanted to.

"I call my last witness, Archangel of the Seraphim, out of the House of Raphael." A note of confidence rang in her voice that hadn't been there for the other witnesses.

My mind buzzed like the angels' auras. Nemamaih practically glowed. Why did my gut feel like it dropped six inches? What else could Raphael add to the other witnesses? Yes, we'd gone to see Queen Alequora together, but I don't recall saying anything incriminating, but . . . did I? OK, I asked if I could incinerate her because I despised her, but what of it? Alequora's totally unlikeable personality got the better of me. Well, really, Lilith's influence. The Alequora from childhood vibrated life and love.

After Raphael's swearing-in, Nemamaih began her questioning, but she altered the order. Apart from minor details, it was as if Raphael and the others read from a script.

Then Nemamaih asked about the meeting with the queen. "Did Chamuel seem wound up to you?"

Raphael replied, "You know Camie, always a bit of a hothead. He can't tolerate the *Father* being ignored."

"Interesting you should choose the word 'hothead.'"

Raphael flushed and stared at his hands.

"Did he say or do anything that caused you concern?"

Raphael mumbled.

"Please repeat your answer clearly for the court."

"He asked if he could incinerate Queen Alequora, but I dissuaded him."

"What happened next?"

"Alequora would not repent."

"How did Chamuel react to that?"

"He said he had a message from the *Father*. He said the *Father* would unleash *His* power so Alequora might know *Him* as the *One True God.*"

"What did you do next?"

"We left, and I returned to my duty of observing Greece."

"And . . ." Nemamaih drilled on

"I took a break and went to discuss with Camie how we might approach Alequora to get her to change her mind, but I couldn't find him."

"So, what did you do?" She seemed like the cat that got the cream.

"I thought he might have gone back to fulfill the *Father's* instruction, so I returned to Atlantis."

"And what did you see?" Nemamaih practically purred.

"I arrived in time to see Camie destroy the temple."

My heart fell through my feet. How did I not know this? Why hadn't he told me? I turned to Satan for reassurance. He shrugged.

Nemamaih continued, glee bubbling with her next question. "And what state of mind did Chamuel appear to be in?"

"Full-on vengeance."

"You're powerful enough to have stopped him. Why didn't you?"

"I had no instruction from the *Father*. I could only watch."

The heartbreak in that last statement pierced my heart.

"No further questions."

Satan studied Raphael for some time before opening his line of questioning.

"Did you lose children in Atlantis, Raphael?"

"Yes, several; my heart still aches."

"I'm sorry for your loss. Is it possible that loss has colored your memory of events?"

"No, my memory is quite clear."

"It's hard to imagine a loss like that not affecting the way we view the world. Can you, before the Throne of *God*, say truthfully that those events didn't color your memories even a little bit?"

Raphael squirmed. He glanced at the dais, where *God* and *Christ* sat. He looked to his brethren.

"No."

"So, it is possible that Chamuel wasn't displaying, as you phrased it, 'full-on vengeance,' but that he might have been, in fact, fulfilling the will of *God*?"

"Possible, but—"

"Thank you. That will be all."

"For my first witness, I call Archangel of the Seraphim, out of the House of Chamuel."

I trembled as I stepped forward to the rail of the dock. Raphael's evidence left my confidence in surviving this in tatters. Satan had done his best, but the evidence damned me.

"Chamuel, did you have an assignment from the *Father*?" Satan took a casual stance.

"Yes."

"Please inform the court what it involved." Satan leaned forward over the lectern.

"I cannot, as *Father* swore me to secrecy."

I held my chin high.

"In other words, you honor the *Father* before preserving your own life. Is that correct?"

"I honor the *Father*. My life is *His* to command."

"And command you *He* did when it came to Atlantis, did *He* not?"

"Yes."

"Would you say your *Father's* command was fulfilled?" Satan's eyes narrowed.

"Yes."

"Did you do it gleefully?"

"No, my heart was torn over the children and the vulnerable and those who kept the faith, but what would be left to them if I had spared them? The world they knew would be gone, and their very survival would have been in jeopardy."

The pain my soul carried over the deaths of the children could not be expressed in words.

"Did you do it because you hold mortals in contempt?" Satan rapped the lectern.

"Do you mean, do I hold mortals accountable for their choice to serve or betray the *Father*? Contempt . . . no; accountable, yes."

"You exacted the *Father's* will to hold the Alanterian society culpable for not serving the *One True God*?"

"Yes."

"Did you follow the *Father's* dictates?"

My eyes bulged. My breath shortened. Why had he asked that? He knew I hadn't. But I had no choice but to answer honestly. My *Father* would know if I lied.

"Before the throne of *God*, I admit, I may have gone too far."

The gallery broke into an uproar.

I paced the halls while I waited for the verdict. Had I damned myself by my admission; or would my telling the truth count in my favor?

The doors swung open, and Zedkiel's voice commanded my presence.

The complete silence in the chamber felt worse than the condemnation I experienced on my first walk of shame to the dock. Even the auras stilled.

Zedkiel's compassionate countenance did nothing to reassure me as I took to the dock. He reread the charges. "How does the Angelic Tribunal of the Heavenly Host find in the matter at hand?"

Raphael bowed. His voice communicated to me the burden of his heart.

"Guilty."

Zedkiel prostrated himself before the dais of the *Most High.*

"Oh, my gracious, merciful *Lord*, you have heard the verdict of your chosen ones, but it is your will and yours alone that determines our futures. Please, oh *Lord*, communicate your will to your humble servant."

The sound of wind through the trees rushed from the dais and swept over Zedkiel.

"Thank you, *Most Holy One*, for your wisdom and compassion."

His first glance was to me; then, he faced those assembled.

"The *Lord* your *God*, first and foremost, wishes these remarks to be committed to the record."

"Archangel of the Seraphim, out of the House of Chamuel, it is not for the destruction of Atlantis that I pass this sentence, but, by your own admission, you strayed from my command. Son, I cannot allow that to go unpunished. As you know, the sentence for such an act is banishment."

My blood ran cold. My heart ceased to beat. *Banishment.* From the presence of the Lord? How would I survive without my connection to *the Father?*

"But because you were fulfilling my command, I choose to be merciful. Zedkiel will pronounce your sentence."

Zedkiel choked as he began. Clearly, the duty didn't sit well with him.

"Archangel of the Seraphim, out of the House of Chamuel, the verdict is this: You will serve one thousand years in a corporeal, mortal form . . ."

Mortal. A thousand years! What's worse banishment or this?

". . . to overcome your disrespect of mortals."

Living as one is going to teach me that?

"During the thousand years, you will experience many lives, each one different and with new lessons. The joys of fatherhood shall be yours, so you will appreciate what you robbed Raphael and others of, but more, so you will appreciate why the *Heavenly Father* loves his Creation."

I doubt a hundred thousand years could explain it to me.

"You will live in many cultures and learn many religions to see how the *One True God* is featured in them all.

"At times, you will be blessed by wealth, at others, poverty. Longevity will grace some lives, but in others, early death from disease and disaster will occur.

"Loved ones will be taken from you. Wars will disrupt your life."

Yes, why are mortals so ready to engage in war?

"You will know what it is to hate and to want vengeance or justice."

Hmm, been there, done that.

"Your body will take many forms—some human, others not, but all will be mortal."

Other forms? what does that mean?

"The sum total of your lives will encompass the mortal experience in order for you to appreciate and understand their fallibility but also their great capability to love.

"When you have proven yourself worthy; the *Lord* most *Holy* has one last mission. It will be revealed to you when the time is right. Suffice to say, the *Father* has great plans for redemption in which you will play a key role."

That, at least, sounds promising.

"Oh, before I forget, when you are in the heavenly plane, the memories of all your lives will reside in you, but when you are in the earthly plane, you will have no memory of any past lives' events . . ."

Oh great, I go in blind every time. Sooo, helpful.

". . . but you will have written on your heart the lessons from each. That is, what you have learned concerning the mortal condition will carry forward."

I suppose that makes sense. Otherwise, it would be a waste of time.

"However, during your last life, to fulfill your mission, key memories will return to you at critical times. Watch for them. Figure out their meaning and put them to good use."

If it didn't sound so cryptic, it might be interesting.

"Do you accept the sentence?"

What choice did I have?

"As I said, my life is the *Father's* to command." Those words were hard to swallow now.

I comprehended why Zedkiel had been chosen for the task. He had a close affinity with man. He understood the plight of man, his struggle since the fall in the Garden, and of all the archangels; he alone knew the ramifications of this sentence.

Chapter 6

Introspection

⊰⩴ ⅃ℐⅎⅎℛℼℿℾ ℛ⅃⅃⊰

'd been back in the Heavenly Realm from my last life for a few days, but I always spent those initial days secluded in my quarters, processing that life and praying to the *Father* for understanding. This one proved conflicting. I understood the devotion to the god they worshipped, and like the *Father,* all deities call for sacrifice, but a suicide bomber? *Father* might ask us to lay down our lives, but *He* would never have us kill innocents in doing so. But then, who am I to talk after what I did to Atlantis?

The years had not dulled the memories—quite the opposite. As always, the *Father's* wisdom prevailed. Throughout my lives as a mortal, certain events gave clarity regarding the extent to which I had disobeyed and the pain I had caused my brethren, not the least of which was the murder of my children when the Romans sacked Carthage. On the return from that life to the Heavenly Realm, I begged forgiveness from the *Father. He* said *He* had forgiven me at the time, or *He* would have banished me. It was not *He* from whom I needed forgiveness. I swallowed. Would they forgive me?

After the *Father* called the angels together, I fell to my knees and poured out my heart, needing them to understand that my suffering had given me insight into theirs. Not that I placed my sorrow higher but that

I had experienced the grief only a parent can know, something of which I was ignorant about at the time.

Raphael spoke for the assembly.

"Our hearts still grieve for our children, Chamuel, and you will find, time does not lessen that. We recall their faces bright with laughter, their childish innocence, and their potential every day, but we would not be worthy of being servants of the *Father* if we did not forgive you, hard as that might have been for some."

He came forward, extended his hands to me, and as I stood, he embraced me. My tears wet the shoulder of his robe.

"Camie, we feel for your suffering but rejoice in your understanding and acceptance of the extent of the atrocity you committed. Come now, join your brethren."

I struggled to look my fellow angels in the eyes as they came forward to greet me. After murdering their children, how could they be so accepting?

But now, I reclined in a comfortable armchair in one of the many lounge rooms throughout the Heavenly Kingdom, chatting with Raphael and Zedkiel. The convivial atmosphere of the room with *Father's* glory streaming in on the brightly colored flowers eased my concerns.

"So, how many lives is this?" Zedkiel asked.

I rubbed my chin. "I've kinda lost count. Fifteen, sixteen?"

Raphael chipped in. "I think it's seventeen. You must be close to your last."

"Possibly, but it's hard to tell with the time spent in the Heavenly Realm between lifetimes. Our time here is so different from Earth's. A millennium might pass on Earth in a blink of an eye here. My first life as a goat herder must have been about eleven thousand years ago, Earth time. I miss the peace and simplicity of that life. Sure, I owned little and slept with my animals, but none of the twenty-first-century issues existed. The air and waters were pure. Nature had its place, and as long as it didn't threaten my goats, I left it in peace. This killing *God's* creatures for sport in the modern world is beyond my comprehension."

Zedkiel leaned forward. "Do you have an affinity with mortals now?"

I sighed. "I have an appreciation of the finite life of a mortal and what it means to exist within the limitations of their five corporeal senses, if *Father* allows. I still can't come to terms with how many reject the Word of the *Father*. Lucifer has a field day down there. Mortals are so easily corrupted. While they have a great capacity for love, once Lucifer turns their hearts, hate reigns supreme."

"Enough of this seriousness; what is your funniest memory?" Raphael asked.

"Now, that would have to be the time I took my laundry to my fiancée's as I had no washing facilities at my rented room. I heard what I thought was my beloved in the kitchen, so I left the scrub room to greet her. I opened the back door, and to my everlasting embarrassment, it was her mother, stark naked. She grabbed the nearest object to cover herself. The dishcloth didn't do much."

Zedkiel and Raphael gripped their stomachs laughing.

Raphael managed to get out between bouts of laughter, "Why was she naked?"

"I have no idea, and I was too embarrassed to ask."

Zedkiel commented, "I think it's funny that whichever culture you ended up in, your name always derived to Camie. Like Kamau in Africa and Kambiz when you were Afghani."

Raphael grinned. "You were Camaraja in India."

"I guess I needed to keep some sense of my own identity."

Raphael asked, "What was the most unusual life?"

"As a werewolf. I was terribly misunderstood. Most of the supposed hermits are actually werewolves. Better to live a solitary life than to be persecuted. I both loved and hated the full moon. I enjoyed the freedom of running through the forest, on the scent of a rabbit, and the joy of being one with nature. Those were great. The fear of discovery was not."

"Saddest?"

"You mean apart from losing my children? I have had many sad lives, but within many, I found peace and joy. Illness, for one, brought me closer to the *Father*. Life as a child beggar in Babylon—"

"Weren't you Kalumtum then?" Raphael interrupted.

"Mm-hmm, but as I was saying, it showed me both the worst and best of human nature. My deformed foot and leg meant I had to walk with a crutch. Since I couldn't work the fields, my father set me to begging to earn my keep. If I didn't bring home enough, he beat me."

Raphael pulled a face of angelic indignation. "Cruelty to those weaker than themselves seems to be a favorite play of Lucifer's."

"Don't I know it; many spat at me as I sat there, but I had regulars who knew of my father's treatment of me. Sometimes, other beggars would ask if I had enough and share their take with me."

Zedkiel's eyes sparkled. "That reminds me of Hebrews 13:16—

Do not neglect to do good and to share what you have, for such sacrifices are pleasing to God—no matter how little we have, we can share."

"Yes, I was struck by how much more generous the poor were than the wealthy."

"Mm-hmm. How often do we hear, 'I earned it. It's mine to do with as I please?' The lure of money is one of Lucifer's greatest ploys."

Raphael's lips bunched like a prune. "But please continue, Camie."

"Sure. My human father didn't know it, but every day after I finished, I hobbled to the temple to make my offering to the goddess, the Queen of the Night. Sometimes, it was a piece of fruit, others a small coin. And I said a prayer of petition to her."

"Then, one day, a priestess approached me.

She said, "Child, I have observed your faithfulness these last three years and listened to your prayers. When many would ask for relief from their suffering, you have prayed for your family. Because of your sacrifice, I offer you a place in the temple as a servant."

"I can't tell you how I rejoiced. I was the happiest girl who served the priestesses and gave thanks every day of my life."

"But weren't you a deity yourself once?"

Zedkiel touched on a bittersweet memory.

"Yes, in Nepal. And yes, my name translated to Camie—Kaamini. At the age of three, I was chosen to be the Kumari, the incarnation of the female goddess Taleju. My life as a living goddess had its strictures. I had to sit calmly and silently when petitioners came. I had to preside over religious ceremonies. My feet weren't to touch the ground, so they carried me everywhere on a litter. But I lived in a palace of great beauty and dressed in fine robes; my face was painted in intricate designs, and I had all my needs taken care of."

"What was it like, being worshipped?" Raphael asked.

"A bit weird, people constantly wanted to touch me to receive a blessing. My silence was taken as their prayers answered. I don't think I ever felt any kind of power, though."

"How long did you serve?" Zedkiel's curiosity tugged his mouth.

"Until I was eleven; once a girl menstruates or cuts herself and bleeds, the goddess's spirit is believed to leave. It's also bad luck for a Kumari to get her period while serving, so they kick you out early."

"Wow, what a comedown, from goddess back to possible poverty."

Raphael had hit the nail on the head.

"All too true; for a start, I could barely walk because I had been carried everywhere. I had no social skills, as silence was my virtue. I couldn't take care of myself, having had everything done for me. My parents were poor, so I went from a palace to dirt floors. But worst, people shunned me, and I could never marry. However, the love of my parents brought me great happiness as I had never experienced such a personal connection."

"Such a contrast to your Babylonian father . . ." Raphael pointed out.

"But such was the punishment. I was to experience the full range of the mortal experience. I've been murdered, killed in war, died prematurely in an accident, and have lived to be a great grandfather. I've been a powerful king. Lots of cultures, but in every one, there is a need to connect with a deity. The *Father* has it ingrained into our subconscious."

"What will you do if this is your last life?" Zedkiel raised an interesting question.

"I know I will miss it. Well, not all of it. Some of it was pretty crappy. But the connectedness to other living souls and the different way mortals relate to the *Father*—that I will miss."

"On a brighter note, if this is your last life, the *Father* has a mission for you. Are you curious?" Raphael asked.

"Redemption; I was a priest once and thought that might have been what the *Father* meant, but clearly, this will be different. I just hope I don't screw it up like I did the last mission."

Zedkiel reached out and patted me on the knee. "I think you have learned your lesson, Camie. All should go well."

Chapter 7

Pain as the Teacher

𝔛𝟩𝟤𝔜 𝔛𝟩 ✓𝟢𝟩 𝟩𝔛𝕏𝟢𝟩𝟤

It began with a single tear, a very human tear. In that moment of introspection, experiencing the moisture forming on my new human visage, I contemplated the meaning of a tear.

What a curious and profound thing a single tear is. Human science can describe it in minute detail. Biology can tell you what it is made up of. It can break down that tear into its various chemical compounds, amino acids, and proteins, but it falls woefully short of understanding its purpose.

In my mortal lives, I had shed many—some for love, others in self-ishness; some in frustration, others in fear. But this tear, this precious gift of understanding of the *Father's* love for the world, represented my acceptance of the mortal condition.

Suspended in the gateway between the Heavenly Realm and the earthly planes of existence, the knowledge that on the other side, humanity waited for me no longer filled me with fear. This time, hope blossomed in my heart.

Cameron's mother, Josie, turned at the sound of small feet to see him dragging his teddy bear by its ear into the living room where she watched TV, his three-year-old face lit with an inner glow.

"Camie, what are you doing out of bed?" Josie asked.

"Dream 'gain, Mommy." Camie put his teddy on the couch as he crawled onto his mother's knee.

"Another dream, my angel?" Josie studied his face, seeking signs of distress, but a calm radiance greeted her.

"Angels fight." He picked up his teddy and cuddled it.

"Now, Camie, we've been over this. There is no need to be frightened. Angels don't exist." Josie stroked his dark hair. She'd lost count of the number of times he'd had this dream.

"Not fright. Good angel win; he on my side." Camie's cherubic face split into a grin.

Josie sighed. His descriptions had been so vivid. A female in black with bat-like wings and an angel in shining white with three pairs of wings. Where he'd seen images of this, she had no idea. She didn't think her mother, even as religious as she was, would show Camie images as frightening as a demon. Funny that he called them both angels, though.

As Camie grew, imaginary friends replaced the dreams. Today, Josie had to pick him up from school because he had punched another boy. And, yet again, he used the excuse, "she made me do it." Maybe she'd been too lenient on him. This time she would punish him—after she'd talked to him, though.

Once she got him home, she sat him at the table in the homey kitchen and asked him to explain what happened.

"Jerry hit me with a stick," Camie said as if that explained everything.

Josie put her hands flat on the table. "And what have I said to do in those situations?"

Camie dropped his head and mumbled, "To get a teacher. That's what he said, but she said I should show him who's boss and hit him. She made me do it."

"How many times have I said that no one can make you do anything unless you want to?" A little exasperation crept into her voice, and she schooled herself to remain calm.

Camie's head shot up, and she inhaled sharply at the intensity of his eyes.

"You make me do things."

Josie admitted he had a point. How could she explain the difference? She took his small hand in hers. "That is true, but there is a difference between a mother's love teaching you things like the importance of brushing your teeth or when you have done something that is not acceptable and saying someone made you do something you know is wrong."

Tears filled Camie's eyes. "But she did."

"No, Camie, you must have wanted to, or she could not have made you do it. And besides, she's just imaginary. You need to take responsibility and say you did it." She got up from the chair and patted him on the back. "But right now, you are to go to your room. I'll be taking your electronic devices. When you are prepared to accept and admit you wanted to hit Jerry, you can come out and tell me. Now, get up and go to your room, young man."

Camie stomped down the corridor.

After his mother left, carrying his electronic games, he flung himself on his bed, his arms folded over his chest.

A dark shape materialized in one corner of his room. She fed his anger. "You don't need to do as she says. You did nothing wrong. Being punished for standing up for yourself is wrong."

A bright shape in the other corner spoke: "Camie, listen to your heart. Deep down, you know what you did was wrong. Sure, Jerry shouldn't have hit you, but hitting him back is not the answer. Violence breeds violence."

"What would that stuffed shirt know? It felt good, didn't it? You showed Jerry he couldn't hit you and get away with it, didn't you?"

"Mm-hmm, I wasn't going to let him just hit me and then run off crying. I'm braver than that." Camie sat up on his bed and turned to the bright figure. "You just want me to do what I'm told. Well, I'm going to do what makes me feel good from now on."

Raphael faded from sight and shot to the Heavenly Realm. He paced back and forth in front of the *Father's* door while he waited for an audience, wracking his brain as to how he'd let Lilith gain such a hold on Camie. He needed permission to intervene or else the darkness would consume Camie.

He'd calmed a little by the time the attendant ushered him into the Holy Sanctum but not enough to prevent him from blurting out the situation before prostrating himself. At his oversight, he blushed and flung himself onto the floor. The *Father* chuckled.

Raphael, I don't think I have seen you this worked up since Atlantis. Please rise and tell me what you think needs to be done.

"I need permission to intervene."

And how do you propose to do that?

Raphael threw his hands in the air, lamenting, "I don't know."

He dropped them to his sides, staring at the floor as if it could give him the answers.

Tell me, what does the mother know?

Raphael studied the delicately carved marble statue of Adam and Eve before the Fall.

"She knows he has imaginary friends and that he blames his bad behavior on one of them."

What doesn't she know?

A star beam illuminated the answer for Raphael.

"She doesn't know who the imaginary friends are." He slapped his thigh.

I give you permission to influence Chamuel's mother to ask more about his imaginary friends. Camie's grandmother will know what to do.

After Raphael took his leave, he dashed through the gateway, arriving in Camie's room in time to hear Lilith say, "You go and tell your mother that you didn't do anything wrong, and you shouldn't be punished . . . that you're not going back to your room. She will have to agree."

Camie charged down the hall and into the lounge and planted himself in front of his mother, hands on his hips.

"Have you come to admit you were wrong?" she asked.

"No. I didn't do anything wrong. I won't be punished." He stamped his foot. "I'm not going back to my room."

The stunned look on Camie's face when his mother's hand shot out, spun him around, and walloped him on the backside brought a grin to Raphael's face.

Josie's neck turned red, and her lips tightened. "You will not speak to me in that manner."

Camie's lip trembled. "She said you would have to agree." He sniffed.

Raphael nudged Josie's mind.

"Camie, go to your room. I need to ring Nansie."

After Camie left, Josie picked up her mobile and dialed her mother. "Mom, I'm at my wit's end to know what to do with Camie. I've never seen him behave like this. He just stamped his foot at me and told me he wasn't going to do what I say. He was so rude, I smacked him. Then he repeated what he's been saying for a long time—she made me do it."

After listening for a moment, Josie said, "No, I guess they don't sound that imaginary."

Josie put her free hand on the back of her head. "Ask their names? I never thought of that. I'll do it now and get back to you."

She hung up and padded down the hall to Camie's room. After she entered, she sat on his bed. "Camie, who are these friends of yours?"

"The angels . . ."

His mother blinked. "The angels?"

"You know, from my dreams."

Her hands gripped the chair's arms. "Do they have names?"

"Yes ma'am. Raphael and Lilith."

Her face paled. "Camie, you must not speak to Lilith again."

"But why? She's my friend!" Camie wailed.

"A friend doesn't make you do bad things, Camie. She is not your friend."

Once back in the lounge, Josie rang her mother again. Her voice quivered as she spoke. "Mom, I did like you said and asked Camie about his friends. He said they were the angels from his dreams. He says their names are Raphael and Lilith. You know how he's always described the female as having bat wings. I thought you'd been telling him tales. I've never believed in angels or demons or, for that matter, God, but is she the demon Lilith?"

After a pause, Josie said, "Yes, changes in terms of how he views them. He used to say they fought over him and the one in white won. He used to be pleased he was on his side, but he seems more and more influenced by this Lilith of late."

She frowned and ran her hand through her hair. "Is that really necessary? It seems a bit drastic and archaic."

She nodded. "If you say so . . . thanks for believing me, Mom."

After she hung up, she went back to Camie's room to tuck him in. She kissed him on the forehead and then laid her hand on his and recited a prayer.

"Now I lay me down to sleep, I pray *the Lord* my soul to keep. If I die before I wake, I pray *the Lord* my soul to take."

She shivered.

Raphael sent her a warm burst to comfort her. He'd stand guard as he had done since Camie had come to Earth the first time.

When Josie opened the door, she did a double-take. She hadn't been sure what to expect, but this young, trendy female standing next to her mother was the furthest thing from the black robe, huge Bible, and enormous cross that she'd seen in the movies.

Her mother introduced the exorcist as Paula, and Josie welcomed her into her home. She asked her mother to take Paula to the lounge while she made coffee.

Once they had their coffees, Paula asked Josie, "How long has Camie had these imaginary friends?"

Josie's brows knitted. "I think he first mentioned them when he was four. I didn't think anything of it as all kids have imaginary friends."

"And when did he begin displaying antisocial behavior?"

"The first time he said, 'she made me do it,' was after he drew on the walls with a Sharpie. He was about five, about eighteen months ago."

"And has it gotten worse?" Paula put her mug on the table as if to emphasize the point.

"Most of it I thought was just Camie being a kid and testing my boundaries, but the incidents have been more numerous, and then yesterday, he punched a kid and knocked his tooth out."

"What did you do?"

Josie ran her finger around the rim of her mug. "I explained that he couldn't go around punching people and sent him to his room and told him to come out when he was ready to take responsibility. Instead, he basically told me he was going to do what he pleased. When I smacked him—and I've never needed to before—he said she told him I would have to do what he wanted. I sent him to his room and rang my mother. She suggested I ask about these so-called friends. I asked him for their names. When he said Lilith, my blood ran cold. Mom suggested you."

"This is important." Paula leaned forward. "Do you think he is possessed?"

At the word possessed, Josie shrank in on herself. "He talks about them like he can see both of them and that they both say things to him, so I don't think he is possessed so much as influenced by Lilith."

"The other being . . .?"

"Raphael."

"Well, that's good news. It means we have a powerful angel on our side. I will need to speak to Camie to assess whether he is or is not possessed. Even if he isn't, we still need to cleanse the house and protect Camie from Lilith."

Josie called Camie to the lounge and introduced him to Paula. Camie climbed onto his mother's knee and stared at Paula across the coffee table.

Paula said, "Please tell me why you told your mother being punished was unfair?"

Camie chewed a fingernail and muttered, "She told me not to talk to you."

Josie dug her fingers into his shoulder as she gripped it. "I told you not to talk to her."

Paula said, "It's OK. Why did she say that?"

"She said you'd make her go away." Camie hunched forward and crossed his arms.

"Where was she when she said this?"

He kicked at the coffee table. "Standing at the head of the bed."

"And the other angel?"

"By the door . . ."

"So, you see them, and they talk to you?"

"Uh-huh."

"What does he say?"

"He says not to listen to her, that she'll get me into trouble."

"And does she?"

Camie scowled and didn't answer.

"I take your silence to mean *yes*. You can go back to your room for a bit now, Camie."

After Camie left, Paula said, "I don't believe he is possessed"—Josie sighed in relief—"but he is significantly influenced by Lilith. I think it wise to cleanse the house, particularly his room, and banish Lilith. It would be helpful if you took him to church as well. He will be better protected if more people are praying for him."

Josie nodded. "Certainly. I always thought my mother was nuts for believing in the tooth fairy, but I clearly have a lot to learn. How does the rest work?"

Paula smiled. "Nothing too drastic now that we don't have to exorcise Camie. I say a few prayers, sprinkle some holy water, and send Lilith back to Hell. Unfortunately, she is powerful and won't stay there for long, but I should be able to stop her from accessing Camie for a few years, at least."

Paula retrieved what she needed from her bag and began.

As Paula prayed, Raphael cornered Lilith. The level of malice demons exuded always took him by surprise.

"Don't think we don't know that thing you worship has something planned involving Chamuel. We're not going to stand idly by and let it come to fruition. If I have to wipe Chamuel from the face of the Earth, I will," she screeched.

When Paula called for the *Lord Jesus* to expel Lilith, Raphael shot a blast of Holy Fire of *Elohim* at her, driving her back to Hell.

Like Paula, he knew it wouldn't hold Lilith for long, but he had strong confidence that Paula had broken her influence over Camie for now, at least.

Chapter 8

Let the Games Begin

7✓ ✓∞7 ⚹7ᒣ 77⋺

News Headline:
Woodbridge Township Times
"Miracle Boy Survives Car Inferno!"

ine-year-old Cameron Rathmeuson survived a fiery crash when the car his mother was driving careened off the I-78 near New Providence, plunging down the embankment before colliding with a tree and bursting into flames.

Cameron, or Camie as he likes to be called, claims an angel wrapped its wings around him, saving him from the fire. When asked about the angel, Camie replied, "His name is Raphael, and he's been with me since I was little. Lilith was, too, until someone got rid of her. She made me do bad things."

Camie was too upset about the death of his mother to say more. Later, Camie's grandmother, Margaret, rocked him while he cried as they sat on the couch in her quaint cottage. She suspected Lilith had been behind the crash but needed to be careful in her approach to asking questions. "You told me that a deer appeared in front of the car, and your mother swerved to miss it. Was there anything odd about it?"

"Its eyes were orange." Camie sniffed and rubbed his nose with his sleeve.

In Margaret's experience, deer eyes did reflect orange, but at least Camie had begun to open up.

"Anything else unusual?" she didn't want to frighten Camie by suggesting Lilith tried to kill him, but to know what extent of protection she needed to provide, Margaret had to be sure.

"It just appeared—*boom*, in front of the car. Didn't run onto the road, just appeared."

Margaret processed this piece of information. Yes, it could be a trick of the car's headlights, but it might be something more. "I see. It just materialized."

Camie nodded.

"Was there anything surrounding it? You know, like an aura?" Although she hoped there wouldn't be, she suspected this to be a critical piece of information.

"It looked like its back had flames dancing on it." Camie shifted to look at his grandmother. His lip trembled. "It was Lilith, wasn't it?"

Margaret bit back the reassuring lie she wanted to tell him, but if Lilith was targeting him, he needed to know. "Yes, but we can have special prayers said to *Jesus* to protect you. And you can add it to your daily prayers. How about I get you a Saint Benedict medal?"

Camie brightened. "Who's he?"

"He's a Catholic saint who protects you from the devil."

"But we're not Catholic? Will he still help?"

"I'm sure he'll be willing to help a nine-year-old boy." Margaret smiled and kissed him on the forehead. "Now, off to do your teeth and then bed. I will come in about ten minutes to say prayers with you."

As soon as he left the room, she began making phone calls.

⚬⚭⚬

With graduation from elementary school just weeks away, Camie's excitement about winning a medal in either math or science grew. He'd gotten *A*s in both subjects all year. He hadn't done so well on the poetry bit in English, not even after his grandmother had pointed out that the Psalms were poetry. Still, he'd gotten good marks in other areas. With his mind focused on his grades, he didn't notice the gang of boys following him across the schoolyard as he headed to the locker room.

He had just fitted the key to the lock on his locker at the back of the room when a sneering voice echoed in the space. "I smell a nerd. Talk about a pong."

"Yeah, me too—disgusting."

His familiarity with those voices caused his gut to tighten. He shivered at the gang's reputation for cornering academic students and destroying their belongings.

Footsteps squeaked on the concrete floor as they approached him. Which way to run? Bodies appeared to his right, so he headed left, only to be confronted by more bodies. Trapped, his eyes grew wide, and his breath came in short gasps.

The leader of the group, Justin, took a step forward. "Well, if it isn't miracle boy."

Mostly, Camie didn't regret his statement about the angels, but at times like this, he wished the article had never been written.

Justin strode up to him and poked him in the chest. "Where's your angel now?"

Camie wondered the same thing.

The other boys closed in on him, corralling him in the center of a circle. Someone shoved him in the back, causing him to stumble toward the boy in front of him, who kicked him in the shin.

Justin flung Camie's locker door open and began rifling through his belongings. "Well, lookie her . . . a Bible!" He ripped out some pages and

66

sidled back to Camie. "How about you tell us a story?" He shoved the pages in Camie's mouth. "Chew."

In Camie's dry mouth, the pages sandpapered his tongue and scratched his throat as he swallowed. He recalled the horror stories of what these bullies did to those who begged or cried. If you stood up to them, then they might be a little lenient. He pulled himself to his full height and eyeballed Justin.

Justin grinned. Not the sort of grin that said *everything's cool*. It was the type of grin that said, *so you want to play it rough.*

Camie took up the challenge. "I'll tell you a story about what happens to bullies in the Bible. It's about a man called Daniel who was faithful to *God*, and *God* delivered him. Daniel lived a righteous life, and his intelligence and integrity shone, so much so that the king promoted him. Those who'd thought they should be in Daniel's position tricked the king into making a law that said anyone who didn't pray to the king would be thrown into the lions' den. They knew Daniel would not give up his faith, and then they waited for him to pray to the *Lord*. The king had no choice but to throw Daniel in with the lions, but Daniel prayed to be delivered, and because he was faithful, *God* delivered him. The king threw his enemies into the lions' den. *God* will deliver me too, and you will get yours."

Justin's face turned puce. He moved to within inches of Camie's face and whispered in his ear, "I know that decrepit thing you worship has something planned for you, but we won't let you complete your mission."

When Justin's eyes locked onto Camie's, the flash of fire in their depths turned Camie's innards to jelly. Between his confusion over the notion of a "mission" and fear of Lilith, Camie's hand rose to his throat, where it contacted the medallion. He grasped it and said a prayer for deliverance from the demon to the saint.

"Now, what are we trying to protect." Justin yanked Camie's hand away. "Ooo, pretty."

As Justin's hand snaked toward the Seal of Solomon sigil that Camie's grandmother gave him for protection, Camie expected it to be ripped from his neck.

Justin curled his fingers around the medal and then wrenched his hand away, pain screwing up his face as he looked at the burn on his palm. "You'll pay for that." One hand balled into a fist and drew back behind his ear. The other gripped Camie behind the neck.

Camie scrunched his eyelids, waiting for Justin's fist to slam into his face. It never came. Instead, he heard a familiar voice saying, "They followed Camie in here."

Justin shoved Camie away, saying, "I will get you someday."

As the teacher rounded the last locker, Justin's gang bolted for the door.

Camie hugged his friend, Ari.

From his perch on the stool at the kitchen bench, Camie watched his grandmother make his favorite snack, pepperoni pizza Hot Pockets, as he related the day's events. His grandmother listened intently without interrupting. When he finished, she handed him the plate and congratulated him on keeping calm.

Camie stuffed the last piece of savory goodness into his mouth, pizza sauce running down his fingers and dripping onto his shirt. He grunted.

She asked if he had said a prayer of gratitude, and he mumbled something around his mouthful. After swallowing, he asked, "What did Lilith mean by 'mission?'"

His grandmother seated herself on the stool next to him and took both his hands in hers. "You know not everyone has angels in their lives like you do. That makes you special."

Camie felt her searching his face, perhaps looking for recognition.

"Mm-hmm, but what mission?"

His grandmother squeezed his hands. "Ever since the accident that killed your mother, I have sought guidance. First, the *Lord* told me you were special and that I needed to protect you to ensure you made it to adulthood. Then *He* told me he had a plan for you. Recently, he told me he intended to . . ."

Camie yelled for his grandfather as his grandmother's face drooped, and she slid from the chair.

His grandfather checked her breathing and pulse and sat her up. He shook her until she woke, then asked her to smile, raise her arms, and speak.

Camie struggled to comprehend that she couldn't do any of those things. "What's wrong with Nansie?"

His grandfather laid his hand on Camie's shoulder. "She's had a stroke, son. Call 911."

Camie thought he heard a female cackle.

Chapter 9

Fair-Weather Friends

As the never-ending wait for news of his grandmother's condition continued, Camie rested his head on his grandfather's shoulder in the hospital's shabby waiting room. He hiccupped from crying, and his nose had been rubbed raw from blowing it. The mental video of the incident replayed over and over as he thought of all the ways he might have prevented it from happening. Maybe if he'd stopped her from telling him about the mission, maybe Lilith wouldn't have attacked her. The coincidence of the stroke occurring just as his grandmother was about to tell him and that cackle after left him in no doubt who had hurt his grandmother.

But why had *God* let it happen? Surely, his grandmother's faith and devotion deserved better treatment than that. Maybe his grandfather could explain it. "Papa, why did *God* take my mother and let Nansie get sick?"

"I don't think *He* did, son. I'm pretty sure it was Lilith." His grandfather put his arm around Camie's shoulder.

Camie wiggled on the hard plastic seat, his dissatisfaction with that answer leaking into his voice. "Yes, I know that. But *God* let it happen." Tears threatened to fall again. "To people I love. Not once, but twice."

His grandfather replied, "You know the story of Job, how *God* allowed Lucifer to torment him because Lucifer claimed that Job was only faithful because of his wealth? Lucifer killed all Job's children, his cattle, and servants, but Job remained faithful. We are like Job. Our faith is being tested."

The unfairness of it rankled Camie; *God* was supposed to be just. He struggled to find the justice in this.

❦

Camie sat by his grandmother's bed in the rehab unit, balancing the iPad on the covers so she could watch the video his grandfather had taken of him receiving the science award. He hadn't wanted to go to graduation, but his grandfather said Nansie would want him to. Now, he wondered if she could actually see the screen.

When it finished, she put her good hand over his and squeezed. She said something, but to Camie, it sounded like the noises a baby might make. He assumed she was saying she was proud or something, so he thanked her and leaned in to kiss her cheek.

He picked up her Bible and read a couple of Psalms. Then he prayed for her. She always seemed calmer after he did that, but the hollow words held little meaning for him.

He prattled on about a movie he'd seen on TV, anything to fill the gap left by his grandmother's inability to speak clearly. His grandfather said little, preferring to massage her hand and arm. Apparently, massage helped the nerves to regain function or some such thing. At least, he sat on her paralyzed side, so Camie didn't have to look at her drooping face.

The doctor stopped by on his rounds, and Camie had to leave the room. He hated being treated like a child and stood by the slightly open door to listen. His heart leaped when he overheard the doctor say that the likelihood of his grandmother going home in a few weeks looked good. That must mean an improvement in her condition. *God* must be answering his prayers. He said sorry to *God* for his grumpy behavior and lack of faith.

As the time approached for his grandmother to return home, Camie's disappointment in her progress grew. Yes, her speech had improved to the point that he could understand her if he concentrated hard, and she could move a couple of fingers a little on her bad hand, but she couldn't walk.

After their last visit to rehab, Camie asked his grandfather about the possibility of his grandmother walking again. He said that given time and lots of physical therapy, she may be able to walk with a frame but only short distances. What came next rammed the truth home. His grandfather said that because she couldn't take care of herself, he'd need to dedicate much of his time to that. Camie only heard "not take care of herself," and his gut told him she might never.

His grandfather went on to say he needed Camie to assist by dusting and vacuuming, making some meals, and doing his own washing. He said he'd teach Camie, but to Camie, Lilith had robbed him of his mother, grandmother, and now his childhood.

⚜

One afternoon, Camie entered the kitchen to find his grandfather brooding over a cup of coffee. His grey skin and the dark circles under his eyes, together with the slumped shoulders, indicated to Camie just how much it took out of his grandfather to look after his grandmother. He cleared his throat to make his presence known. His grandfather straightened, but the smile appeared forced to Camie.

Camie went to him and hugged him, asking, "Is everything OK, Papa?"

His grandfather rubbed Camie's back. "I'm just not getting much sleep, that's all. But I've been neglecting you, I think. So, tell me . . . what's on your mind?"

Camie set aside his misgivings about troubling his grandfather when his grandfather clearly had worries of his own, but he did need to discuss the matter of the mission. "Papa, did Nansie ever say anything to you about *God* having a mission for me?"

"She did tell me you were special in the eyes of *God* and that he had a plan for you, but she never said what, and I think it is too late to ask her."

His grandfather's serious face concerned Camie. "Why?"

"Nansie has significant memory loss. Mostly it's, short-term memory—can't remember where she put things, that kind of stuff—but I've also found some gaps in her more recent memories. Sure, she's fine with things from years ago. The good news is that with therapy, her memory will possibly improve and may even return."

Camie couldn't decide whether his grandfather believed that or not, but right now, it didn't help him. More to the point, he suspected Lilith had stolen those memories.

"Another positive, she can sit in the wheelchair longer. I'm getting a ramp for the front door so that we can take her into the garden."

Camie's smile didn't reach his eyes. While it encouraged him that his grandmother was making progress, the outcome he desired seemed unlikely.

After a summer of pretty much taking care of the house, Camie chomped at the bit to get to junior high. He hadn't had time to visit his friends, so catching up sounded great. It'd give him a break from the glumness of the house, where the brightest room, the lounge, had been converted to his grandmother's quarters since the house only had upstairs bedrooms. But more than the dim light, his grandfather's somber mood, particularly after an exercise session, weighed on the atmosphere. Camie's guilt poked him if he laughed, talked loudly, or played music. The accident that had robbed his grandmother of her independence had robbed them of their gift for living.

Rain pattered on the roof of his grandparents' house and tree leaves on the morning of his first school day. With the collar of his waterproof jacket turned up, he sloshed through the puddles on his way to the bus stop. His grandfather volunteered to drive him, but, in Camie's experience, he also fretted every moment apart from his wife. As the rain trickled down his neck, he regretted his decision to say no. Still, he enjoyed the freedom, the independence of making his own way to school.

After the teachers herded the seventh graders into the gymnasium, Camie scanned the faces of his fellow students. He waved at a few of his friends, pleased to see familiar faces given he didn't know most of the others. Then he spotted one face he'd have preferred not to. Clammy wetness stained his shirt under his armpits. *Justin.* What would Justin do if he ended up in the same class as him? It didn't bear thinking about, particularly if he still danced to Lilith's tune.

After finding his assigned locker, he stealthily made his way to his designated classroom and peeked in the door to establish if Justin's presence dominated the space. When he couldn't detect Justin, he grinned, and his grin widened when he spotted one of his friends. He sauntered into the room and threaded through the desks to take a seat next to Ari. Man, it felt great to catch up with him. The teacher entering the room cut their conversation short, but they had lunchtime to look forward to.

Apart from getting lost on his way to math, his first day lived up to his expectations and even getting lost gave him something to talk to his grandmother about. Given how limited his life had been over the summer break, he'd struggled to know what to say, but today he was bursting with news.

He bowled into the house, dropped his school bag by the bench, and headed to the fridge for a drink. He didn't bother to use a glass but simply swigged it from the bottle, hoping his grandfather wouldn't catch him. Next, he raided the cookie tin. How he missed his grandmother's chocolate chip cookies. The packet ones were better than nothing but not like the crunchy bite of a homemade cookie with its rich chocolate taste.

With one half-eaten cookie in one hand and two in the other, he knocked on the lounge door. When he entered, his grandfather said, "I take it from your grin, your first day went well."

A few crumbs sputtered from Camie's lips as he replied. He plunked himself into the chair next to his grandmother, who sat in her wheelchair, and took her hand before he launched into his account of the day's adventures.

The working half of his grandmother's face smiled when he ran out of puff about an hour later. She locked her boney fingers with his and slurred, "It's good to see you so animated. I worried this might all be too much. It wasn't much of a holiday, but school will do you good."

He had omitted the bit about Justin. Maybe he should have told them, but he didn't want them to worry.

For the first week, Camie and Justin didn't cross paths at all, not even in the cafeteria. None of the split classes included him, and it seemed that Justin used a different quadrangle to hang out in. But in the second week, Camie spotted Justin and one of his cronies sprawled on a tabletop holding court with what Camie feared were recruits.

Another week passed with no issues from Justin. Camie relaxed a little, hopeful that Justin had either outgrown bullying or was picking on someone else. Well, Camie didn't really want another person to suffer, but hey, better someone he didn't know than himself.

After a month, Camie dropped his guard as nothing even resembling a bully attack had occurred.

The following Monday morning, his calm shattered. His knees trembled as he froze before his locker. The words, *I'm coming for you,* scrawled in red ink left him numb. He wanted to run, get away from Justin, and go home where safety enveloped him, but he just wobbled on his jelly legs. A small crowd gathered behind him. An older student patted him on the shoulder and said, "Wow, what did you do to get the dude that riled?"

Camie's voice squeaked, "My medallion burnt his hand, and then *God* delivered me."

The boy scoffed. "Delivered, as in the post? You don't believe that crap, do you?"

"I don't know what to believe after *God* let Lilith hurt my mother and grandmother."

The boy clapped Camie on the back. "You're a weird one, but hey, if you need help with the bully, I'm Lucian." He extended his hand. "Call me if you need me."

Raphael's voice echoed in Camie's mind: "Don't do it. He's bad news; worse than Justin."

But Camie's only concern centered on not getting the crap beaten out of him.

Chapter 10
Bigger Fair-Weather Friends

ᘛᒥᔑᛸᔑᒥᘛ ᒪᛸᕉᗐᗐᒥᘛ ᘛᒪᒪᕉᛜᒥᘛ

A few days later, Justin cornered Camie in the toilet block. As he stood at the urinal with his fly undone, Camie's sense of vulnerability caused his palms to sweat. Before they could reach him, he tucked himself in and zipped his pants.

He stepped back from the urinal and aimed his feet for the exit. With his head down, he mumbled, "Excuse me, I need to leave now."

The wall of five boys didn't shift. Justin stepped forward and raised his arms, pivoting to face his friends. "Do you hear that? He thinks he's leaving." He spun back, using the momentum to punch Camie in the stomach.

Camie doubled over. He couldn't breathe. His innards felt bruised. Was this how it felt to die? The prayer his mother had said the night she found out about Lilith sprang to mind, the ending—*pray the Lord my soul to keep*—seemed fitting.

Justin yanked his head up by his hair and brought his face so close to Camie's that he could smell the booze on Justin's breath. Camie shivered at the malicious look in Justin's bloodshot, glazed eyes. He barely registered the pain when a hunk of hair ripped out as he jerked away, being so intent on escape. He charged at a small gap between the boys, but Justin's foot sent him crashing to the floor. He tasted blood and spat out a tooth.

He tensed his body for the barrage of boots he expected, but a vaguely familiar voice echoed in the tiled space. "What have we got here? Five against one . . . hardly sporting; how about you runts take us on? We'll even give you a few free punches."

Justin and his gang retreated behind Camie, and he raised his head. Lucian. He had four friends with him who all gave the impression of quarterbacks.

"Aw, it seems like your little friends don't want to play. Come on, Camie, let's get you cleaned up." Lucian offered his hand to haul Camie off the floor then escorted him from the toilet block.

Toward the end of the week, Lucian approached Camie, where Camie sat at a bird-pooped table under a tree in the schoolyard. Lucian clapped him on the back as he dropped a backpack on the table. "Had any more troubles with those clowns?"

"Uh-uh, can't thank you enough for rescuing me. I thought I was going to have the crap kicked out of me."

"Well, there is a way you can thank me." Lucian leaned in.

Raphael whispered in Camie's mind: "Don't do it. It will lead to big problems."

Camie responded inside his head: "I owe him."

"Not the amount he wants."

Camie ignored the warning. "Sure, whatever you need."

"I need you to deliver something." Lucian rummaged around in the backpack before producing a small parcel. He placed it on the table in the space between himself and Camie.

Camie's hand reached out for it. "What's in it?"

"Best you not ask."

Camie's hand fell. It sounded dodgy, but he'd said he would do it, so he'd kinda committed.

Lucian dropped a scrap of paper next to the parcel. "Take it to this address and ask for Bernaba. Don't give it to anyone else. Oh, and I'll know if you opened it."

Camie stared at Lucian's retreating back, his gut in knots.

Camie checked the address on his mobile phone. Darn it, across town. He couldn't be too late home, or he'd worry his grandfather. He'd have to cut the last couple of classes. He retrieved his backpack, shoved the package inside, and headed for a bus stop a little away from the school, hoping not to be spotted by a teacher.

The brightly colored poster behind its Perspex frame jarred against the grungy condition of the bus stop. Camie fingered the few coins he had. How he'd get home, he didn't know as he had just enough for the trip there. At least, he hoped he did.

The bus rattled its way into the city, churning Camie's stomach. He'd asked the driver to let him know when they got to the stop he had to change at, so when the driver called out, "This your stop, kid?" Camie scuttled off the bus.

After a ten-minute wait, the bus he needed pulled up. The cleanliness of the bus struck him as he sunk into the well-padded seat. The bus that took him to school had bone-hard seats and graffiti everywhere. This bus even smelled cleaner, and it didn't shudder like the ones he usually rode.

He studied the unfamiliar territory with interest. The city gave way to suburbs with leafy streets and large houses. He imagined what it would be like to have a yard that big or a pool. Compared to his grandfather's twenty-year-old car, the sleek vehicles that lined the driveways looked like they had just driven off the showroom floor.

When the driver said it was his stop, he hopped off the bus. Even the smell of this suburb differed. Freshness and the fragrance of cut grass greeted him. The five-block walk took him into an even wealthier area where the houses sat well back on huge blocks surrounded by high fences and security gates. Given Lucian's comment about not asking, Camie had thought the address would be somewhere seedy. The unexpected nature of the surroundings eased Camie's tension.

When he arrived at his destination, he peered through the security gate set in a two-foot-thick high wall at a circular driveway boarded by a low hedge, beyond which he glimpsed what he could only describe as a mansion. At first, he puzzled over how to make his presence known. Then he spotted the intercom. He pressed the buzzer and waited. Just as he went to press again, a voice spoke, "Name and business."

The abruptness of it took Camie aback, and he stuttered, "Camie. Here to deliver something to Bernaba."

"Wait there. I'll send him out."

A car approached the gate from which a figure more like Camie had expected, except for the suit, stepped out. The brawny Latino even had a gold tooth, which showed when he grinned and said, "You're young for this type of work, aren't you?"

The phrase—"type of work"—confused Camie. What type of work? It was just a package. "S'pose so," he fished out the package from his backpack and handed it to Bernaba through the bars of the gate. Bernaba slipped him a fiver. Camie smiled. That took care of his fare home and a little to spare.

Bernaba called out, "Thanks, kid," as he slid into the driver's seat after pocketing the package.

As Camie made his way home, he ran the encounter through his thoughts. The neighborhood was respectable. The owners of the house were clearly wealthy. It wasn't unusual to hire security guards, and Bernaba dressed well. There couldn't be anything amiss. And yet Lucian's "not ask" and Bernaba's "type of work" set his nerves on edge.

His grandfather didn't comment when Camie arrived home an hour and a half late.

As a rule, Camie didn't read the newspaper, but this morning's edition had an enlarged picture of the house he'd been to yesterday, so he read the headline: "Multibillionaire Murdered."

Cold crept into Camie's bones. What if they connected his delivery to the murder? He'd end up in jail. He told himself not to be silly. You don't even know how the murder happened.

Camie read the article. Poisoned? Poison comes in small packages. At least, that's what they showed on TV. Ridiculous. He'd done nothing more than deliver a small parcel.

He grabbed his backpack and slammed the door on his way out. Reading the article had made him late. Now he needed to run for the bus.

All morning he fretted on the article. Finding Lucian became a priority. But what could he ask him? About poison and murder? What if it were true, and he pushed for answers? Would Lucian kill him too?

At lunchtime, he scouted the quadrangle in search of Lucian. He didn't find him, and when he thought about it, he'd only seen Lucian those three times. Sure, older kids hung out in different places than him, but someone that good-looking and charismatic stood out, particularly given his height.

After a futile lunch break, he headed to class still consumed by the article, and he had a whole weekend to wait now.

He scoured Saturday's and Sunday's papers for information regarding the murder. The police suspected someone on the staff, given the security on the property. The drug had been administered in Mr. Vicario's nightcap. That didn't sound like something Bernaba had access to, and the articles didn't mention his name. Camie exhaled. He worried for nothing.

At the beginning of the school week, Camie searched for Lucian again. He even tried the library, not that Lucian looked like a library geek. He tried the bleachers where the older kids hung out but struck out each time.

Lucian showed up on Thursday, just like last week's encounter. Camie sat at the same table, mucking around with his friends. He caught Lucian's signal and ambled over to him, curious to know what he wanted.

"You did well." Lucian slapped Camie on the arm. "Bernaba's mother was pleased with the gift."

His mother, the gift, all that distress for nothing. Camie beamed. "That's great."

"Now, you've proven yourself trustworthy and reliable. I might have other jobs for you."

Camie basked in the praise. With his grandfather so tied up with his grandmother, he had little time for Camie, and his grandmother tired easily, so Camie welcomed Lucian's attention. The "other jobs" comment conflicted him, though. How long did Lucian expect to claim favors? "Thanks, I appreciate it but . . . other jobs?"

As if reading Camie's mind, Lucian said, "Don't worry. I'll pay you from here on."

"Paid?" Camie didn't quite know what to think. Some extra money meant he could buy stuff he wanted but his grandfather couldn't afford.

"Yeah; delivery men are important for what we do." Lucian extended his hand. "We have a deal?"

Raphael whispered, "No, Camie. Lucian is trouble."

"How much trouble can I get into delivering packages?" Camie shot back through his thoughts.

"It's not the now I'm worried about."

"I can take care of myself. I proved it the other day." Camie's anger at Raphael's interference tinged his words. He took Lucian's hand, saying, "Fantastic. Anytime you want."

Chapter 11

Fork in the Road

T̲wo weeks later, Camie leaned back on the train's faded fabric seat, taking him to his latest destination. Although less opulent than the last house, from Camie's viewpoint, this residence could be featured in a trendy makeover magazine. As he opened the gate, its rusty hinges squeaked, and he meandered along the curved path edged with flowers to the front door. A distant chime sounded after he pushed the buzzer. Footsteps approached, and the door opened a crack. A hand reached out, grabbed his arm, and dragged him inside.

"Hey, let me go," Camie protested.

The man ignored his complaint and drilled Camie's eyes with a cold stare. "You weren't followed, were you?"

"Followed . . . why would someone follow me?"

The man grunted. "I take it this is you they're talking about." The man threw him a paper that had been sitting on the hall table.

When Camie read the headline and first paragraph, his insides went to mush.

"There is a new lead in Vicario murder . . ."

A witness said they had seen a teenage boy handing a packet to one of Vicario's security guards. Although the witness had been too far away to identify which security guard, they said the boy appeared to be about twelve or thirteen. He wore a school uniform and carried a backpack. When asked if the witness could identify the school, he replied that it wasn't from around here. The police are asking for the boy to come forward.

Camie raised his pale face to the man. He held out a trembling hand. "What should I do? Do I go to the police?"

The man exploded. "Don't be so stupid. If you don't get arrested, they'll kill you, and even if you do, they'll probably kill you anyway."

Camie cringed. Kill him. Who did he mean . . . the police? "I . . . I delivered a gift for Alejandro's mother."

The man's intensity lessened. "Is that what they told you? Bernaba got careless. Never do business in public."

Camie dropped his head. "I didn't know. No one told me." Tears slid from his eyes.

The man gripped Camie's shoulder. "Listen, kid, you gotta be careful and make sure no one follows you. Let this be a lesson. Now, where's my package?"

Camie retrieved a thick manila envelope from his backpack. The man snatched it from his hand. As he turned to go into another room, he said over his shoulder, "Wait here. I gotta check this. Make sure you haven't had your nose in the trough."

"No, I didn't." He didn't mean it to, but it came out like pleading.

Once the man returned, he said, "I'll tell the boss you done good kid." He opened the door enough to stick his head out and said, "All clear. Now, remember to be more careful in the future."

Camie scurried away, keeping his head down until he got to the station. Too many questions overwhelmed him, so he squeezed his eyes shut and focused on the safety of his room.

The next time he met with Lucian, his voice quivered as he asked, "Will they figure out it's me?"

Lucian's raucous laughter surprised Camie. "Not likely, and besides, we take care of our own. You're one of the family now."

The positive way Lucian said it infected Camie with a sense of belonging that he missed at home. And the fifty bucks Lucian slung him boosted his spirits. He'd expected five or ten. Fifty was more money than he'd ever had.

During the intervening days between the delivery and meeting with Lucian, Camie had scanned the papers for anything connected to the address or the previous murder. The only article that drew his attention concerned the death of a minor drug dealer, but that was miles from the house.

Lucian's assurances and the fact that nothing bad had happened since the delivery convinced Camie to relax. Besides, if he got fifty for the next job, he'd be able to buy the trainers he wanted. Not even Raphael's pleadings swayed him, but he did give Raphael an assurance that it would only be a couple more jobs.

Raphael had said, "If it was only that simple."

The next job, Camie behaved as if he were in a spy movie, backtracking on his route, taking tangents, and checking to see if anyone had followed. His pride in achieving his objective buoyed him, but when he arrived home, his grandfather called him into the study, and Camie's mood flattened. His grandfather suspected something.

"Camie, I had a call from the school. It appears you have been skipping classes, and your grades are slipping."

His grandfather didn't appear angry, more worn down.

Even though Raphael begged him to tell the truth, Camie leaped on the most plausible lie. "Things get a bit much between school and my chores at home. Sometimes, I just need a break."

Raphael pointed out the slippery slope that started with lying, but Camie shushed him, claiming he didn't want his grandparents to worry.

His grandfather's face saddened. "I'm sorry I can't be there for you the way you need, and I know how deeply affected you are by your grandmother's condition, but please talk to me."

Camie hugged his grandfather. "Thanks, Papa, I will," he said as he hoped his grandfather never found out.

"So, no more skipping school?" His grandfather smiled.

Camie replied, "I'll try," knowing he couldn't fulfill that promise in the short term.

Raphael reminded him of his agreement after the next delivery, so when Lucian approached him again, he said he couldn't do it.

Lucian's mouth hardened into a straight line, and his eyes glittered. Then his expression softened. "Petros told us how well you'd done, and he said he gave you a piece of advice. You've been following it?"

"Yes, after I turn a corner, I walk partway down the street and stop to tie my shoelace or pick a flower and check if anyone has followed."

"That's pretty smart thinking for a kid your age. Be a shame to let all that talent go to waste. We got some jobs coming up that need a person with your abilities." Lucian patted the bench for Camie to sit next to him. "What do you say?"

Having his abilities praised bolstered Camie's flagging ego, but he had promised Raphael and his grandfather. "I can't. I promised." Part of him regretted letting go of something bigger than himself.

Lucian held his gaze. Camie had never noticed before how unusual Lucian's eyes were. The red-amber irises rimmed with black glowed.

Lucian placed his hand on Camie's knee. "Is it the money? We were just about to promote you to the next level with more responsibility and better pay."

"Promote?"

Lucian leaned back against the table, stretching his legs. "Yes, become more involved. Do more than just deliveries. After all, you've earned it. The family is pretty big, so there is lots of opportunity for advancement."

"Like . . . in a business?"

"You could say we're a business, yes."

"What would I be doing?"

"That will depend on the job. How does one hundred dollars sound?"

Camie's eyes widened. "A hundred dollars?" He forgot his promises and agreed.

"Great." Lucian tilted his head closer and dropped his voice. "This Sunday afternoon, I need you to go to this restaurant and sit as close to this man as possible." Lucian palmed him a slip of paper and a grainy photo. "I want you to listen to their conversation and report back. But you mustn't look like you're listening. Play on your mobile or something."

That didn't sound too hard for a hundred dollars. "OK. What time?"

"Not sure what time he'll show up, but if you get there by one, that should be time enough. Here's a twenty so you can buy yourself food and a drink . . . to make it legit."

Camie frowned. "I don't think I can make it by one. We don't get home from church until twelve-thirty."

"You'll just have to pretend you're sick or something and stay home."

"But how do I explain going out for the whole afternoon?"

"Just say you needed some air to clear your head."

If it were only this once, he'd get away with it, but too often, and his grandparents would notice.

"Besides, you don't need that religious baloney. It's for old people and children who believe in fairytales. You're way too mature for that garbage."

Camie straightened his shoulders. Of course, he was mature.

Chapter 12

At the Crossroads

Camie wheeled his grandmother out to the garden one clear, calm spring day. His grandfather had built a path around the garden, which his grandmother walked with the help of a frame. He returned to the house for the walker and assisted her to stand.

Camie strolled beside her. To Camie, she seemed more like her old self, and although still limited, her use of the paralyzed side of her body had improved remarkably. Her speech had lost its slur, and her memory had returned—all but the information Camie still desired.

She stopped to admire a bunch of daffodils. "You know, Camie, you were like a daffodil. Once we rid you of Lilith, you grew straight and strong and blossomed into a delicate, intricate design, but now you seem harder. Your shine has disappeared. And you don't come to church with us much anymore."

Both Camie and his grandfather had praised the Lord when his grandmother asked to be taken to church. Camie accompanied them for several weeks, but then assignments cropped up mostly on Sundays. Lucian deliberately scheduling him on them, given his repeated statements against religion, had crossed Camie's mind. But what did Lucifer gain if he severed him from the church? When he did go, he enjoyed the serenity.

88

He took his grandmother's hand and gave her an earnest look. "I've asked them not to schedule me on Sundays, but I'm too junior to have an influence."

"What is it you do? I know you've told me, but you know what my memory is like."

He squeezed her hand. "It's much better than it was, Nansie. I'm proud of the way you've worked to get better. In terms of work, I pick up and deliver."

"On a Sunday," her brow creased.

"Er, yes. Most of their clients aren't home during the week." Lame but better than nothing.

"Who do you work for?"

"It's a small family firm. You wouldn't have heard of them. But they're too small to afford couriers, so they hire juniors. They've said I show potential, and there might be a permanent job down the line."

"It's nice to be recognized, but just finish school first, won't you?"

His grandfather obviously hadn't told her about the truancy or poor grades, but since he worked mostly weekends, those issues had improved. "Yes ma'am."

She shuffled her frame forward and continued the circuit of the garden.

Lucian's next request raised some flags with Camie. He wanted Camie to be at an address at midnight. When Camie broached the issue of no public transport at that time of night, Lucian arranged for a pickup. He said they needed their smallest team player for this job. Camie pointed out he'd grown an inch over the winter.

Lucian scruffed his head. "Good on you, kiddo, but you're still our smallest."

"What do you need someone small for?" Camie folded his arms across his chest.

"Can't tell you 'til we get there; see you at the witching hour."

Camie chewed over the scant details he had received. He certainly couldn't be delivering something at midnight. Nor would he be information gathering. What would they need someone small for? The only thing he could think of was a small space, but why?

When his grandfather checked on him at eleven p.m., as he did every night, Camie was tucked up in bed. He couldn't know Camie wore his jeans and hoodie. Camie waited for his grandfather's bedroom door to close, and the light to go out, then he crept downstairs, careful to avoid the creaking treads. He checked he had his key and hoped he'd be home before his grandfather rose at six a.m.

A black Mercedes cruised up the street at five minutes to midnight. A passenger rolled down the window. "You Camie?"

It was on the tip of Camie's tongue to say, "Who the heck do you think I'd be, standing on a deserted street at midnight," but he bit back the response.

When he said yes, the back door of the car opened, and he climbed in. The guy in the back flicked his fingers on Camie's arm. "So, you're the imp who's going to get us in."

Camie had no idea what the guy meant but didn't want to appear ignorant, so he simply said, "S'pose so."

"I'm Donato, and this is Agostino and Jacopo."

Camie replied, "Oh," but Donato didn't get the joke.

Color crawled up Camie's neck as he listened to the ribald conversation. Donato's fit of laughing over a crude joke subsided. He nudged Camie in the ribs. "Getting an education?"

Camie squirmed, not wanting his embarrassment to show, but the explicit descriptions left the schoolyard banter for dead.

"Aw, we've embarrassed him. Guess you're still a virgin then."

Camie's whole face glowed red. He turned his head to look out the window as the men launched into stories of their first time.

The car glided through empty streets, the trees making a lit arch over the road until they pulled up near a park.

Camie asked, "This is it?"

"No, we walk from here. Put these on." Agostino slung Camie a balaclava and a pair of gloves.

Camie held them like he would a poisonous snake. Thieves wore these. What did they expect him to do?

"No chatter."

Camie hadn't been exactly talkative, so why did Donato think he would start now?

"And follow my lead exactly. No deviations. We have ten minutes to be over the fence and undercover before the guard does his rounds."

Camie swallowed and nodded. They must have done their homework if they knew the timing of the guards.

Donato retrieved something that Camie thought might be a rope ladder and a thick quilt from the boot. He loaded some torches and tools into a bag, which he handed to Jacopo.

As the men padded silently toward their destination, Camie got the impression they had done this a few times before.

At a corner, Donato gave the signal to stop. Agostino hunched over and crept forward, keeping as close to the fences and their shadows as possible.

A couple of minutes later, an almost imperceptible *phfft* reached Camie's ears . . . a gun with a silencer? *What had he gotten himself into?*

He moved as Donato did, crouched down, edging his way along the fence line until they came to their destination.

Donato threw the quilt up first so it covered the razor wire. Then he launched the rope ladder high over the fence. It had grappling hooks on rope extensions that Camie hadn't noticed at first. The hooks dug into the wall when Donato tugged on the rope. He stepped on the first rung to ensure the ladder held.

Camie tugged on Donato's arm and whispered, "This is break and enter. I can't do that."

"Like you haven't done worse? No time to grow a conscience now. Up you go. Flip over the fence at the top." He shoved Camie toward the ladder.

When Camie hesitated, he growled, "Get moving."

As Camie climbed the ladder, the words "done worse" echoed in his mind. Done worse, how?

Toward the top Camie looked at how high he'd climbed. What if he broke a leg? Did they know what was on the other side of the fence?

Donato tugged at the ladder. Camie held his breath and flipped. Everything jarred as he hit the ground, but nothing appeared broken. He stepped aside for the next man.

Agostino led the party to a clump of bushes into which they burrowed. Camie could just make out the figure of the guard as he passed within fifteen feet. They waited until he moved out of sight.

Agostino moved about thirty feet ahead. When they got closer to the house, Camie heard the silencer a few times and assumed Agostino targeted the security cameras.

Once at the side of the house toward the back, Donato stopped before a two-foot by two-foot grate. He handed Camie a piece of paper and a torch. "Read this."

Camie shone the torch on the paper to find a set of instructions.

20 ft left junction
30 ft grate
Left down hall
639745

What were the numbers, a security system?

Donato bent down and whispered in his ear. "Don't drop the frigging grate."

After Jacopo yanked out the grate, Camie slithered into the tight space. He hauled himself along with his hand and by digging his toes in, pushing the torch in front of him. The distance seemed impossible, and by the time he made the junction, his breathing labored, and sweat poured off his face. Was it left or right . . . *right*.

Ten feet into the next section, his leg muscles cramped. He lay there, fighting tears. Then he inched his way forward.

He came to the grate. Was this it? He had no way of knowing how far he had crawled, so he twisted his body and shone the torch back the way he had come to estimate the distance. It seemed about right.

He pushed on the grate. It didn't budge. He shouldered the grate. It didn't budge. He lay there panting, his mind screaming, *what do I do now?* The only way he could see it working meant using his feet. But how did he stop the grate from falling? Maybe if he shifted it just a little, he could work it out with his hands.

Bent like a corkscrew, he drew his knees as far back as he could and rammed them against the grate. He hit it harder than needed, and it popped out, thumping on the floor. He held his breath, expecting a barrage of feet. When nothing happened, he stuck his head out.

He drew it back in and drove his fingers into his eyes to stop the tears. He was screwed. It wasn't the hall. Did he go on or back? He fished in his pocket for the instructions. *Shoot!* It should have been left.

The second grate came out more easily, and he managed not to drop it. He slid out of the duct and replaced the grate as best he could. Treading as lightly as possible, he progressed down the hall until he came to the door. Sure enough, a keypad secured it. He punched in the numbers and opened it wide enough to stick his head out to look for guards. A movement caught his eye, so he closed the door.

A soft knock sounded. A guard wouldn't knock, would they? He shook as he opened the door, half expecting to get shot.

Donato glowered. "You took your bloody time."

Camie wanted to protest, but the heated expression on Donato's face prevented him.

Donato handed him another piece of paper.

It read:

Wait 20 minutes.

Go back to the cars.

The men slunk inside.

Twenty minutes in the cool night air, in the dark, exposed. He moved to the trees for cover, but even there, he shifted from foot to foot, checked what he could see of the gate, checked the grounds for security personnel. After what seemed an excessive amount of time, he checked his phone. The twenty minutes were up. He figured they'd disarmed the security system so bolted for the gate and kept running until he came to the cars.

The headline in Monday's paper read: "Theft of Priceless Van Gogh"

"A well-planned heist at the residence of Senator Jackson's saw a Van Gogh worth over $50 million stolen."

Camie read on.

Two security guards were shot, one critical, the other serious but stable.

Camie's pulse increased, but he continued to read.

The only clue police have is footage of what is believed to be the same boy from the Vicario murder running from the scene.

Camie ran to the bathroom and threw up.

Chapter 13

Awakening

When Camie spotted Lucian headed in his direction, he folded his arms across his chest, nostrils flared and eyes narrowed. Lucian flipped his leg over the bench seat and rested his elbows on the table next to Camie as if nothing amiss had happened.

Camie spat, "Exactly, who are you people?"

"Temper, temper; first things first." Lucian fixed his strange eyes on Camie. "You were careless running back to the car and getting caught on security footage. Fortunately, the cars were parked in a blind spot, or you would have led them right to us."

Camie had no intention of being chastised. "I was careless? What was I even doing there? What have you gotten me involved in?"

"Come on, Camie. It's not like you don't know." Lucian's voice held a hint of mirth.

"No, I don't know." Camie's eyes blazed.

"You'll figure it out," Lucian gestured dismissively.

"A robbery . . . security guards injured?"

"Let's just say, the good senator owed us money, and the painting is our security. Besides, the guards are not dead."

Lucian seemed to think that that made it all alright, but in Camie's mind, it had gone too far. "I won't be part of it anymore. It's wrong. It goes against what I believe in."

Lucian's eyebrows shot up. "Believe in? You're not still talking about that *God* nonsense."

"Yes, I am."

"If there were a *God*, why did he let you get involved in this, then? Hmm?"

A little of Camie's confidence that he was in the right slipped. "He tried to warn me, but I wouldn't listen."

"So, why didn't he just stop you outright? More to the point, why did he allow your mother to die and your grandmother to have a stroke?"

"She's getting better."

Lucian held up his hand. "Doesn't answer the question."

"Papa says our faith is being tested."

"Papa says? That's a great excuse when things go wrong, and people don't want to admit there is no *God*. They cling to rhetoric like that. No matter what happens, it's *God's* will, even bad things."

"It is *God's* will."

"So, *God* willed you to carry the poison that killed Vicario?"

Camie paled, his anger deflating at the enormity of what he had done. He stuttered, "You told me it was a gift for Bernaba's mother."

"You're so gullible, but back to the question. Is it *God's* will to see you in prison?" Lucian poked Camie in the chest. "Get it through your skull. There is no *God*."

"I still won't be part of it."

"Fine; when you come to your senses, look me up."

Lilith turned round on Lucifer. "I thought you said you had him."

Lucifer shrugged. "I seem to have pushed him too far too soon."

Lilith paced the bright lounge room of the house they had rented. "It's time to take decisive action."

"Such as?"

"Kill him."

"We've tried that before, and he only came back."

Lilith stopped in front of Lucifer as he sat in an overstuffed armchair. "This time's different."

"No guarantee of that. No, we need to crowbar him off his rusted-on beliefs."

Lilith ran her hands through her hair. "I don't think he will ever stop believing in that snake he calls *God*, but we have to convince him that *God* doesn't care."

She began to pace again, and when Lucifer went to speak, she shushed him. Her face brightened. She leaned in and whispered in his ear.

"Sounds good to me; when?"

"I've got just the perfect time in mind."

Camie sat on the dirt, leaning against the wall of the gymnasium. Mostly smokers frequented the narrow space between the gym and the fence. Today, Camie had the space to himself. He sniffled and rubbed his nose on his sleeve. The worst of the crying had passed, but some tears still leaked from his eyes. Raphael had been right. Lucian spelled trouble, and he'd landed right in it. If he kept his head down, it might go away.

Voices carried from the end of the gym. He dropped his head, not wanting anyone to see his tear-stained face.

"There you are. We've been looking for you."

Camie's head shot up. His heart missed a beat. Justin. But then being beaten to death might be justice. He didn't bother to move.

Justin flopped down beside him. "So, I hear you've been working for the mob. Way to go."

Mob. Camie's mind took a moment to catch up. *Holy crap.* How stupid was he?

Justin nudged him with his elbow. "We could use an inside connection. Why don't you join us?"

Camie blinked. He balled his fists. After everything Justin had put him through, he expected him to join them so they could use him? "Not bloody likely. Now get lost."

Justin levered himself off the ground. "Suit yourself." He stalked to the end of the building, his cronies following, then called out, "But you might want to consider my offer."

Camie stared at the blank page on the desk under the window in his room. The teacher expected an essay by tomorrow. He had tried all week, but with his concentration shot, nothing came. At school, he fidgeted and squirmed, counting the minutes until he could escape into the yard where he could work off his nervous energy.

At the sound of a car door slamming shut, Camie bounced on his seat. Loud noises did that to him. He wanted to run downstairs and check the door locks.

His grandparents expected him down for dinner in fifteen minutes, but the thought of eating turned his stomach. He had to force himself to eat, or they'd know something was wrong.

Would he ever be safe? The mob didn't let you go easily. What if got his grandparents killed? Bile rose in his throat.

His grandfather called for him, and he made his way to the kitchen, taking his seat at the table.

"You don't look well. Are you coming down with something?" His grandmother placed her hand on his forehead.

He pushed it away. "Just not sleeping that well."

The hurt look on his grandmother's face cut through him. "I'm sorry, Nansie. I'm just not getting enough sleep."

He so wanted to tell them. But he couldn't.

After dinner, he helped his grandfather with the dishes.

His grandfather asked, "It's your birthday in a week. What would you like to do? Have some friends over? Go out for pizza?"

Camie had almost forgotten his birthday. He didn't really want to think about it and certainly didn't want a fuss. "Maybe order in Chinese."

"I'll drop by the restaurant and get the takeaway menu so you can choose."

As the next week drew closer to Camie's birthday and no one had attempted to kill him, Camie's tension eased. He even wondered what his grandparents would buy him. Not that he needed them to. He had plenty of money he couldn't spend stashed under the floorboard in his closet. They thought he delivered stuff for pocket money, so he only bought himself small things. Still, the idea of a surprise present pleased him.

He had a spring in his step the morning of his birthday. It had been a while since he felt this carefree—years in fact. First, there had been Justin's bullying at primary school. Then this business with Lucian; but today was his day, and he intended to make the most of it. He'd brought extra money to get his friends a bang-up lunch. What good was it if he couldn't share it?

The boys snuck off the school grounds and headed down to the diner.

Camie spooned the last mouthful of his third desert into his mouth. The creamy texture of the mint ice cream floated on his tongue, its chill causing his teeth to ache.

How he'd managed three on top of the hamburger and chips and pizza, he wasn't sure. His friends had the sticky treats smeared over the chins and mouths. He grabbed a serviette and wiped his face then draped his arm along the back of the booth. "Don't know about you, but I'm going to have to roll back to school."

Ari grinned. "Me too." He let out a loud burp. "Hey, let's see who can do the longest, loudest burp."

Hysterical laughter punctuated the obnoxious noises to the point a waitress told them to knock it off. Not that it mattered. They had to get back anyway.

Camie had difficulty staying awake during the afternoon classes with his bloated stomach. The bell rang, releasing him from his torture. As he grabbed his bag, he grinned. It had been a good day.

He whistled as he strolled from the bus stop to his house. The whistle cut short as he turned onto his street. *An ambulance.* He began to run, his mind outstripping his feet. Had the mob hit his grandparents? No police cars. Then what?

His grandfather stood at the back of the ambulance.

Camie yelled from half a block away, "Papa!"

His grandfather turned, a pained expression on his face.

No, she can't be dead. He flung himself into his grandfather's arms, sobbing. "Is she . . ."

"She's had another massive stroke. You'd best prepare yourself for the worst."

Chapter 14

Lost in Rebellion

ᛚᛏᛦ ᛚᛞ ᛏᛣᛏᛣᛈᛈᛏᛚᛞ

After weeks of praying as he had never prayed before, the news that his grandmother would never walk again nor regain the use of her right arm made Camie swear at *God*, threaten Him, plead, cry, and curse, but nothing worked. His grandmother remained trapped in her useless body. She couldn't even talk. And his birthday would ever be a reminder of the day *God* took his grandmother from him. All the fun with his friends at lunch evaporated. It fell into the time before, before his grandmother's stroke. The distant memory of school seemed like a time of freedom and fun. Now, he faced bleakness.

His rational mind said the responsibility lay with Lilith, but his emotional heart blamed *God* for letting it happen and doing nothing to fix it. In the end, in his anger, he told *God* to go to Hell and never speak to him again. Anger wore him out, and he fell into apathy. No matter how many times his grandfather told him how important it was that his grandmother saw him; he buried his head under the bedcovers and refused to get up.

One morning, his grandfather marched into his bedroom, ripped the covers off him, and yelled, "Get up. I've had enough of this selfish brat routine. I expect you to be ready in fifteen minutes, and when we get home, I expect you to dust and vacuum the house, tidy your room, and do your washing. No arguments."

His grandfather's anger infused his words with a hostility Camie had never, experienced.

"Fine!" Camie stomped out of the room and slammed the bathroom door, all the while ranting at his grandfather in his mind. *Do this, Camie. Do that, Camie.* He wasn't his grandfather's slave. He'd show him.

After he completed his chores, Camie headed for the park. He ran as if he could escape the nightmare that trapped him. Nobody cared. Not *God.* Not his grandfather. Belligerent tears burned his eyes. He remembered his mother's love. He recalled his grandmother's gentle voice as she helped him through his time of grief and her love and compassion over the years. He yelled at *God,* dumping all his frustration, pain, and misery on him.

When he arrived at the park, he rocked his grief on a swing. Threads of mucus hung from his nose, but he didn't have the will to wipe them.

A familiar voice sounded behind him. "You look like crap, kiddo."

Camie turned his red-rimmed eyes to find Lucian and a girl about his age approaching the swing. He wiped the snot off his nose with the back of his hand and smeared it on his pants. He missed how unlikely the coincidence of running into Lucian at that moment was, given he'd never seen Lucian at this park.

Lucian lowered his weight into the other swing as if testing that it would hold. "I'm sorry to hear about your grandmother. How is she?"

Camie fought back a fresh wave of tears. His voice broke when he said, "She can't walk or talk. She has to go into a home. You were right. *God* doesn't care."

Camie's chin rested on his chest, so he missed the spark of delight that lit the girl's eyes.

Lucian slapped Camie on the thigh. "Well, we care. You know you were a highly-valued member of the team. I mean, we couldn't have gotten our hands on that painting without you."

Camie muttered, "Whatever."

"We have something perfect for you. It'd take your mind off your troubles." Lucian grabbed the girl's hand and dragged her closer. "This is Lillian. She's a new recruit, and we thought you could train her."

Camie looked up to find a pair of eyes with irises so black the pupil got lost, sparkling at him.

She extended her hand. "Pleased to meet you."

When Camie took her hand, a buzz of electricity jumped between them. So taken by Lillian's charm, he missed the unlikely coincidence that she accompanied Lucian at just this moment. He smiled for the first time in weeks. "Sure, why not. I need a distraction, anyway."

"That's the spirit, kiddo. Meet us at this address tomorrow." Lucian handed Camie a slip of paper.

Yet, again, Camie missed the obvious.

Raphael's voice penetrated Camie's mind. "Don't you see it?"

"What's to see? Someone who's interested in me, wants to be my friend, and thinks I'm of value?"

Raphael pleaded: "There is more to Lucian than you know."

"He's been good to me. Where has *God* been?"

Right here, my son.

Camie felt a warmth fill and envelop his heart.

"Not anymore."

With his new purpose, Camie announced to his grandfather that he intended to leave school and work full-time.

His grandfather's troubled eyes held Camie's. "I feared something like this. I don't know what hold they have over you, but you've changed and not for the better."

Camie dropped his eyes. "I enjoy what I do, and they pay well."

His grandfather pushed himself up from the table and went to give Camie a hug.

Camie shied away. Guilt stabbed him at the look of pain on his grandfather's face. Camie left the kitchen.

<hr />

Working with Lillian proved to be the balm Camie needed. She laughed at his lame jokes, teased him relentlessly, but she also told him in no uncertain terms when he acted like a jerk. She picked up the trade quickly, and soon, Lucian assigned them tasks to handle by themselves.

Although Camie still heard Raphael's voice, the clamor and adrenaline of Camie's new life eclipsed any warnings or advice he offered.

The more jobs they pulled together, the closer they became. Camie couldn't deny his attraction to her, but he'd never had a girlfriend, so he had no idea how to approach the situation. Lillian solved the problem for him.

"How about we catch a movie together? There's a great action-adventure on."

Camie jumped at the opportunity, although still not sure whether it was a date. As such, he didn't even try to hold her hand.

His grandmother died on his fifteenth birthday. He yelled at *God* again. "Ram it home, why don't you? So much for my being special and you having a plan for me . . . you don't give a crap!"

Lucian and Lillian showed up for the funeral.

"See, *God,* my friends care more than you do."

As on all the other occasions, *God* and Raphael remained silent.

A few weeks later, Camie and Lillian's job went south. Someone had tipped off the target.

As per their escape plan, they darted across the demolition site toward the alleyway, where they'd find the door to the building diagonally across from the site open. The concrete blocks provided cover as they dodged bullets. Lillian squealed behind him. His stomach cinched. Shot? He clambered over the rubble to find her foot wedged between two slabs.

"I'll lift. You pull."

Camie's biceps bulged. The veins on his neck stood out. His mouth contorted. Blood spiraled down Lillian's leg. Camie panted as he checked the position of the police. A bullet ricocheted off the block in front of him. He ducked. Camie judged the officer to be out of range of his Sig Sauer 9mm, particularly since he couldn't hit the side of a barn even if he were close, but he fired a couple of rounds to let them know he had a weapon. He snapped in another mag, but if the cops got close enough for him to hit, he might take one down; however, they'd still be captured.

He scoured the immediate vicinity for something to use as a lever—nothing.

He had a decision to make. In this situation, the rule stated he had to kill Lillian to prevent her from lagging and get to safety. He put off deciding and peered around the block—an officer dove for cover. Camie fired. *He cursed under his breath.* They'd gained about fifty feet.

His feelings for Lillian were uppermost in his mind, clouding his judgment. How could he kill her?

But he must. He put the gun to her head, his finger on the trigger. He couldn't look into her pleading eyes, so he focused about twenty feet in front of him. His finger twitched.

Lillian cried.

Then he spotted it. A length of steel pipe balanced on some rubble. It hadn't been there before, had it?

Without a thought for his own safety, he scrambled across the gap. A bullet clipped his arm, nearly knocking him off balance, but he had no time to dwell on the searing pain.

He grabbed the pipe and checked the officers' positions. They were within one hundred yards. He fired about a half dozen rounds to cover his return. That left him with four bullets and no more mags left.

He jammed the pipe under the slab and heaved, pain from the wound rippling through his brain.

Lillian tugged at her leg. "A little more."

Camie felt like his muscles were tearing as he drew on every last drop of energy to force the slab another quarter inch.

Lillian groaned as her ankle bone scraped on the slab; however, her foot came free.

Camie put his arm under her shoulder. "Let's get out of here."

They had fifty feet to traverse before they got to the alleyway. He fired his last rounds, hoping the officers hadn't counted his shots. They might think he intended to ambush them from the lane, and perhaps they'd slow down just long enough for Lillian and him to get to cover.

A bullet thudded into the open door, and the sound of running echoed in the lane. Camie hauled against the door's pneumatics to shut it after him then thrust the lock in place.

By the time police backup arrived, he and Lillian would have retrieved the car from the basement parking and left the building, blending in with traffic.

Once back at base, Lillian threw her arms around Camie and wept. When her tears subsided, she asked, "Why didn't you kill me?"

Camie stuttered, "I couldn't. You mean too much to me."

She raised her mouth and kissed him.

As time went on, Camie and Lillian became inseparable and raked in the money for the bosses.

On his eighteenth birthday, Lucian approached Camie. "I've got great news. I've convinced the underboss to make you a soldier."

A smile split Camie's face. Then his brows puckered. "I thought only verified Italians could make soldier and, more to the point, have proven themselves with several kills."

"Yeah, but the underboss said you're an exception, kiddo. You've made a killing moneywise as an associate. Think of it as a reward."

The night of the ceremony, Camie chewed his fingernail as he waited for the car to pick him up. He tugged at the shirt collar under the tuxedo. The whole outfit restricted his movement, and his shoes pinched.

If Camie thought he'd seen tight security, nothing compared to the manning of the walls of this fortress. The outline of someone stationed every twenty-five feet left little room for a break-in. The car glided through the gates after the driver gave his and Camie's name to be stopped fifteen feet in. The guards patted Camie down and removed his phone then indicated for them to proceed.

Floodlights illuminated the grounds, giving Camie a good view of the formal garden with its fountain, topiary, marble statues, designer garden beds, and immaculate lawns.

A footman opened the car door for Camie, and a maid guided him to the grand drawing room. A trickle of sweat tickled his temple as he stepped into the room after being announced. About forty faces greeted him, very few of whom he knew. Rarely did one meet the family due to the restricted dealings between associates and higher officials.

Names swirled around him during the introductions until the last man—the Don. Camie's knees quivered as if they might buckle. He wiped his sweaty palm on his pants before taking the Don's hand. He bowed. "I am honored."

The Don gestured him forward then placed his hand in the center of Camie's back and directed him to the front of the room. He opened his arms to the gathering. "My loyal supporters, tonight we welcome a new member to the family, Camie Rathmeuson. It is a little unusual that he is not Italian, but I have it on good authority that he is loyal."

Camie glanced at the table to the Don's left—a Glock, dagger, picture card, candle, and what looked like a needle.

The Don picked up the Glock and the dagger and handed them to Camie. "As a member of the family, you live by the gun and the knife, and you die by the gun and the knife."

Someone stepped forward to take the gun and dagger away.

Then, the Don retrieved the needle and the picture card. "Hold out your right hand."

Camie complied, and the Don pricked his index finger, dripping a few drops of blood onto the card. It appeared to be a saint, but Camie's limited knowledge of the Catholic faith left him in the dark as to which one.

"This blood represents your entry into the family." The Don set fire to the card and handed it to Camie. "Now, repeat the oath."

Camie's tongue stuck to the roof of his mouth. His mind fumbled for the words. The Don stared at him.

Camie stuttered, "Sorry, just a little overcome." He then recited the oath. "I pledge my life to the family, to abide by the rules, to not betray them or my fellow members, and if I do, as burns this saint, so will burn my soul. I enter alive, and I will have to get out dead."

The Don stepped forward and kissed him on both cheeks. "Welcome. May you have a long and prosperous life; now we feast."

Chapter 15

A Prodigal's Journey Home Begins

ᔕᒪᎧᏆᒪᏰᎴᏆ ᒪᎴᏂᏕᏴᏆᒪ ᒪᏆᏆᏆᏴᎴᏆ

Camie turned his face away as Donato rammed his fist into the captive's face. Blood poured from the man's nose, his split lip, and a cut above his eyes so badly bruised that only the slits of his whites showed. Camie shuddered as every body blow struck, which left purple splotches blooming over the man's torso. The metallic tang of the viscous red ooze clung to Camie's nostrils.

Donato shoved his face an inch from the man's. "Tell us where he is, and we will make it quick for you."

The man strained to get his words out between shattered teeth. "You might as well kill me. I'm not betraying my captain."

Camie admired the man's loyalty, but Donato's renowned mastery of torture preceded him. Although Camie had taken an oath not to betray the family, he couldn't answer what he would do in a similar situation.

Donato's dagger scraped against the leather sheath as he drew it. He rested the edge of the cold steel against the man's neck and drew a line of blood. "So, you want to do it the hard way. Fine by me." He lowered the blade to the man's chest, slid it under the skin, and began removing a strip of flesh.

The captive clenched his jaw, but a moan escaped his swollen lips.

Donato chuckled. "There is a lot more skin to go, followed by fingers and toes, and I enjoy cutting off toes. Tell us where he is, and I'll put a bullet in your brain. If not, it's death by a thousand cuts."

"Go back to Hell."

"Have it your way." Donato filleted another strip of skin. A ray of sunlight turned a blood drop on the blade into a red jewel as he withdrew the dagger from the man's body. After several more strips, he asked, "What next?" and rattled the tools on the table.

Camie flinched when Donato gripped the man's little finger and positioned the tin snips. At the crunch of bone, Camie curled his fingers around his own pinky.

The prisoner spluttered blood as he stifled a scream.

Donato held up the severed digit. "Look here. I have a diamond ring." He pulled the bloody object off and pocketed it. "Ah, diamond earrings. I might give them to my girlfriend. She won't care, but my wife would complain."

The snips cut through the lobes like a chef's knife carving a turkey. Blood from the man's ears mingled with the blood on his wounded chest.

"You sure you don't want to talk yet? I'm being generous here. Help me out." Donato held another finger between the snips.

"Go back to Hell, you Guiney bast—"

Donato squeezed the tool, and the man screamed. Camie wanted to cover his ears. When the prisoner passed out, Camie threw a bucket of water over the victim. He'd have preferred to give the poor bastard a break, but that would make him weak in Donato eyes.

After another hour, blood pooled under the man's chair, his shallow breathing barely moved his chest, and his head hung loosely.

"Check his pulse."

Camie's shoes squelched in the sticky mess and made a sucking sound as he lifted his foot. His eyes fell on the mangled hand as he felt the man's wrist. A mixture of repulsion and sorrow flowed through his mind. "Barely anything."

"Wrap it up here. Lock the doors and set the building alight."

During the night, Camie dreamed of being tortured. Sweat soaked the tangled sheets, and he woke screaming.

Lillian rubbed his arm. "The first is always the hardest. It will get easier."

Camie didn't know if he wanted it to get easier. He sat up to clear his head, only to be confronted by a pair of enormous aquamarine eyes at the baseboard. They stared at him, through him, and into his soul, sifting for answers. He knew those eyes. "Pi** off, Raphael."

A different season, another interrogation, but this time, one of their own was caught selling information.

The other interrogations had been brutal, but nothing prepared Camie for the level of hatred or the ferocity of the attack this time. Where the other occasions had been a one-on-one situation, this time, each soldier present took a turn at beating the victim. It seemed to Camie that no one cared about getting information. The soldiers wanted revenge. They rendered the man's face a bloody pulp, beat him with pipes, and lashed him with a cat of nine tails. The women seemed more vicious than the men. When not an inch of skin remained on his torso or back, they cut out his tongue and shoved it so far down his throat that he choked, then they left him to die.

That day taught Camie the consequences of betraying the family.

Camie had planned to take Lillian out on his twenty-first birthday, but he got called in for a job. His body sagged at the instruction to assist Donato on another interrogation. The urge to vomit no longer plagued him, and he'd gained the ability to stand impassively and watch, but unlike the others, he didn't enjoy it.

This time, the victim broke. Once he provided the information Donato sought, Donato said, "I will honor my word and give you a quick death . . . Camie."

Camie froze. Surely, Donato wasn't asking him to kill the man?

Donato's eyes narrowed. "Are you disobeying an order?"

Camie's wooden movement propelled him forward.

Donato's mouth twisted, his beady eyes fixed on Camie. "Rumor has it, you've never killed anyone. So how did you, you strano piccolo punk (strange little punk), get to be a soldier?"

The other soldiers cheered.

Camie blanched at the level of aggression against him.

Donato spat in his face. "*Uccidilo adesso, o ti ammazziamo noi; capire!*" (Kill him now, or we kill you, understand!)

People he had worked with, lay his life on the line for, howled and jeered. A few sympathetic faces refrained from joining in, but the majority vented what he could only assume was spite filled hatred.

Donato ordered him to draw his gun. "Kill him!"

The gun wavered in Camie's shaking hand as he raised the muzzle toward the prisoner's temple. His mind went back to the day Lillian trapped her ankle. He thought he hesitated out of love, but now it dawned on him, his cowardice prevented him. Cowardice? No, that wasn't it.

Donato yelling, "Get on with it!" broke his train of thought.

He pulled the trigger. Time slowed. The shower of blood and brain matter that exploded from the shattered skull traced intricate patterns through the air as it traveled away from the head. It splattered the wall with globules of matter that had once been a man's life.

Normality returned, and he vomited, then dropped the gun to his side and ran.

His trajectory brought him to the cathedral in the center of the city. *Confession?* Yes, he needed to confess to *God.*

He pushed to the head of the confession queue, dragged the woman in the box out, and dumped himself on the seat. The partitioning window opened. His words tumbled out of his mouth, semi-incoherently. "I'm not Catholic, but I need to confess. I had to do it. They would have killed me if I hadn't. Maybe, I'd be better dead."

"Slow down, my son, and tell me what you need to confess to *God.*"

"I killed a man."

"You said you are not Catholic, so you don't know the correct form. I need to ask if you are repentant."

Camie sobs shook the box. He choked out, "Yes."

"Is there anything else you need to confess to *God?*"

"No."

The priest prayed in Latin and then said, "Your sins are absolved."

Camie staggered out of the box. Was that it? How could his sin be absolved? He'd killed a man.

He stared up at the crucifix. Memories of attending church with his grandmother surfaced. He recalled the serenity of *God's* love for him, the security it had provided. Images of all the barbarous acts he had committed flooded his mind, culminating in the death of a man.

His heart ached. A hole *God* once filled cried out to be filled again. But how could *God* forgive him?

A whisper in his mind said, *If you are truly sorry, go to the police and confess.*

Camie bowed his head and left for the station.

⚭

"After all I've had to put up with, him pawing at me all the time, you're telling me he's turned back to that sniveling excuse for a deity?" Lilith thrust her hands on her hips.

"Donato threw a spanner in the works. I didn't expect him to force Camie to kill someone. Not yet, at any rate."

Lucifer's calmness only irritated Lilith further. "You're supposed to know these things! Why didn't you?"

He spread his hands. "Some things are shielded from even me."

"We have to stop him."

Lucifer took Lilith's hands in his. "We will. Don't worry about it."

Camie approached the duty desk. "I'm—"

"We know who you are, but we never expected you to walk in voluntarily."

"I'm here to confess to a murder."

"Only one?"

Camie's backside went numb from sitting for hours on the uncomfortable metal chair. His wrists ached in the cuffs, restraining them on the steel table. He guessed the cops had informed the FBI, and they'd send a couple of senior agents. Whoever got the gig expected to make a name for themselves off his back.

An hour into the interview, Camie sighed. "How many times do I have to repeat myself? I am only here to confess to one murder. I am not going to rat."

The agent said, "We sent a team to the location you specified. Nothing there. No body. No blood. Nothing. We need more to go on. And you know you even being here paints a target on your back. Turn state witness, and we will put you into witness protection."

Camie shrugged.

The second agent produced a folder and laid it on the table, squaring the edges before pushing it toward Camie. "Go on, take a look."

Camie flipped the folder open. It contained a series of photos of dismembered bodies. He didn't react. He'd seen worse.

"These clowns thought they could make it on their own after visiting the police. None of them lasted more than a week before they disappeared. You have a chance to start fresh—job, house. Maybe get married, have kids. No looking over your shoulder. You could have a normal life, a clean life. After the crap you've done, doesn't that sound like a good deal? If you go down for the murder, you won't last a day in stir."

Part of him figured being killed served justice, and part of him wanted to live. He bowed his head and calmed his mind. *God, is that You?*

Not because you want to live but because it is the right thing to do for all those others you wronged.

His eyes popped open. "I'll do it but not because you're going to set me up in some cozy house. I need to make restitution."

∞≪≫∞

Shouts woke Camie from his fitful sleep on the lumpy mattress. His hand reached for the gun on his dresser until he remembered the bed was in a safe house, and he had no way of defending himself. The barred windows prevented him from getting out as much as anyone getting in.

A window cracked, and a blinding light lit the hall, followed by a loud bang. It didn't take a genius to work out the family had compromised the safe house. Even as he searched for a method to protect himself, his mind toyed with who they might have sent.

As he dragged the dresser across the door after locking it, upended the bed, and smashed the chair to get a leg, a small explosion echoed down the hall: the front door. Once he'd hunkered down behind the bed, he said a prayer of thanks that justice would be served.

Lucian's voice rose over the gunfire. "I take it you're in there, kiddo. Sorry, it had to end this way."

Camie figured as Lucian brought him in, it was fitting Lucian took him out.

"Yes, open the door, sweetie."

Camie's world tilted on its axis. *Lillian.* The thought of death proved less painful than Lillian's betrayal.

Something crashed against the door and then again. The third time, splintering accompanied the crash, and light flooded in from the hall.

Camie cursed at not having a gun as Lucian's figure silhouetted against the light made a perfect target. The dresser's legs squealed on the wooden floor as it got shoved to the side. He waited until the footsteps indicated they were in the room then leaped over the bed in a vain attempt to strike one of them with the chair leg. He got three steps before the bullet blasted a hole in his stomach.

Lucian and Lillian stood over his crumpled form. Lillian asked, "Is he dead?"

"Not yet, but he will be soon."

Camie gurgled, "Why?" in the hope Lillian might explain herself.

She just laughed and said, "Oh, he's trying to talk." Then she imitated a gurgling sound.

Lucian aimed the gun at Camie's heart and pulled the trigger.

As Camie's life expired and his soul departed his body, Lucian and Lillian's figures dissolved into their true forms.

Camie thought, "I'm a fool."

Chapter 16

Daddy, Can I Come Home Now

𝔛𝔛𝔛𝔛 𝔛𝔛𝔏 𝟕 𝔏𝟕𝔏𝔞

A sense of peace embraced Camie as he returned to consciousness. His heavy lids took concentration to open. When he did, unfamiliar surroundings greeted him. A bright room furnished with comfortable but shabby furniture. Where was he, and how did he get there? He lay there, raking his mind for information, but his memories refused to play ball.

As he attempted to sit, pain ratcheted from his stomach and his chest to his brain. His hand grasped his belly, where it encountered the remnants of a wound. Recollections of the past month swept over him like bats leaving a cave. If he could die again, he thought he might die of the grief which overwhelmed him—Lillian's betrayal, the life he stole, his rejection of his grandfather's love. It gave way to the heavier burden of remorse.

After sitting with his feeling for what seemed like hours, he turned his mind to solving the riddle of where he found himself. Not Earth. Not Heaven. Not Hell where he belonged. Purgatory? Didn't only those who could be redeemed end up in purgatory? How could *God* forgive him for the life he'd lived, for the life he'd taken? He didn't see redemption as a possibility for him, and yet, here he sat.

Over the next few days, he reflected on the past nine years—so many of his actions had led to the death of others. His conscience no longer allowed him to absolve himself by saying he didn't know. From that very first assignment, the murder of Vicario, somewhere in his heart, the knowledge of his complicity had lurked. That time and right up until he took a life, he excused himself, saying he wasn't the one actually doing the killing. Now, he comprehended that his actions formed part of a chain, and that chain bound him to the deaths. The new emotion of shame flooded him.

One sunny morning—it never seemed to rain here—as he walked the formal garden filled with the most exquisite blooms, a voice spoke into a silence only interrupted by bird song and insect noises.

Are you ready yet?

Camie spun around but could find no presence. Then he calmed his mind. In purgatory, one could expect the unusual. "Ready?"

Yes, to confess your sins.

"How long do you have?" Camie followed the path to the center of the garden, where a fountain splashed pure spring water. Benches sat equidistant around it.

The voice laughed.

An eternity . . .

"It might take that long." Camie made himself as comfortable as one can on a backless concrete bench, but the sun shone, and the breeze caressed him. He began his saga in primary school, with Justin and how badly he wanted to hurt him, and continued through his transgressions, culminating in the man's death.

The voice listened attentively, asking questions for clarification. At the end, it said, *You have done far worse, my son. But that telling is not for now. The life of one man is no different from the life of many.*

Camie blinked, "Far worse? What could be worse than killing a man? And when, how?"

118

He opened his mouth to speak, but the voice stopped him. *Not yet. You're too fragile now.*

The truth of that resonated in Camie.

Do you think the murder of the man is your greatest sin?

"Probably denying my grandfather is greater."

Yes, this is about relationships, but not with your human family.

Relationships? With whom, if not his family? He gnawed on the issue, turning it every which way, but nothing clicked.

The voice cleared its throat.

Ahh-hmm.

Like a comet streaking across the night sky, realization hit him. The ferocious torrent of emotions that crashed into his psyche nearly unhinged him. If it weren't for the gentle stream of love and energy flowing from the voice, his mind might have cracked.

After the paralysis of his mind and body passed, he said, "How can you forgive me?"

No soul is irredeemable, but that soul has to be willing and ready to confess their sin and repent.

Camie fell to his knees on the pebbles of the path, oblivious to them digging into his flesh. "*Father,* my sin against *You,* in denying *You,* in breaking *Your* commandments, is beyond what I can expect to be forgiven. Yet, I ask for forgiveness and pledge my soul to You."

I forgive you, my son. Sin no more.

A surge of his *Father's* love, like 240 volts of electricity, coursed through his heart, mind, and soul and blasted away the crimes of Camie's past. Camie wept tears of joy for the first time since his mother died.

When you retire for bed, rise in the morning, or reflect on my creation, praise my name. Go now and rest. I need you to heal before I discuss the remainder.

Several days later, the voice returned.

Are you well, my son?

"My faith is restored. How could I not be well? But I have some questions. *You* knew all this would happen. Why didn't *You* stop me?" Camie stretched his legs in front of the garden bench.

Yes, I know all things, but first, I gave man free will. I cannot neglect that fact. Second, Raphael was your guide. Third, the subtleties of Lucifer's game are dangerous to counter once he has claimed a mind without doing great harm to the human mind itself.

"But I prayed so hard for my grandmother, and nothing happened."

You cannot know what I might have done had you remained faithful.

"So, it comes back to my decision to reject you." He plucked a flower, his mood morose.

Essentially, yes. But that is in the past. Do not dwell on the past, but never forget its lessons. However, I have an important issue to discuss with you . . . or rather, show you.

Camie's thoughts raced back to Earth and his grandfather.

Yes, it has to do with Earth but not your grandfather. I need you to concentrate on the ball of energy that will appear before you. It will guide you to a past that has been hidden from you.

The intensity of light emanating from the globe, which popped into being and hung about five feet off the ground, stabbed Camie's eyes at first. His eyes adjusted, and the myriad of colors that sparkled and danced in the ball mesmerized him. He sensed his consciousness being drawn into the light. Images of the Heavenly Realm and angels flashed before him. He did a double-take when one showed himself. Even though it did not look as he appeared now, his heart confirmed that the angel and he were one and the same. At first, he rejected it outright. He was human. He had lived and died. Angels don't die. And if he were an angel, what was he doing on Earth in human form?

All in good time . . .

Camie's eons of existence sped before his eyes in a matter of seconds—the great battles, the fall of the angels, the creation of Earth. Then the display slowed to concentrate on his part in the destruction of Atlantis.

The impact of that vision jolted Camie back into himself. No, the killing of one man seemed inconsequential against the thousands, and yet, how do you weigh a life?

Now that you have been reunited with yourself, I need to outline the mission I planned for your last life until your free will interrupted it.

The voice detailed his expectations. The concept of the *Father's* plan inspired him, yet his transgressions concerned him.

"I am not worthy. Not after Atlantis. Not after my last life."

Are you questioning my judgment?

Camie stuttered.

"No . . . I didn't . . . I meant . . ."

Understood.

He continued, *I am sending you back to the body you had as Camie.*

"Won't I be buried by now?"

No, only a couple of hours have passed on Earth.

"Will I still be injured?"

That has been resolved. The 'family' situation, on the other hand, has added a layer of complication. Lucifer and Lilith were a given, but I fear there will be consequences from the family. OK, I know. You will have to come to terms with them and not let them distract you from the mission.

Camie didn't like the sound of that.

Ready?

Camie nodded.

<hr />

A noise behind the morgue attendant startled her. She spun her chair away from the monitor where she had been playing a game. She shivered at the sight of a corpse sitting upright. All the stories didn't compare to the chills she experienced or her increased pulse. *Rigor Mortis.* She relaxed and returned to her game.

A moment later, the chair clattered to the ground, and her hand sought something for a weapon. The corpse groaned. *Zombies weren't real, were they?*

The corpse asked, "Is it possible to have some clothes, please? I can't exactly leave naked, and besides, it's cold in here."

The attendant's mouth fell open. Clothes? Leave? OK, it sounded alive and rational, but she pressed the buzzer for security anyway.

A few minutes on, the morgue door banged open, and a security guard stormed in, gun drawn.

The corpse said, "Don't shoot me, again, please. I've been dead once tonight. But I assure you, I am very much alive now."

The attendant sidled toward the trolley. "Keep your gun trained on him, and if he tries to bite me, shoot the head."

The security person stepped closer to the trolley.

The corpse replied, "I assure you, I am not a Zombie. Besides, they don't exist on Earth, only on Lupetor in the Medusian galaxy."

The attendant didn't know which astounded her more—that the corpse was alive or that Zombies existed somewhere.

She leaned as far away from the corpse as possible while extending her hand to take the corpse's wrist. It felt warm and had a pulse. She shone her torch into the corpse's eyes. She'd never seen irises that color, almost violet, but the pupils reacted, so definitely not dead. She lowered the torch to the corpse's abdomen. "Didn't you come in here with a gut shot and chest wound?"

"Umm, yes."

"So . . ." the attendant waved her hand at Camie's belly.

"Part of *God's* gift when *He* returned me to life."

The attendant glanced up at the security person as much as to say, *whacko*. "It's okay . . . I think I can handle it from here," she said to the guard.

"You sure, some of these religious types can be a handful."

"I should be fine, but I'll call if I need help."

After the security person left, the now undead person said, "Now, about those clothes."

"Sure, but you will need to be admitted to check your injuries."

"No need. I feel like I could live for thousands of years. By the way, I'm Camie."

Camie extended his hand. The attendant grasped it loosely, ready to pull it back if necessary. "I'm Fatheha."

Fatheha watched Camie's retreating back as he whistled his way along the corridor toward the exit.

Raphael directed his gaze toward the brilliance of the *Father*.

"But I've been with Camie throughout all his lives."

I understand, and you will still be an adviser, but Satan has more experience with humans and their wiles. He also has a deeper understanding of Lucifer and Lilith.

Raphael tried not to pout.

Satan clapped him on the shoulder. "No hard feelings, Raph, but the better angel gets the job."

The *Father* admonished him.

Satan, apologize to Raphael. I won't tolerate angels denigrating each other.

Satan bowed his head. "Yes, *Father*. Sorry, old chap. No offense meant."

I'll leave it to the two of you to decide your roles and how you will work together.

I stopped short a block down from the hospital. Where was I supposed to go? I couldn't go home as much as I wanted to see my grandfather. I had no money, so getting a room for the night and something to eat was out of the question. What now?

Satan popped in through his portal, dressed as always with casual but impeccable flair.

"There's a homeless shelter five blocks that way. I'm sure there'll be a bed and food there. Not what you're used to but some food to stick to your ribs and somewhere to lay your head. I'll catch up in the morning to explain the financial arrangements."

"OK, thanks."

After Satan popped out, I strolled in the direction of the shelter. For all my familiarity with the city, my true self discerned layers invisible to humans. The history of buildings and the people who had lived, which were hidden under films of grime, revealed themselves like walking through a limestone cave with a torch. Every turn exposed something spectacular. Even the broken had their place.

The shelter's door had nearly closed by the time I arrived. I just managed to get a hand on it to prevent it from shutting. "I'm sorry to be so late, but I am in need of accommodation for the night."

The hostel manager looked me over then opened the door. "I'm Shanice."

"Camie and I can't thank you enough."

Shanice pointed to the house rules. "When you've read them, meet me in the supply room for your bedding and towel."

The rules seemed straight forward—respect, courtesy, privacy, and some practical matters. Next to the rules, a map of the building was pinned to the board. I followed the corridors until I came to the supply room. A pile of bedding sat on the counter. "You were lucky. We had to throw someone out for not obeying the rules, or there wouldn't have been a bed. Room 26, upstairs. Bathroom's at the end of the hall."

I thanked her then said, "I know this is an imposition, and I read the rules for dinner time, but is there any possibility of something to eat, even an apple? You see, I've just come back from the dead."

Shanice took a step back.

124

I pulled up my shirt to reveal the now-sealed wound. "It's true. I've been in the morgue for a few hours, but *God* sent me back. You can ring the morgue if you like."

Shanice pulled out her mobile phone. "Your story had better check out, or you'll leave. We don't take the mentally ill. There is another facility for that."

After being put through, Shanice began, "I'm from the Jefferson Street homeless shelter. I've got this nu . . . guy claiming he was dead, and *God* sent him back." She kept a watchful eye on me.

After a pause, she said, "Camie."

A few moments later, she thanked the person and hung up. "It seems like you're telling the truth, although the morgue attendant wasn't so sure about the resurrection bit."

"Oh, no, I'm nothing like *Christ*. *God* just has a plan for me and returned me to my body so I could fulfill it."

"Whatever you say. I'll get you a sandwich."

I lay on my cot, contemplating who the *Father* would bring into my life to complete the task assigned to me and how I would know them. No secret handshake. No magic signs. I fell asleep with the glory of *God's* plan running through my head.

Chapter 17

One Last Dance

ϡ7ℨ ˥ˇℨϡℨℲ7

I made out two sets of footsteps following me. Not the family, or I'd be dead. I reached for my gun then shook my head. I still had choices—run, turn to confront them, or divert from the path and hope to find someone. I opted to confront them as running displayed cowardice.

Mid-step, I spun then dropped into a fighting stance. There stood two men. First, the guy from the seedy pawnshop I tried to trade one of the three gold coins Raphael gave me as my monthly allowance. He said they were a gift from my Mother, *Shekinah*. The other looked like a common thief, much like the shop owner. Can't believe that shop owner tried to rip me off. Both outweighed me by about forty pounds, but I'd learned a thing or two about fighting over the past nine years.

The footsteps behind me shifted the odds out of my favor. A line of sweat coated my upper lip. Where the two in front remained stationary, the step behind me kept advancing. I risked a glance and cracked a smile.

Satan swung his cane as he commented, "Two on one, not very sporting. How about two on two?"

The thug from the pawnshop sneered. "What's a milksop like you going to do?"

Both attackers pulled knives.

"Just this . . ." A swish announced the rapier's withdrawal from the cane. Satan moved with speed beyond the capabilities of a human and whipped the sword across the backs of the men's hands. The skin parted as the narrow blade sliced through tendons, and knives fell to the ground.

Satan wedged the point of the rapier under the chin of one man and asked, "Any other questions? Now get out of here before I run you through."

The men bolted.

Satan turned to me. "Really, day one, and I have to rescue you. I thought your nine years on the streets might have taught you better?"

I huffed. "I had it under control."

"At least you didn't run. But seriously, you went to that dive of a pawnshop. Try the reputable gold buyers in the city center or, better still, coin dealers. They are, after all, rare Spanish bullion."

"Yeah, well, I knew when he offered me three-hundred. The coin was worth a good deal more than that."

Satan nearly choked. "A good deal more; try twenty to thirty times more."

"OK, I never knew the value of the stuff we stole unless the newspaper ran a story on the robbery, but thank you for cluing me in. Why you didn't tell me that this morning, I don't know."

"Gave you more street cred than you deserve, apparently. Here's the fare into the city and the addresses of some dealers." Satan plucked the paper out of the air. "And try not to get killed again today." Satan disappeared.

My feet hurt from beating the pavement between dealers as I negotiated the best price on one of the coins. The other two I fed through a hole in my jacket pocket so they slid into the lining. With my money in hand, I entered a cubicle in the men's room, took off my shoes, and put the bulk of the cash inside. It didn't help my sore feet, but if someone attempted to mug me, I'd only lose five hundred.

My next task was to ring my grandfather, something I hadn't done in quite some time. The delight in his grandfather's voice pricked my conscience, but from now on, I'd make sure I contacted him at least once a week. It saddened me that I couldn't visit, but once the family knew I was alive, they'd be watching the house.

After a shopping expedition where I purchased a mobile phone cheap enough to switch out in a week, some middle of the road clothes, and a newspaper, I found a quiet café where I researched accommodations. Scanning down the columns of ads, one odd advertisement caught my eye.

"Looking to get away from your old life and leave your past behind, try Savannah."

I certainly needed to do that. Even though the family would find me once Lucifer realized I was back, this might buy me some time. I closed the newspaper and opened a browser on my phone to investigate rentals in Savannah.

I risked going to breakfast at the motel in the morning, figuring that since it wasn't on the family's radar, I'd be safe. Besides, I needed a hearty meal for the trip to my new destination.

As the bus rattled away from the terminus, I took one last look at my childhood city. Several hours later, I stretched my legs in what was to be my new hometown. The fresher air formed only part of the impression of wholesomeness. A quick scan on the Internet turned up two motels, one within walking distance. A phone call later, I had a room. Unlike the sooty façade of last night's accommodation, healthy shrubs lined the walkway to this motel. The fresh-faced receptionist was a far cry from the jaded attendant who had practically ignored me last night. The room lived up to the standard set so far. Sure, I'd slept in better, but the fresh paint, crisp linen, and pine scent invited me in. The hearty aroma wafting from the kitchen of the restaurant made my mouth water.

Belly filled, I retired for the night after giving thanks to *God*.

By the early afternoon the following day, I'd secured the lease on a one-bedroom apartment near a park.

The area near the motel boasted only one furniture store, and although the range came nowhere near the furnishings of my previous apartment, I had fun choosing. The shop assistant raised his eyebrows when I paid in cash and paid extra for a fast delivery.

Back at the motel, I counted out the last of the money from the coin. Enough for a few nights' accommodation, some food for my new place, and a little in reserve, but soon I'd have to trade another coin.

I opened the door to my new abode to await the arrival of my furniture. A fragrance greeted me. The faint scent of rose petals filled the air, and a single perfect white rose lay on the floor in the center of what would be the lounge room, dew still glistening on the delicate petals. *Shekinah Mother,* the *Holy Spirit,* confirmed my choice of apartments, and my spirits rose. To know *Her* presence looked out for me gave me confidence.

As the sun set three nights later, I sat down to the first meal I had cooked since I left my grandfather's at eighteen.

A voice from the lounge room said, "Quaint."

I stiffened until the voice said, "It's only me."

I found Satan reclining on the faux leather couch, legs crossed, arm stretched along the back. "Make yourself at home. Oh, I see you have. Any chance you could act like a normal person and knock? I could have a visitor."

Satan rapped the cane on the wooden floor. "Knock knock. Better? Besides, that wouldn't be anything I haven't seen."

I threw a cushion at him. "You're incorrigible. But what do you think? I know, compared to where I lived last, it's a comedown, but for living a normal life, it's good, isn't it?"

"Certainly inconspicuous. Is there a fire escape ladder at the window for when the family comes through the door? But the *Father* has granted you a couple of angelic gifts." He whispered the list in my ear.

B.D. VANNOY

"Great. I will take what I can get. Have you eaten? I have some chop suey that I made."

"Will it poison me?" Satan smirked.

"I'll have you know, my grandfather taught me to cook just fine." The memory brought a pang of regret.

Half an hour later, Satan scraped his plate and spooned the last mouthful. "I have to hand it to you; that was the best chop suey I've had in a few thousand years. But now to more pressing matters," he pulled the cuffs of his linen shirt out from under his silk-blend jacket, the diamond cufflinks sparkling. "The family went to collect your body only to find out you didn't die. We've had a veil over you these last few days, but it won't hold for much longer."

"And then Lucifer will know where I am." I sighed. "This peace, couldn't it last a little longer?"

"Sorry, old chap. Raphael will keep you updated on their movements. I'm hoping you'll manage the family, but I'll be on hand for any confrontations with Lucifer that you can't handle. Anyway, must fly. Thanks for dinner."

After Satan left, I researched places I might trade the coin. Nothing seemed promising, but I'd do a search of the town tomorrow. After thanking the *Lord* for my new abode, I asked for guidance in my mission, then curled up in my new bed with its fresh linen and fell soundly asleep.

The sounds of birdsong woke me. The inner city hadn't had many birds and none with such glorious voices. I remembered the *Father's* words when I was in purgatory—praise *His* name when I enjoyed *His* creations. I did exactly that.

The crisp morning air invigorated me as I strolled through the park, but it promised to be a beautiful summer's day. I heard the bird song again and scanned the trees. A flash of red flitted from one bough to another—a red cardinal. It had been so long since I'd seen one. A squirrel scampered up the oak tree. I hadn't realized just how much I missed nature, but there were some National Parks close to the town. When I had enough money saved, I'd get a used car and visit.

A little way along the path, an old lady covered in newspapers lay on a bench with a trolley filled with bags next to her. As a youngster, I never came across poverty, and as one of the family, the homeless were a good source of information. We slung them some money, but their fate never bothered me. When confronted by this image, as I thought of my warm, comfortable bed, my heart wept for her.

I made my way to a food van and hunted in my pocket for some loose change with which I purchased a hamburger and coffee. I'd have preferred something a little healthier, but the offerings were slim.

She stirred from under the newspapers as I approached. I squatted in front of her and offered her the food. "I thought you might need some breakfast."

A tear formed in the corner of her eye as she smiled. "Thankin' you. Is not often a handsome young'un pay Mama any attention."

"I'm Camie." Something prompted me to tell her my full name. "Actually, it's Chamuel, but that's a bit old-fashioned."

"Sure don't hear a name like that 'round here." Mama looked like she was mulling over the name. "Seem like Mama heard it before."

I sat with her as she ate the hamburger and drank the coffee. I didn't want to pry into her past, so I asked her about the town, its history, the people, and the weather. She chatted happily about the kind souls who helped her. Then her face went dark. "A while back, some of them newcomer, fancy pants Yankees from up north come down to escape the cold. They tried to have Mama and her friends thrown outta our home. Said they pay a lot of money to get down here and shouldn't have to live next to 'things' like us. What? Like we' some kind of mangy animal or something?

"They call us all kinda terrible things, had their chil'en, tryin' to scare us away. Imagine teachin' youes chil'en to hate like tha'. It's not right, Mama tell you. It's jus' not right."

I patted her knee as she rubbed her eyes. "No, it isn't. Lucifer does a great job getting people to hate each other."

"Wees all be *God's* chil'en. Like the Sunday school song: Jesus, do love the little chil'en, all the chil'en of the world. Red and yellow, black and white, they are precious in His sight . . . wees be all kinds out here an' they be Mama's friends. Wees takes care of each other, way it should be. Color makes no difference to 'ole Mama,"

Mama chewed her hamburger in silence for a few minutes. Then, after eating half the hamburger, she stopped. I asked, "Aren't you going to finish it?"

"No, Mama'll save this for later." She wrapped the uneaten half in a piece of newspaper and placed it in one of her many bags.

As I made to leave, she said, "Thank you for not askin' why Mama is homeless. People think they gotta right to know."

I went back to the house and collected the throw rug off the couch, wishing I had a blanket.

"It isn't much, but it is better than those papers," I said as I handed it to her a few minutes later.

"But this be new. I can't take this." She tried to hand it back.

"My couch doesn't need to be kept warm. You do."

Her faded eyes sparkled as she threw it around her shoulders, preening herself like a young girl. I left her laughing.

It wasn't enough. I turned back. "Forget the blanket. Come and stay with me."

"No. You don' wan' a millstone 'round your neck."

"You won't be a burden, and the *Father* says we are to share what we have. You'll be warm, and the couch is softer than this bench."

"Well, you be a blessing, but I don' think I could live inside no more; Mama been years livin' on the streets goin' on long time now."

"At least eat with me. I would enjoy the company."

"Tell you what, buy Mama a burger tamorra; we'll talk some more."

During my wandering around the town, the thought of Mama's newspapers made me shiver. If she refused to live with me, she could at least be warm. I bought a decent quilt and pillow for her.

When I delivered them to her, she placed her hand on mine on top of the quilt and said, "Someun'll jus steal 'em from me; out here, best to have nothin' of value. You keep 'em for visitors."

I opened my mouth to protest, but she shushed me. She said, "You can't save the world, you know."

"But that's what I'm here for . . . not exactly saving the world. But the *Father* has given me a job to do."

She laughed. "So, you thought you'd start on Mama."

"No. It wasn't like that. I simply thought you might be hungry, but one hamburger didn't seem enough."

"Don' forget; one tamorra, too. Thankin' you for you generosity. Tell you what, bring your ole Bible and read to Mama. My eyes ain't up to it no more."

With every mouthful I spooned into my mouth at dinner, my mind replayed Mama wrapping the leftover hamburger for later. I prayed to the *Father* for guidance over Mama.

Just be her friend.

Chapter 18

Rise Once More,
Mighty Archangel

ㄴㄱㄱㅈ ㅂㄱㄥㅇㄱ ㄴ∞✓ㄴㄱㄷ

The following morning, I scouted farther afield to find a more appetizing meal than a slab of questionable meat and a piece of plastic yellow cheese. A small corner takeaway provided the answer. A bun made of real bread, actual ground beef, crisp lettuce, juicy tomato, and a slice of Jarlsberg cheese filled my requirements perfectly. This time, I bought a bottle of orange juice as well as the coffee.

Mama's eyes lit up, and she grinned, revealing her complete lack of dental hygiene. "Mama knowd' where you got thisun; sometime people generous with their coin an' Mama buy one." The lettuce crunched as she bit into it. Tomato juice ran between her chin hairs. "Mm-mm, real beef, put's others 'ta shame. Not tha' Mama sayin' yesterday's gift were no good. Jus' this here be better."

I opened the Bible. "What should I read?"

"Psalms, dear boy. Mama be partial to praisin' the *Lord*, not tha' Mama done much of tha' in recent years. *He* gave me this here task of bein' in this here park an' wait 'til *He* shew me the way. But Mama bin thinkin *He* forgotten ole Mama 'cause it bin years now."

"Would you like me to pray with you?"

"Mama gave up the prayin' a while back as He don' answer no more. Maybe a Psalm or two put Mama in the mood."

I read from Psalm 25. When I read the verse:

Because the Lord is righteous and good,
He teaches sinners the path they should follow.
He leads the humble in the right way
and teaches them his will.
With faithfulness and love he leads
all who keep his covenant and obey his commands.

Mama said, "Thankin' you, chil'. Mama bin needin' a reminder. Now, I's ready for a prayer."

I held her gnarled hands and thanked the *Father* for bringing us together so Mama's faith might be restored and asked *Him* to show her that *He* has not forgotten her by revealing *His* plan.

Mama's tears glistened on her dark skin when she said, "You pray mighty powerful for a young'un. Mama sure *God* listen to you."

I left Mama feeling like I had begun my mission—one soul redeemed. Now, I just had to find a way of doing it on a bigger scale.

I picked up the local rag from a newspaper stand with the idea of getting to know my new town's people and settled myself into a booth in the sunshine to scan the paper. A voice from the next booth said, "You're new in town, ain't you."

I looked up from the paper. A man about in his fifties smiled such a welcome that I had to smile back. "Just got in a few days ago—seems like a friendly place."

"Yep, we are that. Hey, have you been to Old Savannah?"

"No, not yet."

"The historic part of town . . . be happy to show you."

"If it's no inconvenience, I'd love to go. I'm Camie. Chamuel, actually." I watched for a flicker of recognition.

"Weird name; sounds Biblical. I'm Bobby Joe."

As they left the café, Bobby Joe hailed a taxi. "I'm not sure I can afford that at the moment."

"No problems, my treat."

The historic center's well-preserved buildings delighted me as we wandered in and out of "Olde Worlde Shops" and museums. As we walked, Bobby Joe asked about where I lived, my family, what I'd done as a job, and what I planned to do now that I was there.

I skirted my past employment, saying I was a courier for a family business. When it came to what I planned to do, I said, "I have a project that's been assigned to me, but I'm not sure of all the details. I do know I need to reach a lot of people."

Bobby Joe clapped me on the back. "Seems like we were meant to run into each other. I have just the thing for you. Let's go back to my office to discuss it."

Could this be the contact I needed to make? My hopes rose.

As offices go, it put me at ease being neither too flashy nor too down market. Once I was seated in a comfortable but functional chair on the client-side of an inlaid leather desk, Bobby Joe riffled through the filing cabinet. "Here it is." He produced a shiny folder with the words "Marketing and Promotion" splashed across the front.

Over the next half hour, Bobby Joe elaborated a grand plan for promoting my project. WebPages, networking schemes, old-fashioned advertising, billboards. It seemed a little bigger than what I needed, but the *Father* had big plans.

"Now, here's the contract. Sign here." Bobby Joe blustered as he slid the document toward me.

"Contract?"

"Yes, for the investment and my firm's monthly ongoing fee to manage the services." His friendly eyes turned beady.

My pen hovered over the dotted line. This didn't seem right; however, the *Father* had given me access to money, so perhaps it was in order. The tip of the pen rested on the page, but warning bells from my years with the family sounded. I laid down the pen. "Exactly how much are we talking here?"

"I'm sure a man of your means won't have a problem finding the money, and I assure you the monthly fee only covers expenses. No profit in it for me." His obsequious voice grated.

I tapped my fingers on the desk. "Doesn't answer the question, does it?"

"No need for you to worry about the details. I handle all of that." His right eye twitched, and he rubbed his hands.

"But I do want the details."

"It's a mere fifty thousand up front; then two thousand a month for the life of the contract."

My voice hardened. "And I suspect the contract is open-ended." I shoved the chair back and fairly bristled as I thanked him for the tour, but he could shove his contract where the sun don't shine.

Disillusionment claimed me at the apartment. I had been so sure that Bobby Joe and I had crossed paths for a greater purpose, but clearly, he trolled for victims. I prayed for greater perception and discernment that night and renewed trust in the *Father's* vision.

The following morning, I recounted the event to Mama.

"Tha' ole swindler; and they think us homeless is thieves. He's the biggest one Mama know." She screwed up her eyes and tightened her lips. "If'en you was taken in by tha' . . . tha' rat, Mama know a few people who can gets you money back."

"Thanks for the offer, but my common sense kicked in, and I told him what he could do with his contract."

Mama laughed. "Good for you, chil'. What'd you think you needed ole Bobby Joe for in the first place?"

I sighed. "He said he could help me get the word out about my project. In my last job, I didn't have much to do with computers and the like, so when he started talking websites, networking, and such, I got sucked in. I almost signed." I laced my fingers through the bars of the bench.

"Much to my embarrassment, but I thought the *Father* had brought us together. Bobby Joe said there was a purpose in our meeting, and I wanted to believe he was *God's* contact. He'd been so friendly, so helpful."

"Conivin' snake; takin' advantage of people like that, but there is good people about. Some folks like you, give Mama food or spare change. And bless those souls at the soup kitchin and shelter. Mama tries to make due, but sometime, jus' gotta get a bellyful and somewhere warm."

"My place is warm."

"No, Mama got renewed faith that *God* will shew her the way, an' to do tha', Mama gotta be in this here park. Whatcha plannin' today?"

"I thought I'd investigate getting flyers published. Going to go to some printers and do-it-yourself places to check prices."

"Yeah, you don' need ole Bobby Joe. Mama will hear 'bout it in the mornin'."

I discovered that without exact copy or numbers, the printers could only offer a pricing range, which after five, made my head spin with numbers. DYI proved simpler—per page by volume, color or black and white. Without more details, designing a flyer would become impossible.

Two blocks from the apartment, Raphael spoke to me. "Don't go home tonight."

I came to an abrupt halt, one foot raised, pivoted, and headed back the way I had come.

"Thanks for the warning. All night?"

Might be a few if they leave a man waiting.

Crap, I only had ten bucks left!

"Ok, I'll hole up somewhere."

"Let you know when they've gone."

I sucked in a breath—the jacket.

"Raphael, is there any way you can keep my jacket out of sight? It's got the coins in it."

"I'll do what I can, but I can't make it vanish, and if Lucifer is there, if I try to hide it, he will know and become suspicious."

"Of course, whatever you can, then. I'd best get to the shelter before they're out of beds."

The closest shelter had filled their beds. I hoped the next closest had something as the third would be closed by the time I got there.

Raphael kept a watchful eye on the activity at Camie's apartment. After busting the lock, five soldiers barged into the small apartment, splitting up to take different rooms. Lucifer as Lucian sauntered in last.

"Not here, boss."

Lucifer rubbed his temple. "Did he escape down the fire ladder?"

"Window was closed, so I don't think so."

Lucifer bridled. "Don't think so. You're not paid to think. You're paid to act. Get someone out that window and scouting now."

Lucifer studied the lounge. He glanced at the TV and then wandered into the kitchen and touched the kettle. "Someone must have . . ."

Raphael managed to withdraw farther just as Lucifer peered toward the Heavenly Realm.

"I know you're there, Raphael, but you can't hide him from me forever. I will find him, and I will stop him."

Lucian pointed at two of the soldiers. "You two; stay until he returns." He marched out of the apartment.

One of the two soldiers poked through Camie's draws and cupboards and hooked the jacket out of the wardrobe. He thrust an arm down a sleeve and shrugged into the coat, admiring himself in the mirror.

Raphael ratcheted up the soldier's body temperature until he took the jacket off and threw it into the corner.

My face fell when the shelter worker said, "Sorry, we're full."

"But I don't even have a coat."

The helplessness in my voice must have triggered something in the worker. "I shouldn't, but I'll get you a blanket. Just return it in the morning. If you need a bed tomorrow, be here before five o'clock to join the queue."

I thanked her, but now I had to find somewhere to sleep. I didn't know this part of town, but then, that shouldn't have surprised me given how little I knew about the city. After a quiet prayer, my steps led me to Green Square, where people occupied all the benches and sheltered locations. I propped myself against an oak and tucked the blanket around me. As the night lengthened, I buried my chin under the blanket to stop my teeth from chattering and shoved my hands under my arms. If I thought I understood Mama's predicament, I had a lot to learn. Sometime around three a.m., I fell asleep.

Something tickling my cheek woke me predawn. My hand flicked the offending object off. I scuttled sideways at the sight of a four-inch wolf spider on the grass not far from me. It meandered toward the tree, so I withdrew tactically. At least it had taken my mind off my kinked neck and frozen toes.

When I returned the blanket, I asked for directions to McDonalds as they had dollar burgers. The shelter worker not only gave me the requested directions but also those to the soup kitchen. Between the two, I'd be able to eke out my ten dollars for a few days. I didn't want to think about what I'd do if the jacket disappeared.

After a night in the shelter, Raphael informed me two soldiers had settled into the apartment to wait until my return

Even though I'd expected as much, my mood still fell. "How am I going to get them out? I need my jacket."

"I'll let you know when one of them goes out for supplies. That'll even the odds."

"I hope it won't take too long. I'm nearly out of money."

Lunchtime found me in a queue at the soup kitchen. Some people didn't look homeless, and after a half-hour's wait, when I got served my meal, I asked about them.

"Not everyone is homeless, but many are existing in poverty. By the time they pay rent and utilities, there's not much money, so to feed their kids, they eat their meal here. Same as the shelters, some are domestic violence victims."

That evening, waiting for a bed at the shelter, the sight of a woman whose bruised face contained the futility of life, herding her little ones into line, intensified my disgust at my brother, Lucifer. That he inflicted violence on the innocent via a spouse who'd promised to love and protect them sickened me.

At about two the following afternoon, Raphael let him know one of the soldiers had gone out for supplies.

I busted through the temporary fix to the shattered door, raising my auras as I did so.

The man leaped from the couch, drawing for his gun. He unloaded his clip as I charged toward him, my auras deflecting the bullets as the *Father* permitted. As he fumbled for a replacement clip, I wrestled him to the ground using the enhanced strength given to me.

Once I had him subdued on his stomach, my weight pinning him to the floor, I plucked cable ties and duct tape from the air, grateful the *Father* had allowed this gift in emergencies.

With his face squished into the floorboards, my captive's words slurred. "What in Hell's name are you?"

"Wrong realm. I'm the Archangel Chamuel of the Seraphim. When I release you, you will carry a message to the Don. Tell him that if he continues to attack me, he will bring down the wrath of the Heavenly Host. Further, tell him, Lucian is actually possessed by Lucifer who is using him for his own ends."

"Like that won't get me killed."

"Your choice. I can send you to Hell right now, but I am giving you a chance to live." Not that I had any intention of killing him, but he didn't know that.

After I bound his feet and hands and duct-taped his mouth, I hauled him out of sight, then fleeced him of his replacement clip and removed his knives. I'd search through their belongings for more clips once I took care of the second soldier. Then, I repositioned the door.

Not long after, a knock giving the family code alerted me to the return of the second soldier. The first soldier tried to yell through the gag. "If you don't want me to shoot your friend in the head, shut it."

He quit making noise.

I flattened myself against the wall, gun cocked. When the second man stepped into the room, I jammed the muzzle of the gun into the side of his head.

"No sudden moves. Drop the gun and kick it toward me."

He hesitated, and my experience told me he was weighing the odds of taking me before I shot him.

"Don't even think about it." I tapped his skull with the muzzle.

When he began to bend to place the gun on the floor, I said, "You'll be dead before you get that knife. Drop the gun and stand up."

A metallic clatter sounded.

"Turn around, put your hands on the back of your head, and spread your legs wide." I shoved the gun into my belt and plucked another cable tie from the air. I put one thumb into a thumb lock and twisted the arm down, and then repeated the move on the other. From there, I fastened his hands and retrieved the gun. Keeping an eye and the gun on him, I extricated the knife and checked for others. I shoved him toward the couch. "Sit. I've given your friend a message to deliver to the Don."

"You're not going to kill us?" Disbelief registered on his face.

"I'm not in the killing business, even if you'd have killed me."

"Our orders were to bring you in alive if possible," the first soldier said.

"You and I both know that's the same thing, but killing me here would be kinder than what waited if you took me back."

He grunted. "No more than you deserve."

I ignored his remark. "However, I'm in the saving business. I'm letting you go, and I hope my mercy today will lead you to a better life. But if you do attack me again, you'll force my hand."

I cut them loose, and as I ushered them out of the door, the first soldier began babbling. "You should have seen him. He had these wing things that deflected bullets."

Chapter 19

Welcome to Your New Family

⟨ᛏᚲᛒᛚᛝᚡᛚ ᛚᚨ ᛤᛝᛯᛂᛚᚲᛝ⟩

Mama's relief at the sight of Camie the following morning caused her to throw her arms around him. "Mama bin worried. Where you bin at?"

A serious expression replaced Camie's grin as they sat on her park bench, a drizzle of rain misting the surroundings. "I had a little trouble from my past employers." He sighed and studied his hands as if deciding what he should say.

"These ole eyes seen much. Mama don' judge. Get it off you chest."

"You'll probably think less of me when I tell you." He chewed a quick. "I worked for the mob, and during that time, I did some vile things, including killing a man."

"Nothins unforgivable, chil'. . ."

"I discovered that after the mob killed me, and I ended up in purgatory. The *Father* forgave my sins and returned me to Earth to fulfill the role *He* has planned for me."

Mama's heart fluttered and hope rose within her. "Tell Mama more 'bout this plan."

"That's just the trouble. I don't really know. The *Father* said *He* would guide me, but so far, I think *He* is testing me, as nothing is going right."

Mama searched his face for signs. "He bin testin' Mama for years. Like you taught Mama, don' give up."

Camie changed the topic. "I'm sorry I haven't anything for you this morning. I only have enough money for my fare into the city, but I intend to correct the money situation today. Wish me luck."

Mama elbowed him in the ribs. "You don' need luck when you have the Big Man on you side."

As his back retreated down the grand walkway with its trees draped in Spanish moss, she prayed for the truth to be revealed.

My efforts at finding somewhere to trade the coin proved fruitless. Of the three traders, one specialized in American coins, and the other two weren't able to offer me the value of the coin. Not that they tried to take advantage. They just didn't have the finances.

I must have had a worried expression on my face as I traipsed back through the park because Mama called out, "You look likes the weight of the world is on you shoulders. This morning, you was so certain. What happened?"

I sat on her bench and explained my dilemma of needing to get a good price for something I intended to trade. Given her situation, to have discussed the value of the coin would have been tasteless.

She brightened. "Mama has a friend with a pawnshop; he sure to help. What you got?"

My face flushed as I produced the coin.

"Oh my, tha' is beautiful." She fingered it.

Her total lack of jealousy that I had so much humbled me. "I'm embarrassed. This coin would feed you all year, and yet, I can tell, you don't covet it."

She laughed. "Mama, make herself sick ole woman if she got jealous. But back to you coin. Things like tha' is right up Misha's alley. He trade unique objects. Come, Mama take you to him."

As we walked across the park, Mama said, "Yous bes' be lettin' ole Mama do the talkin'. Misha be wary of outta towners."

"If you think it best, then it's fine by me."

A few blocks back from the park, Mama gestured toward a shop. "This be, 'Misha's Mish Mash'."

First impressions of the shop set next to a vacant block covered in straggly weeds didn't instill confidence in me. Its small façade badly needed a coat of paint. The stock on display behind a dirt-filmed window seemed run-of-the-mill. Bells clattered as Mama opened the door to reveal a cluttered, dimly-lit room. As I stepped inside, a burgundy velvet curtain over a doorway at the back opened, and a stooped geriatric appeared. He eyed me then turned his gaze on Mama, who jerked her chin toward me a couple of times. She appeared to have a question in her eyes.

The man's voice creaked as he spoke to Mama while squinting at me. "Misha not sure, could be, but Misha need proof. Misha bin caught before."

He seemed to be answering Mama's unspoken question on a subject I knew nothing about.

Mama gestured with her hand. "This be Camie, and him is Misha. Camie's full name is Chamuel."

I extended my hand, and to my surprise, Misha's strong grip encircled my hand, squeezing hard enough for me to wince. His eyes seemed to want to penetrate my skull.

"What can Misha do for you?"

Mama spoke up. "Thisun want to trade a coin; shew him, Camie."

I fished the coin from my shirt pocket and presented it to Misha. He popped on an eyeglass and inspected the coin. After turning it over a couple of times, he said, "Come, Misha need to research and discuss in private."

He led us through the curtain, behind which sat a desk with a computer and phone. Two doors at right angles exited the space. Misha placed the key into the door on the right. It groaned as it opened, and as I passed it, I put my hand on its four-inch steel thickness.

The room fairly glittered as light bounced off gold and jewel-encrusted objects. The contrast between the shabby, dusty front room with its tasteless bric-a-brac and this immaculate, well-ordered space about double the front room's size and crammed with valuables astounded me. At first, it struck me as odd that the walls appeared to be metal, and then it dawned on me that I stood in a vault.

Misha pulled books out from under piles stacked around a Louis XIV desk. "Ah, yes, this the one Misha need." He hummed while he flipped through pages. He stabbed his finger at a page. "This is it."

He showed me pictures of the exact coin with its coat of arms and distinctive cross. The caption read:

Carolvj Ji ⵏ Dei ⵏ Grat
1700j M Spain 8e Nge
Charlej JJ

Misha asked, "How did you come across this?"

"My *Mother* gave it to me to pay for expenses while I'm completing a project since I won't have time to work."

"Very generous . . . you know what it is worth?"

"I've traded one coin, so I have an idea of its value, yes."

"Good, then you know Misha not rob you. Please wait here." Misha threaded his way through the rows of merchandise and disappeared behind a screen. A few minutes later, he appeared with a wad of money. He handed it to me and asked, "You sure you not want leave some in Misha's safe? Not get robbed? We keep tally 'til it gone?"

The possibility that I may not see my money again crossed my mind as I mulled over the offer, but Misha seemed honest enough, and Mama trusted him. "Seems sensible. I peeled off six of the eight thousand and handed it back to him.

Misha retrieved a ledger from the desk and made an entry under my name and entered the figures then had me sign it. "Money safe with me." He then gave me a deposit slip with the balance written on it.

As we left the vault, I caught Misha whisper to Mama. "Has potential. Find out more, can't make mistake like last time."

My suspicion fired into action. Had I made a mistake with the money, and what did they think I had potential for? Had I told Mama too much about the mission already, and did I let her know I had heard the remark or just keep a watchful eye out? I opted for watching. Telling her might trigger an unforeseen action.

When Mama asked me about purgatory and being sent back, I spoke from the heart about the *Father's* greatness and *His* capacity for love and forgiveness, but I withheld anything about the mission. I needed to ascertain if Mama and Misha acted for Lucifer or not. Until then, the less said, the better. Not that I sensed his influence about them, but then, I hadn't sensed it with Bobby Joe either, and he was clearly a plant by Lucifer.

I spent my days in prayer and meditation, praising the *Father's* greatness and seeking guidance.

A couple of days later, Mama looked me in the eye and said, "You withdrawn; like there a shadow over us. Why?"

"I am beginning to doubt my ability to see the *Father's* plan."

"Tell Mama more about the plan."

There was that overly eager response. Until I got to the bottom of it, I wasn't going to share what little information I had about the mission.

"That's just the problem. *He* hasn't revealed it to me." I did not lie in this, but I also withheld the word "mission" as I had been since the beginning. Those mortals who believe in *God* also believe he has a plan for them. Even some nonbelievers think that, so I considered "plan" to be a safer bet than "mission" as that implies something greater.

When I asked her about the *Father's* plan for her, she was as equally forthcoming as I had been, other than saying she had hoped it might come to fruition soon and she could go home. She went on to say that was just the beginning of the next stage.

I commented on her excitement, and she replied, "Chil', Mama bin waiting for this, can't recall how many years, so sure Mama excited."

I read the note pinned to my door when I got back to the apartment. My mouth dried, and my hands trembled. They had my grandfather. My tumultuous emotions said to rescue him, but my experience showed me I'd never bust him out of the fortress. The note said to come in quietly, and they'd let the old man go. I doubted that. I'd never known a captive to leave the fortress except in a body bag. But how could I stay here and do nothing? My grandfather, whose gentle soul had never harmed anyone, didn't stand a chance in the hands of those monsters. Right now, all I could do was pray.

When my grandfather's ring finger, complete with his wedding band, turned up in the post, it felt like my grandmother's stroke all over again. I struggled to withstand this test, but the words of Matthew 10:37–39 kept coming back to me. Anyone who loves their family before the *Father* is not worthy of *Him*.

Two days later, a burner phone sat at the door with a note that read: *Be available at 5 p.m.*

I couldn't concentrate on praying. I paced the lounge. I gnawed my lip until I drew blood. I checked the time.

Five p.m. came. I waited as sweat sheened my face. At five past five, the mobile rang. My hand shook as I answered it at the first chime.

Lucian's voice came down the line. "We're waiting. We still have your grandfather. Here, speak to him."

I continued to pace.

My grandfather yelled, "Don't come. They'll k—"

The familiar sound of a fist connecting to the face reverberated over the phone.

I bit on the knuckle I had shoved in my mouth. Tears seeped from my eyes. I prayed for my grandfather's soul.

Lucian came back on. "You have two days."

As much as it cost me, I replied, "*God* has given me a mission, and you won't divert me."

"Then you will carry the responsibility for your grandfather's death to the grave and beyond."

Lucian's words rang true.

"Two days."

The line went dead.

My legs gave way, and I landed on the couch with a thump. What had I done?

That night, I poured my pain out to the *Father*, asking *Him* to give my grandfather a merciful death.

A commotion in the hall outside the Don's bedroom woke him. After requesting his wife remain in their room, he collected his Glock and cracked the door open a fraction. At the sight in the hall, he questioned his sanity. A man wrapped in a glowing shield threw balls of blue light at his soldiers. He rubbed a hand over his eyes. He heard gunfire, but nothing impacted the man. When one of the balls hit a soldier, the blue fire turned him into a pile of ashes in seconds.

The man in the shield yelled, "Call your men off before they all die."

"They're paid to die, so, no."

"Have it your way."

The man in the shield parted his hands. Between them, a ball at least three times the size of the others appeared. He launched it at the three remaining soldiers between himself and the Don. While the three burnt, he created another, which blasted the wall to the Don's bedroom into dust.

Before the Don could blink, the man entered the bedroom and waved a ball at him.

The Don unloaded a clip at the man, but the bullets ricocheted off the shield.

"Who are you?" The Don retreated a step.

The man dropped his shields, and where the Don expected to see armor, the man wore an Armani suit.

"I am the Archangel Satan, not to be confused with Lucifer, who you currently have on your payroll. You know him as Lucian. Lucifer's the bad dude."

"You just killed at least ten men. And you say Lucifer's bad."

Satan waved a hand. "Think of it as divine justice."

"There'll be more soldiers here soon." The Don's eyes darted to the hole.

"Uh-uh. I only want to talk, so let's make this quick. You will release Camie's grandfather, and you will stop pursuing him."

The Don pulled himself up to his five-foot-seven height and lifted his chin. "No one tells the Don what to do."

"Believe it or not, there is a power greater than you, and I represent *Him*. I strongly advise you to do as bid."

The Don folded his arms over his chest and tapped his foot. "And if I don't?"

"Camie sent a message saying the host of Heaven would descend on you if you didn't leave him alone. I'm just one. Imagine a host. I'm sure they would enjoy wiping vermin, such as yourself, off the face of the Earth."

The Don paled. "Release the grandfather, you say?"

"And?"

"Leave Camie alone"

"That's the spirit."

The following morning, Raphael spoke to me.

"Your grandfather is coming to visit."

The words made no sense. The family had my grandfather, and when I didn't show up in a day, they would kill him.

"Not funny, Raph . . .you know as well as I that the family has him."

"Not anymore."

"What? How?"

"Let's just say that the Don is now a firm believer in angels. Oh, and by the way, he won't be bothering you anymore."

I praised the *Father's* name.

Chapter 20

Precious Last Days

ᛓ ᛅᛒᛚᛐᛅᛅᛚ ᛉᛅᛌᛉ ᛚᛚ

Even though the bus wasn't due for another ten minutes, I kept getting up and going to the terminus door to check. At the announcement of its arrival, I shot out the door. I bounced from foot to foot as I scanned the descending passengers. The flow turned into a trickle, and my excitement faltered. What if he hadn't made the bus? Had something happened? Had the Don—?

And there he was. The power of the emotions that surged through me left me shaking. I zipped over to him to assist him down the steps, then I threw my arms around my grandfather, my tears falling on the top of his head, for my grandfather had shrunk. The realization that he was nearing ninety struck me. The loss of those wasted years brought fresh tears.

"I'm so sorry, Papa." I brushed my hand over my wet eyes.

"I know, son. Let me look at you." He stepped back, and with eyes dulled with cataracts, studied my face. "I see you are restored to yourself. That is a good thing."

"Very much so, I have lots to tell you, but let's get your bag and get out of here."

I gave the taxi driver directions to the apartment and sat in the back-seat holding my grandfather's hand. He wanted to know how I became involved in the family, and I explained how I had been recruited by some-one who turned out to be Lucifer.

He nodded. "It seems you have been targeted by Lucifer all your life. I have never understood why."

I almost blurted out that I was an archangel but stopped myself in time, not being sure whether he would believe me or be able to handle the news. Instead, I said, "The *Father* has a plan for me, and Lucifer is determined to stop it."

"Hmm," his old eyes grew pensive. "Your grandmother made mention of it before she had her first stroke, I believe. I often wondered if the stroke was intended to prevent her from telling you."

My vision blurred as tears of remorse formed. "I have brought so much pain to my family; first my mother, then Nansie, and nearly you."

My grandfather patted my hand. "You are not responsible for Lucifer and Lilith's actions. But I take it, you have asked forgiveness from God for turning away from him?"

I brightened. "Yes, I will tell you all about that back at the apartment."

The hours flew by as we reacquainted ourselves. My grandfather paled when I told him I had died, but when I gave him an account of purgatory and the grace of the *Father*, he rejoiced with me.

I cooked him his favorite meal, after which he retired to my room. Even though he argued against it, I could tell he was relieved to have a bed.

In the morning, I bought hamburgers for the three of us, and we sat on Mama's bench in the early light. She extolled my virtues in bringing her breakfast until my face turned beetroot.

My grandfather said, "He always did have a good heart, well, until that filth Lucifer got a hold of him. But even then, it won through when he confessed his crimes. Now, we wait on God's timing to learn of this plan."

Mama said, "Amen to that."

"Papa, you can either wait here, or I'll take you back to the apartment, but I'm going to the tourist information center. I'm going to hire a car, and we're going sightseeing. You too, Mama."

That flustered Mama. She went to speak, but I held up my hand. "No protests."

I came back armed with flyers for all sorts of tours, walks, and drives.

My grandfather said, "I hate to dampen your enthusiasm, but I can't walk far these days."

"Do you think you could manage a tour of the Cathedral? We could do the Laurel Hill Wildlife Drive this morning and the Cathedral in the afternoon. Yes?"

My grandfather looked into the distance and then said. "Yes, it will have seats if I need them."

"Tomorrow, I thought a tour of the old buildings in the town and then a riverboat cruise."

Mama shifted and gazed at the fingernails. "Mama can't be goin' on no riverboat or in no Cathedral."

I raise an eyebrow.

"Well, looks at Mama. I ain't showered in Lord knows how long."

I hung my head. How insensitive of me. Then, I brightened. "That's easily solved. Shower at my place while I buy you something to wear— deal?" I stuck my hand out, and Mama shook.

Mama stood a little awkwardly in her new slacks and top in the doorway to my bedroom. "What y'all think?"

Her transformation left me opened-mouthed. She appeared to have shed twenty years.

My grandfather said, "If I were fifteen years younger, I'd ask you out on a date."

Mama blushed.

My grandfather and Mama wound down the windows to take in the fresh air of the wildlife sanctuary as we meander along Laurel Hill Drive, stopping at viewing points for my grandfather to get a better look. Mama and I took a short stroll along one of the paths that wandered through the wetland. Birdlife abounded—herons, egrets, cranes—and to my delight, alligators. The first one tempted me to take it home, a cute baby about eighteen inches long, but then I saw an adult. Hmm, a bit big for the bathtub.

My grandfather expressed his appreciation of the dedication of Savannah's citizens, who had donated to rebuilding the Cathedral twice after fire damage. He said the story of the first donor in 1898, a little boy who emptied the contents of his piggy bank, touched him.

The following day, I lost count at the number of irate drivers who tooted me as I stopped to gawk at the Victorian era's ornate architectural "painted ladies." By comparison to the McMansion the family lived in, they were small, but they'd been grandiose for their time with their foibles of turrets, gables, and ornate veranda friezes. The variety of complementary and contrasting colors added life to the street not found in modern suburbs, but I'd hate to be the one who had to paint them.

We boarded the riverboat at three p.m. for our sightseeing tour. While we waited for it to depart, I bought an array of sandwiches, some pastries, and coffee. After we ate, I swiped a chair and took it out to the deck so my grandfather could sit through the tour. The narration of the port's history intrigued me but not as much as the views of River Street. I did my best with the phone, but I'd have to come back with a camera.

The imposing cannon at Fort Jackson set high on the stone walls made me glad we weren't a target. I put the fort on tomorrow's plans, particularly when I heard they fired the cannon at eleven and two.

The following day the drive to the fort took us through some scenic country. We ate the picnic lunch I'd packed and then proceeded to the gate. When Mama got to the entry, she said she wouldn't be going in. I asked why not, and she said I'd spent enough already. I smiled and reminded her of the money Misha held on my account.

We poked our heads into the various buildings and wandered through arched corridors. The boom of the cannon at two p.m. shook the ground and hurt my ears. Little wonder artillerymen went deaf. After the cannon display, my grandfather asked to be taken back to the car, and then Mama and I completed our exploration.

Three days of activity had exhausted my grandfather, so while he rested the following afternoon, Mama and I went back to Misha's so I could get some money. When Mama told him about my reunion with my grandfather, he spread his arms and said, "Come to Misha's tomorrow for lunch. We celebrate."

As he stepped out of the car in front of Misha's, my grandfather's face reflected a similar expression to the one I had when I first saw the shop. He muttered, "Food poisoning?"

I patted him on the back. "It'll be fine."

Misha greeted us. "Misha honored to have esteemed grandfather of Chamuel as guest."

My grandfather looked askance at me.

"I'll explain tonight."

Misha directed us through the curtain and took the other door out of the office, which led into the living quarters.

Our footsteps echoed on the wooden floor of a narrow corridor, which ran the building's length on the side adjoining the vacant block. The first section presented a blank wall I presumed to be the vault's location. Through the first door we passed, I glimpsed a neatly made bed and a polished wardrobe.

Misha seemed to be leading us to the room at the end of the corridor.

About halfway down, I puzzled over ornately carved double doors. Why would doors be leading to an empty block?

I counted three rooms before we got to the last.

My grandfather's surprised voice said, "My, what a charming room."

Given how grimy the shop appeared, his reaction to the cleanliness of the room was not unexpected.

A step or two in, I paused, drinking in the exquisite art and rich furnishing with its eclectic taste in antiques and tapestries. The glint of polished steel from a row of finely crafted swords caught my eye.

Misha pulled out a chair for me, one for my grandfather, and one for Mama at a gleaming wooden table in the corner of the room. Silver cutlery, crystal glasses, and linen serviettes graced the inlay of the table's surface. I could get used to this.

I wiggled my butt on a chair from a couple of centuries ago, which I found comfortable even though straight-backed.

"Misha go to kitchen now," he said as he exited the room.

I'd seen no evidence of a kitchen, but maybe one of the closed doors in the corridor hid a kitchen.

My grandfather and I discussed the paintings. "They're clearly European, but I'm not sure where."

"From Misha's accent, I'd hazard Russian." My grandfather pointed to one. "That may be a Bryullow."

I gave him a blank look as Mama nodded.

"One of Russia's finest painters," my grandfather informed me.

This aspect of him was new to me. "I didn't know you knew much about art."

"Before your mother was born, your grandmother and I visited many galleries. We had quite the love of a good painting."

Misha returned bearing silver platters from one of which wafted the delicious smell of freshly baked black bread. The other was laced with ribbons of paper-thin slices of rich, smoked salmon, and aged cured ham served with ambrosia melon.

My mouth fairly watered. When he said he'd get more, I replied, "This is more than enough."

"Nonsense; Misha promised a celebration. Celebration you will have."

After Misha made several more trips to the kitchen, the table groaned under the weight of serving dished ladened with food.

Misha informed us that the blackcurrant marmalade, loganberry jam, and butter had been made on-site, and even the honey was home harvested. I slathered my black bread with butter and jam. The burst of sweetness against the chewy bread demanded I eat more, but the delicate spotting on the quail's eggs called to me. The subtle crack of the shell gave way to a perfectly boiled egg. I bit into its firm texture until the runny center exploded in my mouth—the rich, creamy flavor flowed on my tongue then slid down my throat.

My grandfather said, "You must try the pickled herring. The dill crème Fraiche cuts through the pickle brilliantly."

I set down the now empty crystal ramekin that the herring had occupied and turned my attention to the oysters. As with the herring, the mignonette sauce made the perfect accompaniment. My taste buds danced.

Mama spooned a mouthful of sautéed mushrooms. "Mm-mmm, when you have time to pick mushrooms?" she asked Misha.

"Misha send Sera . . . she like the outdoors."

Misha passed me a plate. "Must try goat's milk cheese. Misha wheedled secret out of Fromager on St Simon's Island . . . have preserved strawberry to go with it."

The soft silken texture of the cheese contrasted with its tart, earthy flavor, and the strawberry gave it a zing.

My grandfather carefully drizzled a sauce over some of Misha's fresh tomatoes. His eyes widened as he tasted it. "This balsamic vinegar is so complex. I've not tasted one like it."

"Ah-ha . . ." Misha grinned. "So, you know good balsamic, sir. It forty years old. Goes well with Misha's prized heirloom tomatoes, no?"

My bloated stomach said it refused to take more, but I had to try some. Thick as syrup, the balsamic drew out the flavor of the tomato.

Mama said, "Chef outdone his self."

"Misha will pass on your thanks. Now, who would like some Russian tea with sweetened cream or perhaps coffee?"

My grandfather shook Misha's hand. "You have been more than generous to a stranger. I can't thank you enough."

Misha laughed. "Well, Hebrews 13:2 say, 'we never know when we might be entertaining angels.'"

My heart skipped a beat. Did he know?

Back at the apartment, my grandfather said, "These last few days have been a blessing. I cannot tell you how it lifts my soul to see you returned to the faith. I can meet my Maker, secure in the knowledge that He is taking care of my grandson." His eyes misted. "I am so glad they didn't kill me. Not that it would have mattered. But I praise *the Lord* that I have been spared these few days with you."

I smiled and said, "You make it sound like we are never going to see each other again."

"That is a possibility, son. I have cancer."

The smile drained from my face. I had just gotten my grandfather back. This couldn't be.

"I know it is not news that you wanted or needed, but we have good memories from these few days, and I am content."

My heart resisted asking, but my reason said I needed to know. "How long?"

"A few months at most," he said it so calmly. "I have made my peace with it and am ready for the onward journey. And I'm looking forward to seeing your mother and grandmother again."

"Do you want me to come home to be with you until . . ." I couldn't bring myself to say it.

"No, son, you have a purpose here I will not interrupt. Don't worry; I have a bed at a hospice for the last stages. I'll be well looked after."

I choked out. "Let me know. I will come to see you before you return to *God*."

"I'd appreciate that."

He hugged me, and I became aware of the frailty of his body.

Chapter 21

Epiphany

ᑎᐧᒐᓄ᙮ᐧᑕ

In the morning, I drove my grandfather to the bus terminus and stood staring at the space long after the bus departed. I vowed to see him again, but anything might happen. At least, the *Father* had given me these last few days.

When I got home, I prostrated myself on the floor and gave thanks to the *Father* for *His* mercy and prayed for my grandfather's safe return to *Him*. As with most of my private prayers, I used the Angelic tongue, given its express purpose is to praise *His* name. The connection between the *Father* and myself deepened when I spoke it.

A sound behind me jolted me out of my worship. I leaped to my feet, and my auras sprang out in an instant reaction to protect myself.

Mama fell to her knees. "You is the one. Praise the *Lord*. Mama's prayers has bin answered. I shoulda neva doubted."

I withdrew my auras and gave her a sheepish look. "The one what, Mama?"

"The one the *Lord* send Mama to the park to wait for, so I's could shew him the way."

I burst out laughing. All this time and the answer was staring me in the face. My excitement overflowed. I pulled her to her feet and seated her on the couch. "What is the *Father's* plan for me?"

"Misha and Mama bin doin' it for some time now but only small scale one night a year, All Hallows Eve. Now's you here, wees can go big time." She clapped her hands. "Mama can't believe it."

None-the-wiser, I asked, "Doing what?"

"Why, chil', sending the travelers home. It make Mama so happy when wees does it. But only on All Hallows Eve."

My frustration mounted. "Who are these travelers?"

"Can't you guess?" Mama's eyes twinkled with mischief.

At my blank stare, Mama asked, "Who need redeemin' most."

"Murderers, child abusers . . . there are too many to name."

The lines on Mama's wrinkled brow deepened. "Seem like we gotta few things to shew you first."

I prayed for patience. "If you think that best."

Her enthusiasm returned. "But now, wees gotta tell Misha." She grabbed my hand and began to pull me toward the door.

"OK, I'll just get my jacket." As I disappeared into the bedroom, I asked, "What were you doing here, anyway?"

"The *Lord* said you needed help, but *He* really wanna show Mama your true nature. Tha' was the Angelic tongue you was speakin', weren't it?"

"Yes. How did you know?"

"Heard it years ago . . . once."

I pressed, but she said no more. I'd taken the rental back, so we walked the few blocks, each deep in our own thoughts.

When Misha appeared from behind the curtain, Mama burst out with, "Is him. Is him!"

Misha looked from Mama to me and back again, as if not comprehending what she said. "Does this mean—"

"Yes, wees can go big time now."

162

Misha's voice held a gentility I had heard often between my grand-mother and grandfather. "Misha was going to say, you can come in from the cold after all these years?"

It touched me that Misha's first concern focused on Mama. They clearly meant something to each other.

"S'pose it do, but tha' not the point. Wees gets to save more of them."

Misha took me hand in his. "Misha cannot tell you how grateful Misha is that you here. Mama has served the *Lord* these last decades, and I praise *His* name that *He* answered her prayers by sending us *His* representative.

"Not just a representative. Go on, tell Misha wha' you is."

"I'm an Archangel of the Seraphim."

"Show him." Mama prodded me in the back.

"What, now? Here?" The idea made me uncomfortable.

Misha pointed to the back. "Come. Come. Not here, too many eyes."

When we returned to the room where we had eaten lunch, Misha looked at me, eyes filled with expectation.

I felt like a freak at a sideshow, but I called on my auras.

Misha's mouth formed an *O*, and his eyes widened.

Mama pointed at me. "See three pairs, Seraphim for sure." Her eyes danced. "He glows when he prays, too."

My auras folded, and I sat at the table. "So, let me get this straight. You've been redeeming people but only at Halloween, why Halloween?"

Misha answered. "Is when veil between realms thinnest, but now you here, we can expand."

"Yes, that makes sense, but how and who exactly?"

Mama said, "We got things to shew you first."

Misha leaned over to her and said, "Mama, you can come home now. No need to be the ole bag lady no more."

Mama blinked. "S'pose not." She shook herself and the years fell away. An attractive middle-aged female with waist-long dreadlocks in neat rows grinned at me, and her fiery emerald eyes captivated me. Her rich, dark chocolate skin glowed as she extended her hand. "I'm Sylviel."

"So, you're an—"

"Yes, an ordinary angel, but an angel nonetheless."

"Mama, there is nothing ordinary about any angel, no matter your rank," I protested.

"Thank you, but I lost my way there for a bit until you came."

My mind took a moment to process this. "It's OK, Mama, I mean Sylviel—"

"Mama's fine."

"We all lose our way sometimes. I certainly have. Spectacularly, but I must ask, why the bag lady routine?"

"When the *Lord* sent me to the park, I went as myself first, only to be hounded out by the regulars. I threatened them, you see. After studying the park occupants for a while, I struck upon an identity that they could trust; one that wasn't too far from my roots. It takes time to be accepted, but after I helped a few out by sharing, they became less wary, and over time, I integrated into their lives. Part of me will miss it."

"How long were you there for?"

"Goin' on twenty years."

"Little wonder you thought the *Father* had forgotten you."

"But *He* has answered them now, and we have work to do, but first things first—the venue. I'll give you a little history before we show you.

"We'd been running a little restaurant in Boston, but the economy slowed, and it couldn't sustain itself. We thought our days were numbered and resigned ourselves to the end. But again, *Father* showed us *He* was not done with us yet."

Misha jumped in. "Mama and Misha want to go to Miami for some time, and now seemed perfect. So, Misha took our little nest egg, and Mama and Misha set out for Miami. On the way, Mama and Misha stop here in Savannah for a few days. Misha heard how it such a wonderful place to visit.

"Close to ocean, good seafood. Misha was told it was haunted place with lots of strange things. They did not know about us, did they Mama?" Misha laughed.

Us? Mama's an angel. What's Misha?

"We found beautiful Victorian B&B called 'The Painted Lady' and fell in love with it. On second morning at breakfast Misha find owners were retiring and searching for old-fashioned couple to sell to that would agree to operate a B&B as long as possible and well, as they say, the rest is history." Misha opened his arms wide and laughed a big, satisfied laugh.

Mama picked up the story. "Things were terrific until we noticed problems with the foundation and contracted an engineering company to help us find a solution. The day in that nice young man's office was very hard for Misha and me. He told us that The Painted Lady had sustained irrevocable damage to the foundations and that she couldn't operate as a business anymore. For public safety, the city tore her down, unfortunately. They were kind enough to allow us enough time to salvage what we could, which is when we discovered the secret door."

Misha pointed at the hall. "*God's* providence was at work that day. The little pawnshop was vacant, and the owners couldn't be located, so the city owned it."

Mama clapped. "They agreed to sell the pawnshop to us for back taxes, out of sympathy, I suppose."

"Misha discover Misha can access The Painted Lady through secret door, even though Victorian house is poof, gone."

Mama said, "Yes, her spirit lives on. Apparently, the basement of the old girl was used as a secret disembarking station on the Underground Railroad that saved so many African Americans escapin' from the abomination of slavery. We believe noble and *Christ*-like work is the reason the *Father* maintains this very special link—or portal—between the planes of existence and allows us to use her in our work."

Misha extended his hand. "Come. Come. Misha show you."

I followed Misha to the hall, where he said, "Open the doors."

When I did, the vacant block filled with weeds filled the view. I closed the doors.

"Now, watch."

Misha recited an incantation unfamiliar to me and tugged open the doors. My eyes bulged.

"Come. Come." Misha stepped down the two steps and beckoned me to follow.

The room I entered must have been one hundred feet by fifty feet. At one end, tables and chairs, some of which were occupied, filled the space; at the other, a low stage, dance floor, and couches occupied the area. A stairway tucked into the right-hand corner must lead to living quarters. I heard the sounds of a kitchen behind the restaurant area. So that's where all that yummy food came from.

Before I could take a step farther, a hand the size of a dinner plate landed on my chest. I looked from it to its owner. His face reminded me of a bison. I guessed he was the bouncer.

"Now, Misha, you know I have to be made aware of any unfamiliar people that might come through the door. I don't want the same thing to happen like the last time, right? *Father* gave me this mission, and *He* put me here with you, Mama, and everybody for your own protection. I have sworn to *Him* on my dying breath to do just that."

Mama stepped forward to smooth things over using very formal English. "You are absolutely right, dear boy. I don't want that either, and I thank you for being more reserved this time. I am so very sorry, and I promise that it will never happen again. I sincerely and unreservedly apologize for any disrespect, Gerry."

Gerry removed his huge hand from my chest while showing what I think was a faint smile of approval. "OK, then, Mama. Bring your little friend in; we need all the help we can get, anyway."

Misha touched Gerry's arm. "It's alright, Gerry. This is Camie. He the one Mama been waiting for all these years."

Gerry stepped back as if I had a contagion. He bowed his shaggy head. "I'm sorry. I meant no disrespect, your holiness."

"Gerry, is it? First, I am Camie."

Gerry grinned and offered his hand. "Camie."

"Thanks, Gerry. Second, the only *One* who is *His Holiness* is the *Father*. I'm here to help, but I can't do that if people don't treat me like normal."

"Sure thing. Welcome to The Painted Lady." Gerry swept his hand around the room.

Mama bustled past, smiling at Gerry as she went. "Good to see you being as thorough as always, Gerry. Let's sit over here."

"Mama, I mean Sylviel, he called me little, I'm not little." I feigned protest.

"My brother, to Gerry, most other beings are little."

Sylviel good-naturedly poked me in the chest and smiled.

I sat back in one of the comfortable high-back chairs, finished in rich, supple, fine-grained leather, as Mama continued, "The room holds a secret. She pointed to a pair of ornately-carved cedar doors that were an exact match for the secret doors from Misha's Mish Mash. They somehow appeared on an opposing wall in The Painted Lady but then vanished again just as quickly.

"I was told never to call them until the passing, but I needed to show you so you would understand. They lead to the Holy Place," she said. "I'm not to call them unnecessarily because once the doors are called, The Painted Lady and everyone in her becomes visible to the forces of darkness."

They seemed familiar to me, but I wasn't sure why. I understood why Lucifer would want to shut this little operation down, but what wasn't making sense had to do with why a person needed to be sent through a portal, for that's what it seemed to be, when they did that when they died. I expressed my confusion.

Misha laid a hand on my arm. "Misha and Mama got more to explain, but that probably enough for one day."

I opened my mouth to protest but then remembered these were the *Father's* chosen guides, and I needed to accept their wisdom.

"This calls for celebration." Misha crossed the room to a cupboard near the kitchen and returned with a portable humidor. From the variety of cigars revealed when he opened it, I concluded Misha must appreciate his cigars.

"Ever have one of these, Camie?" Misha asked as he offered me my pick.

"I knew someone who smoked them, but I've never tried one." I smiled.

"Try one of these. You like it, son." He handed me a cigar about six inches long and as big around as a quarter.

"It's a Kuba–Kuba, one of my favorites."

"OK." I held it up to admire the color of its decorative maker's label.

"Ah, you notice color, like color of your blue glow when your auras out, hmmm?"

I just held it, not sure what to do next except perhaps smell it. "Oh, I like that. Reminds me a little of home . . . herbs and spiced-infused . . . kind of similar to the consecrated incense in the tabernacle. Wow, it's been some time since I smelled that."

"Home," Misha leaned forward, keen interest on his face. "You have up there, Camie?"

"Angels don't, no." Disappointment crossed Misha's expression, so I added, "I really couldn't answer for the other inhabitants of Heaven, as I don't have much to do with them."

The cigar forgotten for the moment, Misha plied me with questions about the *Father* and Heaven. What did the *Father* look like? What was it like to be in *His* presence? Where did one meet with the *Father*? What was the room like? Was Heaven like a city? Did people get wings there? The questions seemed endless.

I explained that the magnificence of the *Father's* presence is beyond words. I rattled off words, awe-inspiring, majestic, grand, serene, loving, accepting, amongst others, then said that no human word came close to covering the resplendent nature of the *Father*.

Mama nodded, and Misha said, "Misha knew it; too big for limited words."

I described *His* Holy Sanctuary and the room of judgment, as well as Heaven generally.

After I finished, Mama and Misha's face glowed. We sat in silence for a time. Then Misha's attention returned to the cigar in his hand.

"Here, Camie. Watch me." Misha deftly used a cigar cutter tool to trim the closed end and open the airflow to facilitate a smooth draw.

"That is a rather impressive-looking cigar you have there. What do you call that one?" I asked, my curiosity piqued as this pageantry unfolded before me.

"This is one of Misha's favorites, Chamuel; it a Fuente Opus X, Double Robusto."

Misha held it out for me to inspect. "Misha save these for very special occasions, like come face to face with Seraphim of *God*."

He slapped me on the back, then took out a box of old-fashioned wooden matches. "No use fluid lighter, Camie. Ruin flavor."

Misha's well-aged fingers still held the skill and dexterity to gently roll the cigar back and forth, holding it up to his ear. "I listen to any dried-out crunch sounds. Not properly stored in humidor."

Misha placed the finely-crafted cigar in his mouth and struck a match against the flint on the side of the box, taking a moment to let the sulfur burn off, he brought the flame close but not touching the front of the cigar. "No let flame touch end too long, or it scorch it. Like burn Béchamel, just throw out and start over." He took several long draws as the flame caused the tobacco to smolder in a smooth, even flow.

"Just like that," he said as he sat back and sighed, satisfaction in his eyes. "Now, you try."

I did my best to imitate him but to no avail. I got it lit but gasped and choked as I took too much smoke into my lungs. Mama was trying her best not to laugh at me.

"Mama, our new friend change color from human to blue to green." Misha gently tapped me on my back to help me expel any residual smoke. "Misha sorry; Misha should start much milder, natural wrapper. Sumatra very strong."

He retrieved a cigar, which he indicated was milder, started it, and handed it to me.

"Slow. Like Misha." He drew on the cigar. "No inhale. Hold smoke in mouth get flavors. Then, blow like this." He blew large smoke rings above his head.

I tried again with better success, and by holding the smoke, I discovered the aromatic, spicy, sweet flavor pleased me.

After a period of companionable silence, I took my leave. I had much to think about. "See you tomorrow."

Chapter 22

Unveiling

϶ᖇㄱㄒⵝㄒᖇ϶

That night, although I really wanted to ask *Him* to hurry Misha and Mama up so they might let me in on *His* plan, nothing hastens the *Father*, so I thanked the *Father* for finding me an apartment close to the park, for assigning Mama those long years of service that led her to me, and for Mama and Misha's dedication to the work the *Father* had given them.

My morning walk across the park seemed emptier without Mama to chat with. I did buy the hamburger and did give it to another unfortunate soul, but the gift lacked the same connection. On the other side of the park, I stepped up to the edge of the sidewalk to cross the road to go to Misha's when a garbage truck careened onto the footpath, heading straight for me. The driver turned toward me. He had no face, just a black oval void.

Satan yelled, "Watch out."

But my momentary hesitation trying to comprehend the face left me vulnerable. Satan's superhuman speed collided with me, forcing me out of the way.

As I lay winded on the pavement, the sounds of screaming, gears grinding, and then a crash flowed around me. I said the first thought that sprang to mind.

"Is anyone injured?"

"What, no thanks for saving your life?"

I glanced over at Satan and saw him taking in his unusually rumpled appearance. "Sorry, bro, and sorry about the suit, too."

Satan grimaced. "What a waste of fine Seville Row tailoring!"

"But, yeah, thanks. I got stuck on the faceless driver. Lucifer sending his minions now, is he?"

"Yes, it appears that my duty to protect you from Lucifer has escalated. As to the injured, I can't detect anything other than some minor scrapes and bruises. The lack of a driver has caused a stir, though."

He shot off and came back a moment later. ". . . just pretended to be a witness who saw the driver running away. That has calmed the hysteria for the moment. But I must pop back to give a description to the police. I know, I'll describe Lucian. His eyes are distinctive. Wouldn't it be funny if they picked him up for questioning?"

We both laughed.

Misha greeted me in the shop. "Here our hero."

"Hardly a hero. I don't even know what I'm supposed to do, let alone have done anything."

At morning tea, I stuffed myself on blueberry pancakes. When Misha reached for the vodka, I raised an eyebrow.

"Is okay, son, Misha's getting little long in tooth. Sometimes, it take little of Mother Country to get ol' ticker going." He tapped his broad chest and smiled.

I beamed back, then said, "There's something that's been puzzling me. OK, a few things, but as you said, all in good time. When you mentioned Savannah being haunted, Mama said something like, 'They don't know about us.' Are you an angel, too, Misha?"

Misha laughed with robust joy. "Misha not angel; Misha something better. At least, Misha think so."

At my puzzled expression, Misha left the table and moved to a large space in the center of the room.

Mama said, "I can't wait to see the expression on your face, Camie."

My eyes widened as Misha took off everything but his underwear and got down on all fours.

Mama laughed, pointing to my face. "Priceless . . . and you haven't seen the best part."

Misha's skin began to ripple. His limbs bulged. His body seemed to grow and change shape. A memory of a werewolf surfaced. I went to dismiss it, but the *Father* had advised me to pay attention to such memories as they often held the key to the situation. Could Misha be a werewolf? Even though my experience prepared me for the rupturing of the skin, I still inhaled sharply.

When the transformation finished, he had cloven hooves, the body and legs of a horse, and a man's torso, all twelve feet of him, from head to swishing tail.

"You are a centaur?" I sat back in my chair, running my hand over my head.

The look on my face must have been one of astonishment because Mama chuckled. "I knew you'd be surprised."

Misha took a few prancing steps, locking an arrow in his bow. "Magnificent, no?"

Mama grinned at him. "Oh, Misha, please stop showing off."

"Well, princess, he asked, did he not?" Misha laughed a great, Russian laugh. He placed his hands on what would have been his hips but was now horse muscle. "What do you think?"

"Spectacular. Now I understand my life as a werewolf."

Mama blinked. "Werewolf?"

"Yes. I will explain that and how I came to be here later. Right now, I want to hear about Misha."

"My new friend, Misha, created by *Father* just as you but for different purpose—to teach humans to live off blessed lands, grow things in abundance. Beautiful things, nourishing things, wonderful fruits and vegetables . . . how make wines, ales, and delectable beverages."

Holding up his beloved vodka, he continued, "We show them how grow or find herbs that heal, herbs that flavor and preserve. We taught them about ones not good; how you say . . . *poison*, to leave alone or extract toxin help protect homes, families, and lands from attack."

As Misha moved around the table, he crafted detailed images with his words of an era I had only heard about

"We showed how and where identify in meadows, how find and identify roots, tubers, berries, and nuts and in forest, how preserve food supply help them survive harsh, unforgiving Russian winters. We taught bow, spear, hunt, fight, survive, fish with nets and baited rods, fashion and use tools, to make useful things, beautiful things—for farming, protection, for shelter.

"We help him open third eye, to different world, wonder, enchantment, music, song, and dance. Wonderful melodies and songs give praise, honor, and glory to *Father*. We taught select few sacred wisdom of King Solomon, King David's son, and others as the *Father* allowed."

"You know of Solomon?" I asked, trying to get my head around this race of creatures.

"Mine an ancient race, one of oldest in all *His* creation. Like your family, Chamuel, mine created before man. We taught man give back praise and worship to *Father* using *God*-given reason, curiosity, and intellect.

"We taught man enjoy very short lifespan with much enjoyment of *His* blessed Earth. We not immortal Chamuel; not like you." He waved his hand down my body.

Pride rose in his voice. "Misha's race once free wild, in Russia and Siberia countless millennia. We is children of forest and meadow but compare to angels, we very short-lived, few hundred years or so."

His voice saddened. "We result of union of most corrupt fallen angels and animals."

I couldn't look him in the eye for the shame at what my fallen brothers had done.

Putting his hand on my shoulder, Misha continued. "From ignoble beginnings, corrupt, detestable, *God* turn it around and make a race of beings of stature, grace, honor, and nobility like Misha. We swore allegiance to light, to *Father* for eternity, to somehow amend for our origin."

"Misha, you have nothing to apologize for. It is not your fault. In fact, I lay it squarely at the feet of my brother, Lucifer, the start of it all . . . all the pain, all the corruption, all the horror of mankind through all time is on him."

"Chamuel, thank you; Misha never thought quite that way." For the first time, Misha accorded me the courtesy of a bow as he returned to human form and gathered his clothes.

Mama just smiled at me as she playfully hit me on the shoulder. "You did good, kid. Is that 'brother Lucifer' more than a generic term?"

"To my shame, yes; he is my actual brother. Before the *Father* sent me to Earth, I had much the same disposition as Lucifer toward mortals, but over my experiences, I have mellowed."

Mama sipped her tea. "It sounds like you have been to Earth before this. Why?"

Although the *Father* had forgiven me, the destruction of Atlantis remained a stain on my conscience. I bowed my head and picked at the remains of a pancake on my plate, but in the interests of honesty, I began, "I committed the sin of disobeying the *Father's* instructions. In doing so, I destroyed Atlantis."

Misha and Mama's mouths fell open.

"For my punishment, the *Father* sentenced me to live a thousand years as a mortal. *He* could have banished me, given how great a sin I committed."

Mama said, "The *Lord* is merciful."

I nodded. "Over that time, I have come to understand the *Father's* love for his Creation, although there are still elements of human nature I struggle with."

Misha said, "You're not alone there. Misha, not understand why humans reject *Father*."

"My thoughts, exactly, but the *Father* says *He* gave mankind free will, and if they choose not to worship *Him*, *He* accepts their decision. But I blame most of it on Lucifer. I mean, look how he sucked me in."

Misha gave me a blank look.

"Of course, I only told Mama. Lucifer recruited me into the mob to stop me from fulfilling my mission. It nearly worked, but the *Father* had other plans."

Misha smiled. "And here you are, but tell me more about these lives and mob."

"Not much I can tell you about my past lives as I don't retain those memories in human form. I do as an angel. The *Father* did say I might have memories arise while undertaking the task assigned to me, and I do recall being a werewolf."

"A werewolf; so, you're not unfamiliar with other mortals, then?" Mama asked.

"True, but I wasn't expecting my guides to be non-human. That did come as a surprise."

"From what we know of werewolves, they lead lonely lives," Mama commented.

"Yes, many of them become hermits due to the fear of discovery. I experienced that fear, but the freedom in wolf form was awesome. I got caught out one full moon, and humans killed me. The myth that werewolves attack humans frightens them. Sure, they will attack if cornered, but the drive is to run free." I studied my fingernails for a moment. "As to the mob, what would you like to know?"

A couple of hours later, I had sated Misha's curiosity about the mob as well as confessing my sins.

Misha called for lunch. I laughed. It seemed Misha's solution to all problems involved feeding you.

Chapter 23

Love Hurts

᠘᠌ᠵ᠊   ᠌᠌᠌᠌᠌᠌᠌᠌᠌

Misha waved his hand at me. "Come. Misha go to The Painted Lady now. Have business to attend to, but you meet some of the staff."

Once inside the venue, he directed me to an occupied table removed from the others and said he would send a staff member to take my order.

I wandered across to the table and waited a couple of minutes to be acknowledged by any of the four occupants. With no response forthcoming, I pulled out a chair and took a seat.

"Excuse me, buddy, but this is a private table."

The staff member arrived, interrupting the protests of the beautiful honey-colored woman seated on my right.

"May I please have a glass of your dark ale?"

"Hey, I'm talking to you." The woman's eye burned, and her mouth formed a hard line. "Don't bring this clown a darn thing."

At the staff member's awkward half step away from the table, I felt sorry for her.

The woman continued her attack, "I told you to leave. This is a private table for employees only."

I thought to calm things down, so I said, "I'm new here. I'm Camie." I offered her my hand.

She batted it away, the claw-like fingernails, scratched me as she did so. "I don't care who you are. I told you to leave. Don't make me get Gerry, or you'll be sorry." The woman tapped two red fingernails on the table while trying to outstare me.

I smiled, which only seemed to infuriate the woman more. "By all means, call Gerry over. He'll explain."

She turned toward the door and bellowed, "Gerry! Where in the world is Gerry? I need Gerry over here now!"

Gerry sauntered over, just as my drink arrived. I got a hand to it before the woman swatted it off the table.

"Ms. Dia, that you bawling? What's the problem?" Gerry fixed his eyes on the woman he called Dia.

"This excuse for . . . I don't know what he is . . . thinks he can just sit at our table. No by-your-leave. Just plunks himself down."

"In my defense, I did wait for someone to acknowledge me, and Misha did say I could sit here."

"I don't give a crap about that. I don't want some upstart thinking he can muscle in." She fairly spat the words.

"Please, Ms. Dia, don't speak to him that way. This is Camie. The one Mama has been waiting for." Gerry placed his great mitt on the back of Dia's chair. "You need to show him some respect."

"So, you're supposed to be the chosen one?" Dia sneered. "Someone who doesn't even have the courtesy to ask if they can sit?" Her liquid-green eyes blazed as she planted her hands on the table. "Come on, oh *great one*, if you're going to perform the Great Tikkun, show us those pretty pink and red auras you're supposed to have."

Dia's smug smile enlarged as confusion spread across my face. I opened my mouth to speak, but she cut me off. "I thought as much. Doesn't even know what I'm talking about." With a huff, she turned her back on me and continued to talk to her colleagues.

The person to my left said, "Don't pay Dia no mind. She's not much for change. I'm Freya, and I'm very pleased you're here."

Freya and I chatted until Misha called for everyone's attention. "Misha invite all to dinner. Then, it time Camie meet the family."

After a shuffling of tables to make one large enough for everyone, waiters brought trays piled high with delicacies. Misha said grace, thanking the *Father* for the blessing of food and friendship, for the task assigned to them, and for my arrival.

Before I sat at the table, Misha introduced me to Sera, his adopted daughter. Something about her felt familiar, and like had happened with Mama, we made an instant connection.

I could tell by the good-natured banter that this group considered each other more than friends. As Misha said, they formed a family. Sera and I exchanged stories throughout the meal, and then at the end, I disgraced myself. With my tummy fit to burst, I leaned back in my chair and burped a long, loud burp. "Sorry, not in China."

Sera laughed and let a ripper of a burp go too.

"Everyone, it's time for the unveiling. We need full disclosure to Chamuel. There can be no secrets within the family. Please step forward and reveal your genuine nature to the newest member of our family."

One by one, The Painted Lady's staff, from busboy and hat-check girl, all the way up the line to the chef de cuisine and maître d', calmly revealed their true nature just as Misha had done. Many took off their clothes, saying a little embarrassment saved a lot of money. Laughter echoed in the venue as my expression repeatedly changed throughout the parade of different life forms, some of which I never knew existed.

Gerry revealed himself as from the race of Geryon the giant Minitours *God* placed as the guardians of Hell itself. His massive double-bladed ax gleamed in the light. As I had discovered, the *Father* had assigned Gerry to guard the supernatural family. Now, I understood why.

Shape-shifters, gnomes, elves, banshees, ogres, werewolves, dryads, cyclopes, gorgons, griffin, and more revealed themselves to me. They vied for the best poses to display their unique features and weaponry, many demanding I pronounce them the most impressive.

Mama asked, "So, Camie, what do you think of your new family so far?"

Words failed me. "I don't know what to say. I'm astonished, but I know one thing, my *Father's* creativity has no limits, has it?"

Mama nodded her head in approval. "It sure doesn't, Camie. Dia, you haven't revealed yourself yet."

Dia scowled. "If I have to." She stomped to where I sat, and unlike the others who took time with their transformations, she flashed into herself.

The creature before me awakened something within me that was unprepared to be woke. I knew this kind, somehow. A succubus—a beautiful, beguiling creature, originally wrought from the union of my fallen brethren and human women. They evolved into creatures who seduced humans, taking their life-force through the bodily secretions produced during a sexual union and the sacred exchange of energy. How did I know this?

My face paled, and my body stiffened as the torrent of a memory so powerful, it thundered through my body, leaving me shaking like a leaf.

"Camie, are you okay, son?" Misha's concern showed on his face.

"Misha, I knew one of her kind very well. Her name was . . . is Naamah. She was the—"

Dia interrupted. "That is not possible, Naamah is my ancient—and I do mean ancient—sister. She was the original, the first of my kind, mentioned by name in the Bible, for goodness sake. You couldn't possibly know her. That would make you older than dirt."

Suddenly there was a great hush in the room as all eyes focused on me.

"Camie," Mama said. "Please, full disclosure here. They all need to know who will stand beside them when the going gets tough."

"You know I can't reveal my genuine nature here. It would vaporize everybody in the room."

"Wow, we think a lot of ourselves, don't we, big guy?" A cracking voice echoed down the stairway.

"Drake, there you are. Misha was about to send Gerry down there to drag you here by the tail like he had to do the last time you were late for a family meeting." While Misha's words held a reprimand, a hint of playfulness underpinned them.

I looked at Gerry, whose golden-brown eyes twinkled under his mop of unruly hair. He turned his bull-like head toward Drake and pulled a comic face, displaying his affinity with the boy.

I did not doubt his loyalty. Gerry would lay down his life to protect the family but particularly Drake . . . and I hazarded Sera. As he had displayed at the door, he took his duty from the *Father* seriously.

Mama turned her attention back to me after the interruption. "Camie, we know you are the chosen one, the archangel, the Seraphim, sent here to be the difference in the war, son. As a sign that you are with us, all we ask is that you show us that which only an archangel can."

Misha added, "We prepared. *Father* give us method of separating us so no harm come when you call Holy Fire of *Elohim* into yourself. Go ahead, son. We go over here." Misha motioned for the others to join him near the staircase.

I couldn't see anything special about the area they had chosen, and I couldn't fathom what might protect them from my holy fire.

When everybody was safely in place, Sylviel lay prostrate on the polished wood floor and spoke a special invocation of protection in our ancient Angelic tongue. Her own angelic spirit came back into her.

When I felt that familiar soft, summer breeze and inhaled her fragrance of rose petals, I rejoiced that *Shekinah Mother, The Holy Spirit,* had placed herself between the rest of my family and me as protection.

It's OK, my son, you may call the Holy Fire of Elohim *back into yourself so that they may believe in you and be encouraged to follow you in your mission and their labors.*

Her voice caressed me like the petals of an orchid.

When my angelic eyes picked up the shimmer of her protective barrier, I relaxed and closed my eyes as my heavenly spirit temporarily returned to me. When I opened them, I exhaled. No harm had come to my new family. If my aura shone bright, my face shone brighter as I cringed at everyone bowing low before me. "I am only a servant of our *Father,* just like you. Please, my family, you must not bow to me but only to *Jehovah.*"

With that, the Holy Fire of *Elohim* left me, and the scent of rose petals dissipated, leaving only a single perfect long-stemmed white rose freshly cut and still glistening with the morning dew on the floor. My family came forward, embracing me and pledging their gifts to the mission. Even Dia came over, but her skepticism hadn't shifted much.

"OK, you're an archangel, but there are a dozen of those. I'll reserve my judgment, for now."

Now that her anger had dissipated, the startling resemblance to Naamah rocked me. The honey skin, perfect lips, curvaceous body all tapped into a past that held power over me.

"Careful, Camie, I know that look. We don't need to complicate things right now, brother." Satan chimed into my thoughts.

"No, it's not that look. It's a memory."

Dia gave me a curious glance.

"Sorry, Dia, you remind me of a fierce and noble African queen from long ago when my spirit was known by another name. She was the love of my life then." I thought it might improve her view of me if I told her the story, so I said, "Come, sit while I tell you."

I fiddled with a fork left on the table. "We shared a human lifetime as a Natufian king and queen. Her name was Nemea, and I loved her more than life itself. We reigned as equals, sharing the joys and hardships. Our love produced many children, and they, in turn, produced our grandchildren."

Others had seated themselves at the table to hear the story.

"But tragedy struck when I was away from the village on a hunting excursion. Raiders from a rival tribe attacked our village. Nemea and a few old men fought them off. She took several arrows but lived long enough to kill the rest of the raiders. She saved our people.

"She died in my arms that night." At the unfairness of it all, I stabbed the fork into the table, marring its surface. "It's a night I will always remember with bittersweet feelings. I thanked the *Father* that *He* blessed me with such an incredible human lifetime, shared with somebody who was my true soul mate, but I remained angry at *Him* for a very long time for taking Nemea from me that night.

"I can even say that I fell so far from *Him* that I actually grew to . . . . I'm sorry *Father* . . . hate my *Heavenly Father* for what *He* allowed to happen.

"We were still in our prime of life. I never remarried. I even tried to take my own life several times, I was so broken, but *He* wouldn't allow it. *He* always brought me back."

Dia blushed and then said, "I'm sorry, Chamuel. We can all see that you still hold great sorrow over that experience. What an extraordinary love that must have been." She rested a hand on mine. "I think we have all experienced feelings of distance from the *Father* at some point in our lifetimes. I can't say we could ever understand what it must have been like for a Seraphim, like yourself, but for humans or even . . . well . . . beings like ourselves . . . um, what is that saying? Oh yes, 'you are closest to the *Father* when you are angry with *Him.*'"

It pleased me that she had mellowed some. "Call me Camie. Everyone calls me that, and yes, it was extraordinary. I don't recall my other lives, but I doubt I ever had a love like that again."

Gerry piped up. "Well, let me tell you about my first love. She was a cow. No, I mean a real certified Holstein; she had the biggest brown eyes . . . sigh."

As the group around the table laughed, my gratitude to Gerry for breaking the somber mood grew.

People chimed in with their worst love, best love, true love, and thought-it-was love stories, and the laughs kept coming.

It had been an emotional day, and I needed time alone to process it, so after another hour or so, I thanked everyone for their well-wishes, particularly Mama and Misha, and headed home.

Scorch marks pockmarked my door and the walls around it. I slid the key in, ready to trigger my auras as I entered the apartment.

"About time." Satan sounded irritated.

"Hi. What happened?" I surveyed the damage to the apartment. "Well, there goes the deposit."

"While you were gallivanting around town, I have been stuck here for the last hour fending off a horde of demons intent on frying your butt."

"Sorry, and sorry about your suit again; those scorch marks aren't coming out."

"I'm adding it your bill, which I must say, is growing by the day. How goes the mission?"

"I just met the team, or, more correctly, family, and no, not *the* family. They're all supernatural creatures. I'm talking centaurs, Minitours, griffin, Cyclopes."

"Interesting. So, what's with the Dia chick? You seemed quite taken with her."

"She's Nemea's descendant, and the likeness got to me." A fresh round of memories made my eyes cloud.

"You still carry a torch for her even after all these years, don't you?" Satan's voice held a smidge of sympathy.

"I always will, I think."

"Don't dwell on the past for too long. It isn't healthy. By all means, remember the good but don't dwell. I'm off now. Get some sleep. Never understood it, personally, but then, we don't sleep, do we, bro? Oh, that's right, you're human."

After Satan left, I sat in the dark, nursing a port, as I thought over the events of the day, starting with Misha's revelation through to the memory of Nemea. Was there more to it than just her being Dia's sister?

When I thought about my relationship with Lillian, whom I thought I had loved, I scoffed at my lack of understanding about what a relationship could and should be in the light of my memories.

My prayers were both joyous and confused, but I went to sleep, content in the knowledge that I had experienced pure human love once in my many lives.

Chapter 24

Sylviel Restored

ꌦꍏꌅꌅꌦꍏ ꉓꌦ⎐ꈤꍟꌅꌦꌗ

The tense atmosphere at Misha's when I arrived in the morning prickled my nerves. What Gerry could tell me didn't provide me with much information. Mama had slept in after last night's exertions and had woken screaming. When Sera went to help, Mama said that she remembered, and she wanted Misha. She and Misha had been holed up for the last hour.

I asked for directions to Mama's room, thinking my angelic presence might calm her. I expected to find Mama distressed, but when I opened the door after knocking, she beamed at me and said, "I have news that I must share with the family. Camie, please ask them to gather in The Painted Lady."

"Sister, our Angelic tongue?"

"Yes, my brother, *Father* has restored me completely and much more!"

"They'll be relieved. They've been quite worried."

"Please let them know I am OK."

The gathering in The Painted Lady kept pestering me about what Mama had said. I lost count of how many times I said, 'I don't know.' I saw eyes take furtive looks at the stairs and heard theories ranging from the *Father* intended to shut The Painted Lady down to revelations about an attack.

About three-quarters of an hour later, Mama and Misha came down the stairs. A silence fell over the room as all heads turned toward them.

Misha said, "Call the kitchen staff. Everyone needs to hear this."

The kitchen staff came out bearing platters of food.

Gerry got up to help Mama to a seat. "Are you alright, Mama?"

"Yes, Gerry; I've just had part of my memory restored to me, and I wish to share it with you, or, at least, have Misha share it with you."

Misha bowed to Mama and held out his hand. "Misha been waiting for this day, the day Mama's memory come back. May Misha present to you Duchess Anastasia Nikolaevna, rightful heir to Russian throne."

A few gasped, some mouths opened, then someone applauded, and the momentum swelled. Gerry stood, and others followed.

I certainly hadn't seen that revelation coming.

"Oh, yes . . . now, story of how Duchess and Misha became acquainted." He lovingly kissed her on the cheek. "Misha sorry, princess . . . Misha mean Mama. Some habits die hard.

"Eat; eat, while Misha tell you." He drank a mouthful of orange juice; actually is was probably more of the "Mother Country" with just enough juice to change the color!

"My race been around almost as long as yours, Camie. We belong to the same realm as Fae and all other created beings mankind calls magical."

The other Fae staff's diverse array of humanoid-, equine-, canine-, amphibian,- reptilian-, and aviary-based laughter bounced around the room.

"My kind lived millennia on great plains at foot of Ural Mountains between Mother Russia and Siberia. We thrived during that time; enjoy rich blessings of our lands that *Father* gave to us. We hunted our beloved brown bear, elk, reindeer, and roe in dense forests of Central Valley. We fished Techa and other rivers and lakes for salmon and trout and all way to Caspian for sturgeon, which . . ." His expression changed to a combination of anger and sadness. Misha sighed, a great sigh of loss. "From time of the Garden, Lucifer influence man so he not live in harmony with all of glorious Creation.

"Now, man is short-sighted, greedy, and stupid. He brought great species to extinction."

He took a moment to collect himself then continued.

"We trap ermine and sable to trade with humans *Father* brought to our valley. We learn quick to hide true natures." Misha looked at his large extended family with hope. "Misha pray someday soon, man be ready to accept all as *God* intended, without having to protect small minds from illusions of superiority."

He made quotation marks in the air with his fingers, bringing laughter of agreement from the group, including, Sera, who quipped, "Too bad the rest of the world can't accept you as I do. It makes me embarrassed to be a human sometimes."

Misha just smiled at Sera and reassured his young charge. "Misha's precious Seraphina is true; you human, but you so much more."

Misha returned to the story. "My family serve Romanovs during entire three-hundred-year rule, and before that, all human royal families in aristocracy of Mother Russia.

"My family royal too. We kings and queens of Centaur race, so it appropriate we serve, instruct, and protect human royal families of our lands. We chosen by *God* to guide and instruct them. Makes good horse-sense." Misha couldn't resist a well-timed joke.

"Oh, Misha," Mama laughed.

Misha followed the thread.

"One July morning in Yekaterinburg, so long ago now seems, little Anastasia wandered deeper into forest than she should, Misha guess . . . but everything for reason, da, yes?

"She surprise Misha as Misha come 'round ancient oak with morning catch. Misha not much success at morning fishing since, hmm . . ." He stroked his white goatee.

"Papa . . ." Sera shouted at Misha's unnecessary and somewhat annoying dramatic pause.

Misha started again, with a wink in my direction, telling me that it was definitely a dramatic pause done on purpose.

"Oh, sorry everyone. Now, where was Misha? Oh, yes, the oak. Little Anastasia was strong and brave, even at tender age.

"She did not run from Misha when she almost collided into Misha—the true, unveiled Misha—but she screamed so loud she made Misha drop fish."

Misha let out a great, Russian belly laugh. "Then Misha remember that moment of silence. She bend down to pick up Misha's fish. Took all she had to catch as it flopped around, but she did it. She clutched to her chest and offer to Misha. Probably ruined beautiful white, summer dress . . ."

"It did," Mama laughed. "Nanny was so angry at me but never told Mother and Father that I had wandered off. It hurt so much when I learned she had been. . ." Mama couldn't quite bring herself to finish.

"That's OK, princess. You know she home with *Father* ever since."

Mama just nodded as she wiped away a faint tear or two.

"Well, then," Misha went on. "Over next several years, Misha and Mama become best friends. She visit me in forest when she can, but Misha's family always know where she and her family were. It our sworn duty and honor for their protection.

"Everything is as it should be until . . ." Misha faltered in his telling.

Mama comforted Misha. "It's OK, Misha, I'm right here." She hugged her champion.

"Misha sorry everybody; some wounds never quite heal, da?"

I looked around at the family. Most everyone was nodding in contemplative agreement. All aware of the respective history of being hunted by the worst predator of all—man.

"Camie, you know that *Father* allows suffering in all *His* children, in every plane of existence as a way of instruction and purification."

Satan whispered in my mind. "Yes, I guess I do at that, my brother."

I glanced over at Sylviel to see a knowing smile. She heard Satan, too.

Misha took a moment to stave off the anger that one could see welling up inside of him.

"Then they came. Those bloody Bolsheviks. We hear sounds of war, of revolution. We try to get to palace, but we not fast enough; and many Misha's family die trying."

Misha was now himself, wiping away the tears as he continued.

"By time Misha get down to the basement, it too late, Misha too late. Misha's sweet innocent princess gone. Such evil, such horrible evil! For what? Illusion of power, greed, avarice, jealousy. Then, Misha hear something. Misha hear faint whimpers of female human child. Could it be Misha's little princess? Had she survived somehow?

"I pull dead bodies of family off to find who it is. Misha's heart leaped. Misha's princess; Misha check for wounds. She shot, bad.

"Misha moment of joy short-lived. Misha hears soldiers coming back. Why? They not satisfied?

"Misha could hear them talk about dousing bodies of royal family with lamp oil and set them ablaze—such foul cruelty. My righteous anger was at full boil. Misha unveil to true form, and back then, Misha in prime. Misha would stop them or die trying.

"Misha charged out the door, surprising them."

Misha got to his feet to reenact those terrible and heroic early morning hours moving with a grace and power that did not match is many centuries of life.

"The first fellow never knew what hit him as Misha catch him square in head with my front hoof, completely smash head in. Misha grab his sword. Others drew rifles to open fire. Misha feels surge of power come into him that not his own. Misha raged with ferocity of a wolverine and power of a bear; Misha charges, brandishing sword. From that moment, all Misha remembers is the after: the blood, so much blood, and body parts—arms, legs, heads, brains, innards."

"Eww, Papa," Sera interrupted. "Please, we did just eat sausages. We didn't need to be hearing about innards, OK?"

Her comedic relief timing was impeccable. Everyone laughed.

"Oh, Misha sorry, everyone!" Misha continued his fascinating, albeit gruesome tale.

"Misha pick princess up; she barely alive. Misha had to get her away before more sinners come back. Misha galloped like never done before or since, not caring who saw. Misha tell Anastasia to hold tight, and she did."

Misha stopped for a moment to rub his right shoulder.

"Funny, only seem to hurt when about to storm real bad. To this day, Misha don't remember getting shot by rifles there." He pulled down his shirt collar to show one of his many scars.

"Misha made it to forest, to safety, but Misha found same couldn't be said for Anastasia here. She alive, somehow, but as Misha feared, she fatally shot. Misha mind race. Misha heart felt like it going to explode. Misha remembers tasting own blood; Misha getting weak from wounds. All appeared lost—*was this it?* We were alive and safe in deep woods, but for how long?

"Misha and Anastasia have no family left. We surrounded, and Misha knew—yes, Misha knew, we prey now . . . we being hunted. Misha smell humans around us. Misha see castle but no smoke. They know Anastasia escape. She not found there in castle with others.

"Misha couldn't go farther; Misha collapse just inside the woods under cover of spruce and pine near an open meadow beside my beloved Techa. Misha pray to *Father* to save my princess.

"Misha and Anastasia alone, then someone there . . . Misha and Mama's destinies truly joined when I first saw Sylviel."

Sylviel looked at Mama as she took Misha's cue to continue. "That is when Misha first saw me Chamuel, your sister, Sylviel.

"Misha had been assigned as the princess's guardian from the moment of her conception. Then there in those woods, I was given a new assignment.

"The soul of the human, known as Duchess Anastasia Nikolaevna, was to be reassigned to another life. That is all we were told. Her Ruach, her spirit, the eternal child of *Elohim* would continue in the corporeal form you see here," Sylviel said as she moved her hands up and down her front.

Misha added. "Misha continue role as guardian from that day to this; nothing too good for the two ladies in Misha's life. Three with Sera; Camie is that not what man is supposed to be to woman he love—guardian, supporter, to show woman unconditional love of *Father*?"

"Misha my new friend, suffice it to say that you are more of a real man then any human man I ever encountered in my many lifetimes of exile."

The entire family nodded in silent approval and respect.

Mama patted Misha on his back and ushered him to a seat. "Misha has dedicated his life to Anastasia and me in service to the *Father*. Without his faithful service in protecting Anastasia, he and I would not have met. Then, we would not be here today, engaged in the work we do. I think the *Father* gave me this memory now to demonstrate *He* has *His* hand on all aspects of our lives. It is time we gave thanks to the *Lord*. Misha, will you lead us in prayer, please?"

The humility of Misha's prayer, thanking the *Father* for directing his life, guiding him to Anastasia that fateful day, and giving him the strength to defeat the enemy, without once giving credit to himself spoke of his devotion to *God*. He thanked *God* for allowing Sylviel's vessel to be used to hold Anastasia's spirit. It touched me when he prayed for my role in the work they did, but Misha's praise for the *Holy Father's* glory inspired me most. It came close to how the angels praise *His* name.

Chapter 25

Mission Defined

ᴢᴜᴜᴢᴢᴂ ᴣᴂᴢᴣᴜᴢ

Mama gave me a mischievous look. "Have you worked out who our travelers are yet?"

I scratched my head. I'd pondered that question last night 'til my eyeballs hurt. "I'd say other mortals, but they die like humans, so it doesn't add up. I'm still at a loss as to who it might be."

Mama chuckled. "Who would Lucifer least like to lose?"

"Least like to lose?" My mind ran through all the historic and import-ant people I knew to be in Hell. "I can think of quite a few bigwigs in Hell, but none so influential that Lucifer would care if they got out, other than he hates to lose."

Mama tapped the table. "I had the same issue at first. I couldn't see it because I didn't believe in its possibility. Who are the most unlikely beings you'd think the *Father* would redeem?"

I shook my head. I didn't speak for fear of yelling, "Just b'well tell me!"

"Who are most in need of a second chance where Lucifer is con-cerned?"

I flung myself back in the chair and clapped my hands over my eyes. The thought seemed too impossible to be correct, but Mama had said that. "You don't mean . . ."

Mama beamed. "Mm-hmm, I didn't think we'd get any takers, but we've had a steady stream."

"How many so far?"

"Fifty or sixty, not enough given their numbers, but our numbers are growing each year, and every one that was fallen and has now been redeemed is one for the *Father* and one less for Lucifer. It's exhilarating work." Mama's eyes shone with the light of the love of *God*.

"I can't wait to learn the ritual. If we're going to do it on other nights, we'll need to advertise, and we might have to get more beds. We'll need—"

Mama held up her hand.

"Whoa there, Nellie; we don't even know what powers you have or need training in. We have no idea of when or how many you can handle. Let's get some basics down before we worry about advertising."

"So, how long will my training take?"

Mama plucked at a thread on her cuff. "That will depend a little on what you know already, how well you connect with the doors, and a host of other variables. This is new ground for me, too, you know. But given the *Father* sent you, your eventual ability to open the door is a given. We just need all the pieces."

"We'd better get started. When should we aim for? New moon, symbol of rebirth?"

"Sounds like as good a time as any. How about we start your training tomorrow? I'm a little drawn after this morning."

Mama's usually vibrant complexion appeared dull and her energy with it. As we relaxed, Drake darted through the venue with Sera on his heels. A ball of blue light left her hands and zinged past Drake's head.

I sat forward in the chair, watching to see if it happened again. "Mama, is that what I think it is?"

"Yes, but she doesn't know."

"You have to tell her. Those things are deadly, and an untrained and undisciplined Nephilim of Illumination can create havoc—that I know. But how?"

Mama folded her hands on her lap. "Her mother, Abigail, came to us not long after we bought The Painted Lady. She had no one and being pregnant, she struggled to get work. Misha and I prayed on it, and the *Lord* directed us to give her shelter and a job. She worked hard and seemed happy, but she never talked about the child's father, and she always appeared to be on high alert. When Seraphina arrived, we welcomed her. Talk about having people wound around your pinkie. We literally had to shoo Gerry out of her room so she could sleep. She looked like a china doll in his hands, and he treated her like finely spun glass. When Sera could manage sitting and holding on, Misha would prance around with her on his back. The only shadow—Sera had been born deaf. Would you get me a cup of tea, please?"

I came back from the sideboard where a constant supply of tea and coffee waited and said, "I hope I made it to your liking."

"Anything will be fine right now." She took a sip, and her eyes got that cross-eyed look as she peered at the cup, her lips turned up at the corners. "Oo, that is good, thank you. Now, where was I?"

"When Sera turned three, Abigail fell pregnant again. We couldn't work out how, as the only place she went regularly was to her art and design course. She didn't have a boyfriend that we knew of, and she rarely socialized, but we didn't pry or judge.

"She dreamed of becoming a world-class fashion designer. And she dreamed big—Paris, London. She had the talent, too. She'd tell us of the houses she'd buy us because we took her in." Mama stifled a sniffle.

I patted Mama's knee. "Our pains make us who we are."

"Thank you." Mama sipped her tea. "This part is sad. When she was eight months pregnant with Drake, Abby was assaulted. The hospital put her in an induced coma, but she never woke up. She survived long enough to deliver Drake." She blew on the tea before sipping again. "While they monitored her vitals, the system picked up ghost heartbeats on a number of occasions. Unable to fix or explain it, the nurses called IT, who were none-the-wiser." She paused to let me think about it. "I believe it to be an angelic imprint as the angel poured their spirit into Drake. Do you think that is possible?"

She paused to let me think about it.

"I often wondered how the Nephilim came into being. That makes the most sense."

"Not long after, someone or something healed Sera's hearing, and about the same time, we noticed the beginning of the energy balls."

"Do you have any idea which angel we are talking about?"

"Nothing proof positive, but my heart tells me it is Raphael." Mama studied my face. "You alright, son?"

"No, it's fine. Raphael had children on Atlantis on whom he doted. It doesn't surprise me he wanted more. But how are Sera and Drake in your custody?"

"Seemed like Abby knew something was coming for her as she made a will nominating Misha and me as guardians in the event of her death. Took some months, but we got custody."

"That's great. The kids seem so happy here." I allowed her a moment to appreciate the praise. "You said, 'something coming for her,' because of the children?"

"If it were coming for the children, there would have been more attacks. No, I think there was more to Miss Abigail than met the eye. But something did come. On the second night after her death, someone or something attacked the morgue.

"The morning shift arrived to find the two guards and morgue attendant slaughtered. Their mutilated bodies had something highly corrosive poured over the parts. When they checked the chambers, the only corpse defiled was Abby's. Forensics had no idea what acid could dissolve a body, not immersed, overnight. What are your thoughts?"

"I can think of a couple of creatures from Hell that could do it; Apopsis for one or possibly something even worse, a Danella—very foul and disgusting they are. Dull-witted and quick-tempered. There are some minor demons, but that'd take a couple."

"I wonder who Abby really was if demons tried to kill her."

"Sadly, we'll never know. So, is it time to tell Sera and Drake?"

"As much as I want to preserve their innocence as long as possible, yes, I think it's time, given they will lead the family into the future.

"Wise choice. I will support you however I can."

"That's a relief. Will you take responsibility for their formal instruction . . . please, Camie?"

If a fish hit me in the face, I'd be no less surprised. Me and my big mouth. "I'd be honored." I just hoped the pair didn't have Lucifer's and my dispositions. We gave our instructors some tough days. Where to start? I guess Atlantis is as good as any. After that, I'd need Raphael and Satan's advice.

The kids were at the far end of the venue, bickering over some trivial issue. They had no idea that our conversation would turn their world on its head.

As they approached after Mama called them, I heard Sera say to Drake, "What have you done this time?"

"Me? It's you who is always late for work." Drake punched Sera on the shoulder.

Mama said, "Neither of you is in trouble, but I have something important to tell you. I've sent for Misha. Gerry and Alexi will be joining us, too."

Sera and Drake exchanged glances, clearly puzzled and a little nervous.

Sera blurted out, "It's not about Papa? He's not dying, is he?"

Mama reached across the table and took her hand. "Your Papa is getting old, but the *Lord* will see to it that he is around for the time he needs to be."

Misha joined them. "I agree, Mama. Now, we have Camie to guide them. It is time."

Gerry and Alexi joined the group. Alexi said, "This is exciting news."

I could tell the comments perplexed both Sera and Drake by the looks they gave each other. It pleased me that they had a strong bond. They'd need it. Sera and Drake's eyes looked from Mama to Misha and then focused on Mama.

Now everyone had gathered; Mama began: "You know your mother was unwed. Your mother may have been more than she appeared as there was an unpleasant incident after her death. Suffice to say, we believe a demon desecrated her body."

Given Mama's work, neither Sera nor Drake appeared shocked at the mention of demons. On the other hand, the cry in Drake's voice aired his horror at the notion that they might have attacked his mother. "Demons attack her, but why?"

Misha said, "We never know now your mother is dead. Misha and Mama regret not talking to your mother about her fears while she lived."

Mama continued, "The demon is not the reason we wanted to talk to you, though. Your mother never talked about who fathered you, but we believe we have an idea of who that might be."

Sera's face gave no clue as to what her mind contained. "Go on."

Mama said, "We believe you are special, too. Yes, we always tell you that you are special and unique, but we mean differently."

Gerry entered the conversation. "That is why the *Father* assigned me to guard you."

Mama hesitated. "There is no easy way to say this. We believe your father was an archangel."

Sera slammed her hands on the table. "That's ridiculous. Why would you even think that?"

"Do you remember being deaf, Sera?"

By the darting of Sera's eyes, Mama's change of tack had caught her off guard.

"Vaguely. I was only a toddler."

"Then you were healed. Have you ever wondered how it occurred?"

I appreciated how Mama guided Sera to the truth—gently and logically.

Sera's downcast eyes indicated her faltering confidence. "I thought you did it."

Mama chuckled. "That is way, way above my pay-grade. No, it required something or someone with significant power to achieve a miracle like that. And not that you probably remember, but that coincided with when the energy balls began."

Sera's face showed her reflecting on that statement. "I have a memory of thinking how pretty they were. I'd clap as they danced in the air."

"And your hearing? Would you say it is better than average?"

"Well, I can hear dog whistles. When I was at primary school, I didn't understand why no one else could."

"All these things point to heavenly intervention, which is why we think it was an archangel."

Drake had remained quiet until now. His plaintive voice asked, "What about me?"

"Ah, when someone is in a coma, the equipment monitoring the life support systems is always on. One day, I caught an IT person checking out the monitor. I asked what he was doing. He said the machine kept producing odd readouts as if a second heartbeat was present. I believe that was an archangel transferring his essence to you."

A touch of disappointment echoed as he said, "But I don't have super hearing, and I can't throw energy balls."

"No, but your IQ is off the scale, and you're a whizz at computers."

"I'd prefer the energy balls."

Mama reached for his hand. "When you have time to reflect, you'll realize that isn't true. Your passion is your laptop."

"One more thing, young man; your true nature is the stuff of fairy tales and the greatest legends of old." Misha added.

"S'pose."

I caught a look of rising anger on Sera's face, so it didn't surprise me as it did Mama when she went on the attack. "And just how long have you suspected this?"

I'm glad Mama went with the truth.

"From the time of Drake's birth."

Sera folded her arms across her chest. "And you waited 'til now to tell us?"

Misha entered the conversation again. "We appreciate you are angry, Sera, but Mama and Misha did what we thought best. Tell me, what difference would it have made to you knowing?"

Sera's anger gave way to tears. "I might not have felt like a freak all these years."

Mama got up and moved to Sera to hug her. "Oh, baby, we didn't know. I'm so sorry." She let Sera sob for a while then said, "If we'd known, we might have spoken earlier."

Drake asked, "So what does it actually mean?"

Misha said, "You Nephilim of Illumination with special gifts. You will need training, which is why we now have Camie, and we decided to tell you. Camie will instruct you."

Drake brightened. "I've heard of the Nephilim of Illumination. They're way cool."

To lighten the mood, I chipped in, "I hope your better students than Lucifer and I were. We gave the tutors such a hard time."

Sera said, "Lucifer?"

Drake said, "You had to go to school?"

Of course, they didn't know Lucifer and I were brothers. "Yes, Sera; Lucifer and I are brothers, and before the Fall, he was, as Drake says, cool. And yes, Drake, angels have to learn to master their skills, too."

Chef Alexi had been quiet until now. "So, come on, Camie, spill. Did you cut class often?"

"Hey, that's a loaded question. If I say 'no,' it implies I cut class sometime, and if I say 'yes,' I'm judged by my own omission."

Mama got down to the practicalities. "We will need to draw up a schedule to allow for Camie's training with me and your training with

Camie that doesn't interfere with study and work. I'll let you know when it's done."

Sera said, "Hang on a minute. You haven't said which archangel."

Given I knew him best, I answered. "We think it is Raphael. He loves kids. He'll have been watching over you all of your lives. He is one of the greatest of us all!"

Sera thought for a moment. "I think that's true—the bit about a guardian angel. I often feel their presence. Nice to have a name to them."

Sera and Drake had more questions, which we answered to the best of our abilities.

At the end, Mama went to lie down.

Chapter 26

Target Practice

s I neared my apartment that evening, after crossing Goodwin Street, I became aware of the presence of someone behind me. I monitored the speed of the steps to estimate when they might attack. Since *Father* forbids us to use our almost limitless angelic power while in human corporeal form, my choices were limited—make a run for it and try to get to the entrance to the apartments or find somewhere to make a stand. As I increased my pace, I found an empty car space backed by a brick wall and ducked in. It meant my attackers had to confront me face-to-face, and the space limited them. Three men blocked the parking space entrance, and behind them, I caught the shape of a female. *Lilith*. If she controlled the humans, I expected they'd keep attacking until I incapacitated them.

The skinny guy on the right peeled off, I assumed to flank me by squeezing past the cars, but given the tight space, I'd see him coming. The other two began to approach, the beefy one grasping a knife. He telegraphed their move by glancing sideways, enabling me to prepare. I inched closer to the car on the left so they couldn't attack me on both sides. As the big guy charged at me, I spun my body parallel to the car, grabbing his extended arm, and using his own momentum, smashed his face into the wall. The impact knocked him off his feet, and he dropped the knife as he fell. I heard it bounce but had to keep focused on the second attacker, so I couldn't tell where it landed.

The second attacker took his time. He extended out an ASP as he stepped within range and took a swing. On the first strike, I leaned back, and it missed me by a fraction, but being pinned against the car, I needed to take the fight to him. My instinct screamed *no*, but I had to step in toward my attacker. I had to limit his range of movement with the ASP. As he drew his arm back for another swing, I lunged forward, striking him in the throat with my hand. He choked and raised his hand to his throat. While he was distracted, I grappled the ASP out of his hand. It rolled under the car when it fell. Then I rammed my heel into his knee, snapping the bone. He crumpled to the bitumen but still kept grabbing at my legs. I moved to his side and kicked him in the head hard enough to knock him out.

The big guy began to stir, so I booted him in the head, too, then searched for the knife. Just as I bent to grab it, the skinny guy squeezed past the car and rushed me. He collided with me and forced me face-first to the ground. As he sat on my back, pounding blows on my head, my fingers reached for the knife. The tip of my middle finger touched it, and I flicked it toward me a half-inch, just enough to be able to drag it all the way to me. With it in my grasp, I bucked, dislodging my assailant, then scrambled to my feet. I held the knife so its hilt sat at my thumb, and the blade protruded past my little finger. As he dove at me, I arced the edge right to left across his throat, severing the arteries. Blood spurted from the wound, decorating the car like a Jackson Pollok. The warmth of the blood splattering my face reminded me of the first man I'd killed. Did self-defense justify killing?

Lilith appeared at the opening to the space. "Killing . . . *tut tut*. But it seems some of the family rubbed off on you." She walked up to the body and poked it with the toe of her boot. "Useless. Next time, I'll hire professionals." Then she vanished through her portal.

✧⟨❈⟩✧

I wrestled the bedcovers most of the night so when I turned up to Misha's, Mama commented on the dark circles under my eyes. After I recounted the events of the previous night, Mama said, "It's a war. People die in war."

"But Lilith had control of them. They had no choice."

Mama shook her head. "Lilith wouldn't have picked them if they hadn't done similar jobs before. They may have been innocent on this occasion, but they weren't innocent. But I need you to put it out of your head so we can begin training."

"I need a strong coffee first." I returned from the coffee maker with a brew so thick it could dissolve a spoon.

"Ugh. How can you drink that?" Mama turned up her nose.

"The same way you drink Russian tea so strong I could use it as a paint stripper."

We both laughed.

"I'll give you a little background first. A series of messengers, including Gabriel, provided us with the *Lord's* instructions on how to accomplish *His* holy work. The details were specific, covering which Psalms to read, the incantation to open the doors, the candles to use, and when to light them and when to anoint the traveler, right down to their clothes. When the messengers delivered the holy oil, my skin tingled. It became real then. Here, let me show you."

Mama rose and went to a cupboard at the far end of the room. She returned, holding a flawless white alabaster vessel, topped with a stopper fashioned in equally pure alabaster. My spirit reacted with pointed reverence to the precious oil contained within the vessel.

"You recognize this, don't you, Camie?" Mama smiled.

"My spirit does. It is the same consecrated oil recipe that *Father* instructed Moses to make for his brother Aaron to use in the new temple."

Mama nodded. "You know the best part? It keeps replenishing itself."

I tapped the jar. "The *Father* provides." I waited while Mama returned the jar and then asked, "Which Psalms do you use?"

"Selected verses from Psalms 25, 28, and 40 . . . and 49, 50, and 73, and Psalm 32 and 130."

"A beautiful selection; these I know by heart, so there is no issue there. I take it, we say them in the Angelic tongue?"

"Yes, everything is spoken in the Angelic tongue. Do you need a break, or are you ready to learn the incantation?"

"I think some fresh air before we start might clear my head. It's still a bit groggy from last night."

When I returned half an hour later; Mama sat in front of me. "I can't write it down in case it falls into the wrong hands. Sorry."

"That's understandable."

She continued, "The incantation itself isn't difficult. The inflections are. Once you have memorized the words and can say them fluently, I will teach you the inflections. Ready?"

I nodded, and Mama recited the whole incantation. Then she broke it into phrases, which she had me repeat. After an hour, I pretty much had it, and Mama said, "We'll see how much you remember tomorrow. Now, I believe you have your first class teaching Sera and Drake what it means to be Nephilim. Where are you starting?"

"I think it is important they understand the potential for disobeying the *Father* that they carry, so I'm going to start with end days of Atlantis."

"Won't that mean you have to tell them what you did?"

"If they are going to trust me, and their trust is essential for what I have to teach them, I need to be honest. It is part of who I am. If it weren't for that incident, I would not have the understanding and appreciation of humans that I do."

"The *Father* has a way of working things out, doesn't *He*?"

"Yep, but I best not be late for my first class."

When Drake and Sera clattered down the wooden hall and into the upstairs sitting room, I indicated they sit at the table.

Drake said, "Don't tell me we have to take notes. Are we going to be tested on this?"

I laughed. "If taking notes helps you remember, by all means, do so. As to being tested, when we come to the skills part, I will know what you have and haven't taken in. However, today is more of a story, so you can just listen."

Sera asked, "Can we get comfortable on the couches, seeing as we don't have to take notes."

"As long as you don't fall asleep."

Sera and Drake occupied one couch, and I sat on the other across the coffee table. I chose the sunny side as the warmth streaming in through the window might put them to sleep.

"I'm going to tell you about the end days of Atlantis as I need you to be aware of the potential for corruption that resides within you. The Nephilim of Illumination were blessed with many gifts, but in the end, they misused them."

I recounted Lilith's part in Alequora's rejection of the *Father* and where that led to denying *His* greatness, how she murdered the righteous and defiled the temple. I told them of the cruelty of the experiments and the abominations that resulted and how those creatures were inflicted on the innocent.

When I had finished, Drake asked, "Atlantis sank, and no one knows where it is. What happened?"

"Because of the hard-heartedness of the Nephilim of Illumination against the *Father*, Atlantis was destroyed." I paused. "I destroyed it."

Drake's eyes widened. "Wow, you're that powerful."

Sera asked, "The only way it could have been destroyed is if the *Father* willed it. Did you have *His* permission?"

I swallowed. "No, and for that, I have been punished."

"Is that why you are on Earth as a human?"

Her perception pleased me. "Yes, the sentence dictated that I spend a thousand years as a mortal to learn why the *Father* loves his Creation.

I have had many varied lives, and my attitude to mortals has softened, but there are elements I still have difficulty with. I will tell you of those another time. I think that is it for today."

Before Sera left, she laid her hand on my arm and gazed into my eyes. "Thank you for being honest. It means so much to me, and I feel so much closer to you."

I tried not to read anything into it, but the way she looked at me had me worried.

When I made my weekly call to my grandfather after I had dinner at my apartment, the phone rang out. I tried several times. In the end, I rang the neighbors, who told me he had gone to hospice. At my pause after the news, his neighbor asked, "Are you OK, Camie?"

I wiped the back of my hand across my eyes as I croaked, "As okay as I can be."

In his wisdom, my grandfather had given me the details of the hospice. When the nurse advised me that my grandfather's condition was serious, I tried to rejoice that my grandfather would soon be home with the *Father*, but the prospect of losing my last human family member weighed heavily on me.

I wrestled with my emotions as I prayed to the *Father* for a peaceful passing for my grandfather.

Chapter 27

Escalation

I willed the bus to move faster, but it seemed to dawdle as it meandered through nondescript towns. I'd rung the hospice before I left, and although they said my grandfather's condition was stable, every five-minute delay seemed like an hour. My eyes refused to focus on the book I'd brought. My mind couldn't recall the incantation to practice. I didn't see the ever-changing landscape. All I thought about was getting to my grandfather in time to say goodbye.

The hours crept by, and I seemed no closer to Woodbridge Township. The fading light told me we must be nearing the end of the trip. We'd just passed the Trenton turn-off when my restlessness began to fade. I closed my eyes to prepare myself for seeing my grandfather close to death. At the screech of brakes, my eyes shot open. Just before the bus slued to the side, I caught a glimpse of someone on the road. Then they were gone.

The grinding of metal on metal as the bus destroyed the guard rail, careening out of control, underpinned the passengers' screaming. It plowed into the culvert, the tires on one side airborne, and then the shattering of glass and grating of metal filled the cabin as the bus flipped onto its side. As the bus skidded on, a stabbing pain ripped through my upper arm. I'd been hit by luggage flying off the overhead shelf. I tried to move the arm, but it hung limply at my side. As I moved, something under me groaned. I'd landed on top of the passenger by the window. I used my good arm to try to haul myself up by the back of the seat in front, but I had no purchase for my feet with the bus on its side. I did glimpse bodies in the aisle, and when I glanced at my neighbor, dark stains on his clothes indicated blood. I apologized as I settled back onto him, but he seemed to be unconscious.

Groans and whimpering mixed with screams and crying came from the tangled knot of passengers. As I lay there, I cursed Lilith. It had to have been her. That she wanted me dead, I understood, but all these innocent people. Not that either Lucifer or Lilith had any sympathy for mortals.

The wailing of sirens carried the hope of rescue. Flashing lights bounced off the ceiling of the bus, and voices calling out commands reached me through the walls.

Then, there was the smashing of glass, which I assumed to be the windscreen being staved in. Sparks fell from the ceiling as firefighters sheared open the roof. The noise of the cutter drowned out the other sounds as I watched its laborious progress along the top edge. Then the jarring noise of metal peeling back signaled liberation.

After being pulled clear, a paramedic examined my arm and confirmed the break. He assisted me into a sling and gave me a blanket and some painkillers, then asked me to join the other injured who could walk. As I made my way to the group huddled near the emergency lighting, a body bag drew my attention. I counted three. In the back of an ambulance, my fellow passenger lay on a stretcher, the bloody stump of his arm being triaged.

Pale faces under the bruising and lacerations peered at me as I joined the group. Slings, bandaged hands, and legs leaking blood prevailed. The driver stood alone, either having been ostracized from the group or not willing to join it. As I approached him, he lifted his head, and an angry gash above his eye glared at me, but his face held a pleading expression.

I kept my voice low as I said, "I saw her, too."

His face crumpled. "She was there, wasn't she? I didn't imagine it. She was there, and then she was gone."

"If you need me to verify it, I am willing to do so."

He gripped my good hand, then pulled me into a hug. "I thought I was going mad."

I walked back to the group, and one of them snarled, "What were you doing talking to him? He's the reason we're in this mess."

"No, he isn't. There was someone on the road. I saw them. He swerved to miss them."

"I don't believe you."

"I know, in circumstances like this, we want someone to blame, but in truth, you can blame this on Lucifer." A babble of voices greeted my comment. I held up my hand. "OK, you think I'm a religious crackpot, but I can assure you, the devil had a hand in this."

I walked a short distance from the group wanting to call on Raphael to heal me so I could continue my journey, but the appearance of an archangel might be more than the injured could handle. Like the rest, I'd be taken to the hospital and wait for treatment. My grandfather dying before I got there plagued my mind.

Thirty-six hours later, I left the hospital and got into the cab provided by the bus line. When the driver pulled up in front of the hospice, I threw a fleeting thank you over my shoulder as I clambered out and hurried to the entrance. There was no one at reception, so I rang the metal bell on the counter. The chime didn't get a response, so I hit it a few times. Then I hit it a few more times. Someone appeared from a back room, trying to cover their annoyed expression with a smile. It came out as a grimace.

"Can you tell me which room Peter Rathmusuen is in, please?"

"Room 22, Rose Ward. But—"

I didn't wait to hear the rest. I followed the signs, moving as fast as I could without actually running until I found his room. The door was closed, so I knocked. A murmur of voices carried through the door. For a moment, I thought it might be my grandfather speaking. The door opened, and a man blocked the entrance.

I pushed past him, muttering, "I'm his grandson."

My grandfather's gaunt face appeared above the bedcovers. His breathing came in irregular gasps. I reached for his skeletal hand and held it gently in mine. As I went to say I was here, his breath crackled and rattled in his chest. Then he stopped breathing.

I shut my eyes. I wanted to yell, but instead, I said, "I'm sorry I didn't get here in time, Papa."

Then I vowed to make Lilith pay.

Chapter 28

The Student is Ready

y heart filled with gratitude at the number of members from my grandfather's congregation who attended the service. The minister spoke from the heart about my grandfather's unwavering devotion to the *Father* and his participation in the life of the church. If he had been there, he would have enjoyed the funeral.

On the bus back to Savannah, my heart accepted his passing and gave thanks that he was one with the *Father* now, but a steady rain beat on the window like a drum tattoo, exclaiming my aloneness.

The apartment's still, cold air reminded me I had been away for nearly two weeks, and with the new moon fast approaching, we needed to prepare for my first attempt at opening the door. I rang Mama and asked to meet early the following morning to pick up my lessons.

After we discussed the funeral and my emotional state, she prayed for me that I would be ready to resume the undertaking the *Father* had given me.

The day dawned bright, washed clean by the previous night's storm. It lifted my mood, so I had exercised my melancholy away by the time I had walked to Misha's.

I sat on the couches in The Painted Lady, enunciating words as if learning a language for the first time. After the twentieth or so attempt, I threw my hands in the air. "It's hopeless. I'll never get it right in the three days we have left."

Mama fixed her gaze on me. "The *Father* gave you this mission. If *He* didn't think you were up to it, *He* wouldn't have assigned you. Have a little faith in *Him* if not yourself."

Mama's words hit a nerve. I had been relying on myself rather than *Him*. "Thank you for reminding me I am not in this alone. I will pray on it tonight, but for now, my mind is drained, and I have the kids to teach."

Sera's eyes were bright with tears as she expressed her sorrow at my grandfather's passing. Then she wrapped me in a hug that lasted a little longer than was perhaps appropriate. I disentangled myself and thanked her. I didn't want to say anything in case I had misinterpreted her meaning, but I had the distinct impression she was developing feelings for me. At eighteen, she was a babe in arms compared to my millennia of existence. If my suspicions were correct, I needed to be careful in my response to her.

The lesson covered the various skills and gifts of the Nephilim of Illumination, and we discussed how I intended to test for them. Sera and Drake seemed both excited and daunted at the same time.

The following day Mama and I practiced the incantation until my tongue stuck to the roof of my mouth, but Mama did say my performance had improved. Then she told me more about the ritual. "We light candles of specific colors with each Psalm—black for banishing negativity, purple for spiritual healing, blue for forgiveness, and yellow for joy and manifestation. We inscribe them with the names of the *Father—Yahweh, Shaddai, Elohim, Tzabaoth*. The candles are set in each corner of the room to signify the four elements. The traveler carries a white candle signifying purity, peace, truth, and hope. We do not inscribe it as the passage is consecrated ground. When the last words of the incantation are said, the portal opens to a brilliance that only the angelic traveler and I can bear. After the last traveler has passed through the portal, the cedar doors close behind them, then the doors themselves go home with the traveler in a brilliant blue flash of the *Father's* Holy Fire of *Elohim*. The travelers prostrate themselves to show submission to the *Father's* will. We can only fit five at a time. I'm not sure what we will do if we get more than that number. Even holding the portal open for five puts us at risk of discovery."

"I'm sure the *Father* has a plan if the numbers grow. Like you said to me yesterday, have a little faith."

On the morning of the new moon, we stood in the Holy Place, and I practiced the ceremony, pretending to light the candles before each Psalm, moving to each corner of the room and giving their meaning then reciting the incantation. I needed to time the incantation so it coincided with the moon's crossing the meridian. Mama said I had done well.

As the timing of the crossing occurred at noon, we scheduled our trial for then. My hands fluttered as I lit the candles, and my voice broke a couple of times as I recited the Psalms. I concentrated on the pattern of inflection Mama had taught me as I delivered the incantation. On the final words, I held my breath and looked at the doors in expectation. When nothing happened, I glanced at Mama for confirmation that I had performed the ritual correctly. She said, "Perhaps the new moon is not the right time. We'll practice some more and try again on the full moon. Let's get something to eat."

Sera joined us for lunch and asked how the attempt had gone. After I expressed my disappointment at my failure, she extolled my virtues to the point of embarrassment. I shifted uncomfortably as Mama looked between Sera and myself; I figured I had best talk to Mama about my growing suspicion.

After my lesson with Sera and Drake, where Sera hung on my every word as if it was a pearl of wisdom, I sought Mama out. I indicated to her to follow me outside where inquisitive ears couldn't hear us.

"Tell me I'm not imaging it." I couldn't even name the emotion for fear of conjuring it.

"No, I saw it too. She's young and impressionable. You are an archangel of immense power. Of course, she's drawn to you."

"But what are we going to do about it? I mean, she is so young, and I'm, I'm ancient." I needed a solution as I didn't like the awkward position I found myself in and also didn't want to hurt Sera.

Mama patted me on the arm. "I'll have a word with her and explain the situation."

If I had hoped Mama's talk with Sera would solve the situation, I had a thing or two to learn about youthful crushes. The next time Sera and I crossed paths, Sera's first words were, "I don't care how old you are; I know I can make you happy. Please just give us a chance."

My mind hung, suspended in space like a fly caught in a spider's web. At my inability to form an appropriate response, her eyes filled with tears, and she burst out with, "I love you." Then she fled. I remained stationary for a moment then beat a path to Mama's door.

Mama's advice didn't alleviate my agitation since she said I had to talk to Sera, but with the full moon a day away, I didn't have the time to do that yet.

Expectation buzzed as the countdown to midnight began the night of the full moon. The family had gathered in The Painted Lady and waited in the same area as they had done when I revealed my angelic self. As on that occasion, the fragrance of roses lilted in the air as I entered the Holy Place. Protected by *Shekinah Mother's* presence, the family had the freedom to enjoy the moment when a soul went home.

This time my nerves didn't trouble me, and I executed the ceremony to the second, my final word reverberating with the grandfather clock's last chime. I thought I spotted movement in the doors, and my mouth twitched up at the corners, but in the next breath, it turned down as nothing happened.

I turned to Mama and ran my hand through my hair. "What am I doing wrong? I mean, I timed it to the second, said the incantation perfectly, but nothing happened. I must be missing something."

Mama's face grew thoughtful. "There was something about your aura glowing pink, which hasn't happened yet. That might be it, but I don't know what we have to do to achieve that."

I mulled over the pink aura as I walked home in the drizzling rain. Mine tended to be blue-green, a far cry from pink.

That night, every dream I had featured an intricately inlaid box.

Chapter 29

Boxed In

ᒷᎱᔦᎩ Ᏽ

The following night, when I had the same dream, telling Misha and Mama seemed the logical thing to do.

Over a scrumptious breakfast of eggs Benedict, garlic and herb sausages, sautéed spinach, and pan-fried tomato, I related my dream. Mama and Misha asked questions about the size and shape and pattern.

As the box kept changing size, I couldn't tell them much on that front, but the design clearly indicated the Orient.

Misha said, "Misha might have this thing." He scurried out of the room toward his vault and returned fifteen minutes later, holding a polished jewelry box inlaid with a scene of a crane on a pond. He passed it to me. "Does this look like it?"

"It's beautiful, but no. The box didn't open, and the inlay seemed to have tiny diamonds. It was a bit battered, and some of the inlays had come out."

"Misha think you mean a puzzle box. Japanese make them one hundred and fifty years; popular in America before Great War. About 1980, started to appear again. Some open easy; others very hard. Misha get picture."

After retrieving a book from the shelves, he showed Mama and me a picture of a puzzle box.

I said, "Yes, that's it" at the same time Mama exclaimed, "I think I have one of those."

When she returned some three-quarters of an hour later, she was clearly flustered. "Thought I'd lost it, had to dig through all the bag lady bags. I wondered why I kept them. Now, I know. Is this it?" She handed it to me as she explained how she came by it. "About five years ago, a well-dressed lady approached me with the box in her hand. She held it out to me and said, 'It's not for you to open, so don't even try. One day in the future, it will be essential to what you are doing.' I admit I did try to open it. Fairly frustrating experience. Then I shoved it into a bag and forgot about it."

I turned the box over. No visible seams appeared on its surface to look at, so I ran my fingers over it. Even then, I couldn't detect anything. I pushed at the sides, but that had no effect. "So, how do you open it?"

Misha said, "Misha believe trick panel hidden in design. Find panel, find key to opening."

Mama added, "Easier said than done."

Sera entered the room. It was the first time I had seen her since her declaration. She ignored me and focused on the box. "Ooo, I love these," she said, reaching for it.

"Can you open it?"

"Probably not, but Drake might be able to with his genius mind." She gave it back to me and trotted off to get Drake.

I handed it to Drake, who turned it over and said, "Not my specialty. If it were a Rubix Cube, I could solve it mathematically, but these defy logic." He handed it back. "Sorry. Looks like you will have to get your pals upstairs working on it, Camie, old son."

Mama and I went to The Painted Lady for my session. She outlined the procedure of the three days the travelers spent with the family before the ceremony. Fasting and meditation played a big part in it, with a full fast the day of the ceremony. The linen used in the simple robe they wore had to be handcrafted. Mama sourced it from AIIORA in London and had it made by a tailor friend of hers. The travelers bathed in purified water, and Mama anointed them with the holy oil, much like *Yeshua HaMeshiach* was anointed before his crucifixion. No one but Mama and Misha saw them before the ceremony. They brought the travelers all their meals and tended to their other requests. The travelers were not to speak except in prayer during the ceremony, and no one was to speak to them. Mama assumed I could take over some of Misha's duties as age had caught up with him, given my connection to the work, but she suggested I not reveal my true self as some of the travelers might be afraid of me.

When we finished, I went to my lesson with Sera and Drake. Sera pointedly continued to ignore me, so it had come to the moment where I could no longer avoid speaking with her. After the lesson, I asked her to remain.

Drake teased his sister. "Are you in trouble or what? Love to be a fly on the wall for this one."

Sera sat on the couch, staring out the window, refusing to make eye contact with me.

I fumbled over my approach, but given I was the adult in this situation, it was up to me to do something. "Sera, I am flattered that you have affections for me—"

She grunted and folded her arms, sinking low on the couch, slouching.

"No, seriously, I am. You are an attractive, personable, intelligent young lady—"

"Young? That is how you see me. I'm eighteen, an adult."

The hard edge to her voice told me she was angry, but I needed her to understand. "And I am a few millennia old, so yes, by comparison, you are young, but it is not only the age difference. Dia stirred a memory in me of my one great love. I don't think you were there when I told Dia about Naamah's and my relationship and how she died. I mourned the loss of my soul mate for years and became so angry with the *Father* for allowing it to happen, I rejected him. In my other human lives, I had no recollection of her, but now I do. My heart belongs to her, even after these thousands of years. I am not in a position to give you what you need. I will be your friend, and I will support you, but I cannot return your affection."

"So, you won't even try?"

It seemed she had rejected my reason out of hand. "Please understand. My heart is given. Please take a few days to reflect on what I have said. And believe me, it is not you. Whoever you eventually chose will be a lucky person."

She left, and I sat there wondering what else I could have said.

At my apartment that evening, I messed with the box, pushing and tugging at it, trying to find the hidden key. After a frustrating two hours, I went to bed.

The following night, I threw the box across the room, knocking over a vase that smashed on the floor. I stomped to the cupboards on the lounge wall where I kept my few tools and snatched a hammer. After placing the puzzle box on the kitchen bench, I brought the hammer down on it with as much force as I could muster. When the hammer connected with the box, my wrist jarred as the hammer ricocheted off, leaving the box undented.

Satan lounged on the couch.

"Temper, temper, Camie. You know what happened the last time you lost your temper."

I snapped at him. "Can't you use the door?"

"Why would I when surprising people is so much more fun? But you know that box is a gift from *Father* so trying to smash it won't work. You'll need to control your frustration and temper and then center your focus to open it."

"That isn't going to happen tonight."

"No, probably not; by the way, do you have any of the great chop suey left? I'm starved."

"Nope, but I have a good chili con carne."

While we were eating, I asked Satan if he knew what the puzzle box was about or anything about a pink aura. He replied, "Not specifically, but I hazard a guess they are connected."

Why hadn't I thought of that?

After he left, I sat the box on the coffee table and went to bed.

I couldn't concentrate with Mama the following day. All I wanted to do was get back to the box to solve the mystery.

"Are you listening?" Mama poked me in the ribs.

"I'm sorry, but my mind is on the box. Satan said that the pink aura might be related to the box."

"Satan?" Her brow creased.

I jumped in with an explanation. "Satan is not the devil. The Church has it wrong. Lucifer is the fallen angel. The *Father* assigned Satan to me as my mentor. I hope that clears up any misunderstanding."

Mama beamed. "No, it couldn't be more right. Part of the message about the archangel being sent included a part about Satan being his guide." She jumped to her feet. "Just wait 'til I tell the others."

After much elation from the family at the further confirmation that I was indeed the archangel they had been waiting for, I escaped to my apartment.

With the box on the coffee table, I focused my mind, letting go of all preconceived ideas and random thoughts. I considered a key. A key was small and went into a lock. Did that mean the key on the box was a little panel and had a lock of some sort? At least it was a place to start.

I tried the different sections of patterns first, pushing my index finger in both directions. Then I contemplated each side's sizes and concluded that it had to be on the short ends of the box if the key was small. I started at the top of one end and progressively moved my finger down, pushing in both directions—nothing on the first end, but bingo on the other. In my excitement, I expected the box to just open.

After rotating the box in all directions and finding nothing more, I turned to the Internet for information. Puzzle box sale ads came up first.

I reviewed one page, and when I read fifty-two steps, my elated mood flattened. It had taken me three days to crack one move. Fifty-two! The *Father* wouldn't be that cruel, would *He*? I did find a couple of pictures of moved panels that gave me a clue where to go next.

Two panels later, in quick succession, my confidence that I had the hang of it blossomed—only to be knocked down after an hour with no progress on the fourth. I put the box down and made lunch.

Chewing on my sandwich, it dawned on me that my mind had been running the show, and I needed to allow instinct and my fingers to do the work. I dropped my half-eaten sandwich on the plate and swiped up the box. I closed my eyes, cleared my mind, and let my fingers explore the inlaid panels while allowing my intuition free reign. Within a matter of minutes, I had the fourth level open. It took a little longer for the fifth, but then progress steadied. Within an hour, I had worked twenty-one steps, and my fingers felt a piece of paper.

My eyes flew open, and I lifted the folded note out of the secret compartment. I hesitated to open it, my pulse racing and my hands shaking. When I did, another riddle confronted me. The note read:

The rose blossoms
But in vein you seek
The answer is crystal clear
But you must dig deep within

What did that mean? I hoped Misha or Mama could shed more light on it, so I headed back to Misha's with the note in hand.

Chapter 30

Crystal Clear

Misha and Mama called the family together to brainstorm the meaning of the riddle. Sera refused to help. I guess she was still hurting from my rejection. When Dia, Gerry, Alexi, and the others had seated themselves around the table, Mama read the riddle.

Gerry offered the first insight. "I think 'rose blossoms' has something to do with the color pink . . . like his aura is supposed to glow."

I hadn't picked Gerry as the thinking type, which just proved I had fallen for the stereotype of dumb security. Embarrassed at my own prejudices, I thanked Gerry for his insight, agreeing that that was a good explanation.

'Digging deep within,' everyone agreed had to do with my relationship with the *Father*. That puzzled me since I classified my current status as excellent.

Mama asked, what could be 'crystal clear,' given the message was cryptic?

Alexi chipped in with my role in the ceremony.

We debated that for a while, but it seemed to fit with the notion of the pink aura.

The 'in vein you seek' had the family stumped, and we threw ideas around for about an hour. Then Gerry commented, "Isn't vein spelled wrong?"

Why hadn't we noticed that before? I said, "Vein and crystal have to do with rocks."

Dia added, "'Digging deep within' might have to do with rocks as well."

Gerry and I said at the same time, "I/he's looking for a crystal at a mine site."

Misha added, "A pink one."

Gerry said, "Rose quartz is pink."

Alexi began searching on his mobile. "There's the Hogg Mine in Georgia that has rose quartz."

"Looks like I am going mining; where exactly in Georgia?"

After we checked the website to get times and dates, we struck it lucky and found a machine dig scheduled for Saturday next week. Gerry agreed to go with me in case there was an incident. We had to be there before 9:00 a.m., which meant staying overnight somewhere. Dia organized accommodation. We still had to print out the indemnity forms, but that could wait until Drake got home from school.

The buzz in the room electrified me.

On the Friday before the dig, Gerry squeezed himself into the small seat of the rental I had organized, and we waved goodbye to the family. With our trunk filled with the required equipment I had purchased, we were ready for anything. The hour-and-a-half drive passed quickly as Gerry and I speculated over the possibilities. I laughed at the idea of speculating given it was a term used for mineral exploration. Gerry didn't get the joke.

Up bright and early on Saturday morning, we headed for the mine, having skipped breakfast. We arrived at 7:00 a.m. to be the head of the queue. Fortunately, we had reached LaGrange yesterday in time to pick up some food, so while we waited, we tucked into some homemade quiche.

Once the queue began to grow, our fortitude at standing in the cold for two hours seemed worth it. We picked up our buckets and staked out a claim. Gerry wielded the mattock like it was a toothpick. I shoveled the fallen dirt out of the way while scanning it for crystals. After a couple of hours, we had accumulated a range of minerals but nothing that said *I am special.*

Just as Gerry moved away from the mining face to our picnic basket to get a drink, the earth trembled, and the wall of the dirt quarry gave way. I jumped back but not far enough to escape the avalanche. A ton of rubble smothered me, but my head lay in a pocket of air formed by the overhang of a boulder. I prayed to the *Father* for my rescue and hoped Gerry could dig me out in time.

After several minutes, I heard the sound of the digger. I fully expected the blade to rip my body to shreds, but instead, the weight of earth lifted from me. Then Gerry's voice rang clear. "I can see him."

A few minutes later, Gerry pulled me clear.

I listened to the various accounts of the landslide and rescue, but one thing that stood out amongst all the stories was the presence of what looked like fire on the ridgeline. That could only have been Lilith. My relief that she had targeted me must have been clearly expressed on my face as Gerry commented, "We can give thanks no one else got hurt."

When I had gathered my breath, Gerry and I continued our quest. I clambered to the top of the fall and cleared away the dirt. Gerry asked if I'd found anything. I called down, "Nothing yet."

I had just decided to go back down and join Gerry when I scraped away another layer of dirt. The sun sparkled on a pink stone the size of a grapefruit. It shouted, *Me Me.* I whooped in delight and yelled to Gerry, "I've found it!"

Once I scrambled down the slope, I showed Gerry the crystal, and even in its raw form, Gerry's face lit with delight. I gathered our haul, and we left with our prize.

On the drive home, we discussed how Lilith's attempt on my life had backfired on her. Gerry recounted his fear for my life, and I thanked him for his prompt action in organizing the digger.

The family gathered to see our treasure. Much *oohing* and *aahing* swirled around us, but when I looked at Dia, her expression contained disdain. I had to ask, and she responded, "Sure, its size and facets make it pretty, but in my time, I've seen many such crystals. If you can turn this into something more than a lump of rock, I might see its value."

That got me thinking, and the next day, I purchased a rock tumbler and the necessary grit, pellets, and polishing material. I set the machine up in Misha's shed at the back of his store and loaded it with the crystals from the dig and the precious stone as well as the grit and pellets and set it to run for seven days.

Over the next week, while the stones tumbled, I visited the shed a couple of times a day and had to refrain from stopping the machine to check on the stone. On the final day, with half an hour to go, I paced back and forth across the small shed. My watch beeped, and I flipped the off switch. Pawing through the material in the tumbler, I struggled to find the crystal. I shoveled handfuls of grit, pellets, and stones out, not stopping to admire the beauty of some.

Then it appeared. With a sharp intake of breath and a shaking of my hand, I picked up a perfectly spherical stone. Even unpolished, its beauty stung my eyes. How it had formed such a faultless shape when the other stones were irregular, I could only put down to the *Father's* intervention.

I loaded the machine with the stones and polishing material and set it to run for the next few days. Even with my lessons with Sera and Drake, the time dragged.

Days later, at the end of the polishing time, when my watch alarm sounded, I yanked open the door and flung the unwanted stones out of the way until I found my prize. The star in the rose quartz dazzled me, and the whole form of the crystal screamed perfection.

I burst through the backdoor to the living quarters and bellowed, "You've gotta see this."

Mama gave thanks to the *Father*. Misha capered about like a teenager, Gerry slapped me on the back so hard, I nearly dropped the sphere, and Alexi searched the Internet for comparisons. He barely contained his excitement as he read that the largest known rose quartz sphere, which belonged to Michael Scott, was only three and a half inches. Ours exceeded four. Alexi said we needed to call the *Guinness Book of Records*, but Mama pointed out we couldn't afford that sort of attention. The disappointment on Alexi's face hurt even me.

Dia's continuing derision of my status had begun to feel personal when she said, "So far, it's just a pretty stone. His aura is not pink, and I doubt he can make it so."

As she turned away, she cast a disdainful glance over her shoulder. I uttered a prayer of praise to the *Father* for providing this incredible gift. Her demeanor changed at the sight of my intense concentration.

The family crowded in as the crystal began to glow, their faces taking on a pink cast.

Dia stuttered, "Your a—a—aura. It's glowing pink."

Mama drew her eyes away from the crystal to study me. "Praise the *Lord*. I think we have found the missing piece of the puzzle."

The rest cheered, and Dia said, "I'm sorry I've been such a jerk about it, but I've been let down too many times in the past."

I held the crystal out to her and replied, "No more letdowns now."

At the sound of pounding footsteps on the stairs, I turned my head in that direction to see Drake balancing his laptop as he yelled, "You won't believe what just happened."

We waited until he joined the group and pointed at his screen, then the family squeezed together to see what it was he pointed at. I saw a bright spot on the map of America situated over Savannah. "What are we looking at, Drake?"

"It's a vortex that opened about five minutes ago."

At my puzzled expression, he elaborated. "You don't know about the algorithms I developed to track the Earth's magnetic fields and weather patterns, but this anomaly is what they were designed to discover." The pride in his voice was unmistakable.

"What does it mean?" I asked.

"Well, did something happen five or so minutes ago?" Drake asked.

Mama said, "Yes, Camie activated the crystal."

"Crystal?" It was Drake's turn to be puzzled.

Misha said, "Show him, Camie."

I held out the crystal and explained how my aura and it glow synchronously.

Drake beamed. "That would be it. Activating the crystal must have activated the vortex. I'll keep monitoring it, and if there are changes, I will let you know."

He waved from the stairs when Misha called out, "Well done, son."

Chapter 31

First Strike

ㄱ옷ㄱㆍ ㆍ옷ㄱㅂㄱ

ㄴucifer leaned back on the plush leather couch, feet on the glass coffee table. "You really are making this harder for me, you know. If you'd left well enough alone, Camie wouldn't have the crystal."

Lilith's eyes blazed red. "How was I supposed to know? And at least I am doing something. I can't help it if that cretin who calls himself a deity somehow managed to turn Camie's death into a positive."

Lucifer chuckled. "After all these years, you haven't worked out that that cretin regularly turns our actions against us. However, we need to be prepared for Camie's next attempt. Have a force ready to mobilize the instant something happens."

※

I stood before the doors in the Holy Place, the crystal in hand, and as my true archangel self, ready for the last full moon trial before Halloween. This time, my spirit floated free in the knowledge that the *Father* had provided me with everything I needed to complete *His* will.

I focused my attention on the perfection of the star crystal, and it began to glow. My aura tingled as it responded in harmony. My voice rang with certainty as I recited the Psalm. The light from the candles shone more intensely. The incantation flowed easily from my lips. The crystal flared a dazzling rose-pink at the last words of the incantation, and as the rays struck the sacred doors, they swung soundlessly open.

At the sight of the glory of the *Father* streaming through the portal, my heart yearned to be in *His* presence again, but it also rejoiced that I had been given such an honorable task of sending the travelers home.

At the sound of cheering from the family gathered in The Painted Lady, I grinned. Then Mama's voice cut across it. "Close the portal, Camie. The Painted Lady is exposed."

Shoot! In my elation at my success, I had forgotten the risk. I extinguished the star crystal, and the portal closed. At the same time, I reverted to my human form.

As I exited the Holy Place, the family surged toward me, faces lit with pride, joy, and reverence. Over the babble of excited voices, I heard an explosion, and the building shook. I yelled, "We're under attack. Get ready to defend yourself."

At first, only Mama reacted, changing to her angelic form. The remainder of the family looked at me with puzzled, confused expressions. The second explosion snapped them out of their daze.

Clothes ripped as they transformed into their true selves, their weapons of choice glinting in the dim light. Gerry strode to the doors of the pawnshop. "The attack is coming from in here." He recited the invocation, and the doors opened. Then he bellowed like a bull and charged out.

I grabbed Sera and Drake. "Under no circumstances are you to leave here. I'll get Mama to close the doors to protect you."

Drake began, "But—"

"No buts. We can't have the only two known Nephilim of Illumination killed. You are destined for bigger things."

Mama and I were the last ones out of The Painted Lady. She nodded to me once the doors were sealed. "Let's go kick some demon butt." She raised her hand, and I slapped it.

The wall of the hall to Misha's living quarters showed the aftermath of fighting—scorch marks, missing plaster from blade strikes, the splattering of both black and red blood.

"Hang on a moment."

Mama's brow creased as I headed toward the breakfast room. Her expression cleared when I held up the superb sword from Misha's collection.

Moving toward the entrance, my foot kicked the severed head of a demon, blood-black veins squirreling out of its neck like chewed string. Its frozen grin, which revealed the shark-like teeth beneath its black lips, reminded me that I hadn't confronted demons in their true form in many millennia. Doubt at my ability to overcome them ate at my confidence, particularly given I couldn't use my full Holy Fire of *Elohim* as that would kill the family.

One of ours slumped against the wall, a nasty gash in her belly, her ax still clutched in her hand. I bent to the dwarf to check for a pulse. I felt it and thanked the *Father*, but I couldn't stop to assist her now. I prayed for her to survive long enough for help to arrive.

Black guts spewed over the wooden floor. The stench made me gag. With sticky blood and spiraling entrails splattered across the boards, I watched my step so as not to squelch through the mess, but my heel squished part of the intestine. My body lurched as my foot slipped on the slimy mess. I thrust out my auras to keep my balance, but the corridor's narrow width prevented me. My knee landed with my full weight on the creature's stomach and ruptured it, splattering my white robe with green goo. I sighed but expected that before this night was over, I'd be covered in more than that. Pity Heaven didn't have dry cleaning.

As Mama and I ran through the shop, I caught glimpses of charred and smashed objects, more demon bodies, and shattered glass from the windows. The chaos in the street left me uncertain where to go first.

Mama said, "You go right. I'll go left."

Before I could say we might be stronger together, she had darted away. Just as I went to follow her, I caught sight of a succubus holding an elf in a death grip. As I approached, I had to admit to the succubus's attractiveness, and part of me sorrowed at destroying something beautiful, but it had to be done. I drove my blade into her neck, severing the artery. She released her grip on the elf, who slumped to the ground. The succubus clutched her neck, blue blood bubbling out of her mouth.

I checked the elf. He still had a life force, but whether it was enough for him to recover, I couldn't tell.

I spotted Gerry surrounded by six demons. He kept them at bay with his double-headed ax, but he needed help. I stabbed and cut my way through the line of Hell's spawn until I reached his location. I got to the manticore first and slashed at its wing. It roared as it spun toward me, its unshorn main rippling with the sound. Three-inch ivory canines warned me not to get too close to its jaws. Unable to fly, it used the power of its hind legs to leap at me. I drove my blade into its exposed chest, cracking the breastbone as I did so. The momentum of the creature continued, and I found myself pinned under its ten-foot body, blood oozing onto my face. Its body pinned my arms, but even though I could move them, I'd never shift its thousand-pound weight. It began to crush my ribs, making it difficult to breathe. I gagged for air. If something didn't occur in the next couple of minutes, I could kiss fulfilling the *Father's* assignment goodbye.

Then the weight shifted. My blurry vision made out Gerry. I'd gone to rescue him, but he'd ended up saving me. He held out his hand and hauled me to my feet. I doubled over and dry-wretched. Once I gained my breath, I thanked him, and we rejoined the fight. I hoped I would get the chance to hear how he'd extracted himself from the other five demons, but right now, we had a horde to slaughter.

To my left, the scream of the banshee blasted open the head of her attacker. I thanked the *Father* she was on our side.

As I impaled my fourth demon, it occurred to me that these were all lesser demons with limited powers. Not that they weren't a force to be reckoned with, but in terms of the attack, why hadn't Lucifer sent a stronger one?

At the cry of a gnome, my attention reverted to the present. I'd seen him minutes before using his clawed rod to effect, clutching onto the legs of the enemy, causing them to topple so another member of the family could finish them. Now a praying mantis-like monster held him with its spiny claws. An ogre, whose name I thought was Estefan, ran in to help and hacked at it with his serrated sword, but the plate-like exoskeleton deflected the blows. The mantis extended its other front limb and thrust its claw down the gnome's throat. I raced from my position to try to stop what was coming and managed to slice off the limb, but not before it had wrenched the gnome's stomach out through his mouth. The organ hung from his broken jaw like a balloon half-filled with water, wobbling for a second before the mantis dropped the gnome.

My anger boiled over then. I hadn't known the gnome well. In fact, I didn't even know his name, but he'd been just a boy of about sixteen. I sliced at the mantis's legs then thrust my sword through its jaws, piercing its brain.

I bellowed for the family to get to protection. The demons surged past me, chasing the retreating family as I expected. I smelled the fragrance of roses and appreciated that *Shekinah Mother* had anticipated my intention and come to protect the family. I called on my Holy Fire of *Elohim* and focused it to form a ring around me. Then I unleashed it. The brilliant blast of pure blue energy shot out like a tidal wave from an earthquake, incinerating the remaining demons.

Slow clapping echoed in the ensuing silence. I pivoted my head in its direction. Lilith stood just out of range of the blast. "Seems like you still have trouble with that temper of yours."

"Dam— you." I activated a ball of Holy Fire of *Elohim*, but before I could launch it, she passed through her portal, calling over her shoulder, "I thought I already was."

Once I had returned to my human form, those uninjured of the family came out. Dia's awed expression mirrored many. She clapped me on the back and said, "You certainly don't disappoint."

I scanned the faces: Mama, Misha, Alexi, but no Gerry. My voice faltered as I asked, "Is Gerry . . ."

Mama said, "He's wounded pretty badly, but he's alive, unlike a few others."

I learned the gnome's name had been Tamil and that we had lost an apprentice chef and the head waiter. My concern returned to the injured, so I called for Raphael.

Raphael assessed the most urgent and tended to those first, the dwarf in the hall being one. He laid his hands over the rent in her belly and recited ancient words in the Angelic tongue. His hands glowed, and her body radiated light as it knitted itself together. Her eyes fluttered open in her pale face. She tried to move, but Raphael placed his hand on her shoulder. "You need to rest for a few hours until the healing takes. Someone will carry you to a bed."

Gerry had a deep gash on his thigh, which Raphael healed. When he came to the elf the succubus had attacked and whom someone had dragged to safety, he shook his head. "Too much of the life force has been drained for me to be able to restore it. Make him as comfortable as possible and stay by his side to pray."

After an hour, when Raphael had finished, he raised his drained face to me and said, "This time, you used your anger the right way."

I grasped his hand. "Thanks." I dropped my gaze, both conflicted by my past and relieved to have gotten it right. "Good to know I didn't overdo it like last time." Then I grinned.

"But there are some people who'd like to meet you," I told him.

Mama clapped her hands. "An excellent idea." She went to the doors and spoke the invocation. "Come, come." As she stepped into The Painted Lady, Sera and Drake raced over to embrace her.

"We didn't know what was happening. Is Misha alright?"

Mama nodded. "Nearly everyone is OK. We did lose a few." She named them.

Sera shook when she said, "Not Tamil. He was my friend."

I took a couple of steps closer and said, "I have someone here who I think will cheer you up." I gestured toward Raphael.

Joy and trepidation chased each other across his face as he stepped forward. He held out his hands as he said, "Sera, Drake."

Sera's eye widened. "Is this who I think it is?"

Raphael nodded.

Sera flung herself into his arms. "Why have you waited so long to meet us?"

Raphael replied, "I wanted to sooner, but I needed to wait until you knew what you were, and that could only happen when Camie arrived." He held Sera at arm's length. "Such a beauty. Just like her mother."

He turned to Drake. "Come here, son. You have no idea how much I have dreamed of this. I've watched you both since you were born."

"Yew, creepy," Drake said.

"No not like that—as your guardian angel to keep you out of harm's way."

In his usual style of trying to play it cool, Drake said, "So tell me, Dad, what is the Big Guy up to?"

I left them to their reunion and went to the bar to get a drink. Mama joined me.

"That won't be the last of it, will it?" she asked.

"No, now that they know where we are, we can expect more. I can only hope they still don't know what we are doing."

Mama agreed and then said, "I am so pleased Sera and Drake have met Raphael. I hope he can play a greater role in their lives now."

"I'm sure the *Father* will make time for him to do just that."

"Only ten days to Halloween. Then, you get to send the travelers home."

Raphael drew me aside before he left.

"So, you must know what your mission is by now; spill . . ."

I asked him the question Mama had asked me.

"Who is the least likely being you'd think the *Father* would redeem?"

"Lucifer?"

"Not quite but close . . . our fallen brethren. Can you believe it? *Father* is giving every fallen angel a chance to return to *Him*."

Raphael said, "*His* love truly knows no bounds."

Lucifer set down his glass of single malt on the coffee table, the ice cubes clinking on the crystal. "So, now we know what we're up against. Who'd have thought mystical beasts live in the city?"

"I'd like to know how you didn't know. Or did you and you just didn't tell me?"

Lucifer looked her over. She'd become quite ill-tempered since he'd made her date Camie. If she wasn't such a good asset, he might consider disposing of her. But she had her uses yet. "I had my suspicions, but no, I didn't know for certain."

"Great. I only get half the information. Do you know what they are up to?"

"In truth, no; I've heard rumors over recent years but nothing confirmed. However, I have my spies and the means to find out."

Chapter 32

Blown Cover

𝓍𝓁 𝓎 𝓁𝓪𝟕𝓮

I knocked on Gerry's door before I entered. The morning sunlight fell on Mama as she sat by his bed. The two faces looking at me couldn't display more different emotions. Gerry brimmed with life. Mama's drawn face spoke of more than tiredness or concern for the wounded. Something deeper troubled her, but now was not the time to ask.

Gerry's deep voice rumbled. "There's my savior."

"Your savior; I think it is the other way around. You pulled that dead weight off me. If you hadn't, I'd have suffocated."

"And if you hadn't drawn him away, I wouldn't have gotten the distraction I needed to finish off the other five."

"Ok, we'll call it even. Good to see you so chirpy."

"I don't know what Raphael did, but I feel twenty years younger. I keep telling Mama, I'm fine to go back to work, but she insists I rest."

"And you'd better listen up, too. I'll leave you two to catch up," she said.

I caught Mama's hand as she walked past and raised an eyebrow. She shook her head and muttered, "Not now."

After an hour in which Gerry regaled me with a gory account of his twenty-plus kills, I struggled to reconcile the gentle giant who took care of Sera and Drake with the bloodthirsty warrior before me. "It seems to me that fighting suits you, which is probably good because I know one thing, Lucifer is not going to take what we are doing quietly."

"I did fight the French as a dragoon in my youth. Toughened me up, as they say . . ."

I laughed. "Tough is right.

Gerry's expression became serious. "I'll be with you whatever happens with Lucifer. The *Father* gave us this post, and I won't fail *Him*."

I expressed my gratitude and headed downstairs. Sera and Drake's animated conversation carried up to me from The Painted Lady.

Misha called out from the table where he sat with the family as I entered the room, "Here's the archangel of the hour. Three cheers for Camie."

I bowed, then pulled out a seat and joined them. After the ruckus died down, I said, "I think the award should go to Raphael. He did the best work."

Dia reached across the table and pushed something at me. "I believe this belongs to you."

The crystal; in my haste to stop the attack, I'd forgotten about it. "Thanks for keeping it safe. I will be more careful with the *Father's* gift in the future."

As the star in the rose quartz flashed, Drake's excited voice cut across the general conversation. "I nearly forgot. You know how I said I found a vortex and would monitor it. Since last night when Camie opened the portal, it's been getting bigger. Like really fast."

Misha asked, "What does that mean?"

"I'm not sure exactly, but by my calculations, it will be at its biggest at midnight on Halloween—really huge. Something big is coming."

Mama and I exchanged a glance. "Good work, Drake. You'll be able to tell us when the vortex is right for future ceremonies."

"Hadn't thought of that, but yes, I will." He poked his tongue out at Sera. "See, I told you it was important."

Sera turned to me. "Why did you have to say that? His head is big enough already."

Mama admonished her. "Sera, don't be nasty to your brother. He is, after all, your only real family."

Sera smiled, "We've got Raphael now."

I answered for Mama. "True. But an archangel isn't like a human or even Nephilim of Illumination, so Drake is still the closest to you."

Sera and Drake went back to their animated conversation, and I asked Mama what she thought it meant.

"It could be good or bad. Given it is the first time we have had the vortex, I can't say, but we had best be on our guard."

Three days before Halloween, the travelers began to arrive. I happened to be in the pawnshop when the first came. She looked as human as any of us, but she gave Misha the passphrase. He asked her to wait and then called for Mama.

I watched Mama scan the woman then nod, at which point, Misha escorted the female to The Painted Lady. After they left, I asked Mama what she had been doing.

"I'm gifted at reading aura signatures, but I'm not the only checkpoint. Gerry can identify the spirit of any being from any plane and determine whether they are angel, demon, fae, or something we may not have run across yet. That way, we don't get infiltrated by humans. A human shows up as a void to Gerry. Ask Drake about the one who tried to cross. He loves telling that story."

"So, from here, they go into seclusion, yes?"

Mama nodded.

"Which of Misha's duties did you want me to perform?"

"I thought you could make dinner deliveries. Misha gets tired by the end of the day."

On the first night, we had only one guest. One the second night, my legs got a little more of a workout on the stairs because we had three guests. The third night, we had four. Mama fretted at what we'd do if too many more showed up. But I reminded her that the *Father* would provide, and maybe the large vortex meant we could take them.

I had to admit, my calves grumbled as I carried the fourth tray to the last arrival. I knocked at the door and waited while footsteps approached. The door opened a fraction, and an eye appeared. I pointed to the food tray. After a pause, the door opened.

I'd prepared to smile as I had with each of the other guests, but when I looked at the traveler, the power frequency and energy contained within her aura overwhelmed me. It seemed like time itself came crashing to a halt. The essence of that energy signature had been seared into my angelic memories millennia ago.

My eyes widened, and my mouth fell open. She looked at me, her expression puzzled. I wanted to shout for joy. I wanted to take her in my arms, but all I could do was pass her the tray. Naamah had not recognized me. My heart contracted at the thought that she may have forgotten me, but then I reasoned: I looked nothing like the me of those thousands of years ago. It still stung, though.

I bound down the stairs, my face radiant, and rushed to Mama. "You'll never guess who's here. N—"

She held up a hand. "No, Camie, we don't use names."

"But I have to tell someone."

"From your face, I think I can guess. That would certainly be quite an achievement. Maybe, that's what the large vortex means."

The bell for the shop rang on Halloween morning, and Misha went to serve the customer. He eyed the young man. He couldn't put his finger on it; but he sensed something was off about him, even though his presentable attire gave the air of respectability. When the young man gave the passphrase, Misha's eyebrows shot up. "Misha doesn't usually get travelers this late, hardly time for preparation before journey. Travelers meant to fast and meditate three days."

The youth grunted.

When Misha went to get Mama, he whispered in her ear, "Check out carefully. Misha not feel good about him."

After Mama scanned the male, she frowned and signaled Misha to the backroom. "I understand what you mean. His aura doesn't have the bright edges of other travelers. We need to ask some questions before we admit him."

Misha nodded and held open the curtain for Mama.

With a demeanor that spoke of nothing out of the ordinary, Misha asked, "Please tell, what bring you?"

The young man stiffened a little. "I heard you helped fallen angels."

Misha couldn't tell whether the stiffness was from nerves or resistance. "Help . . . how?"

"Go."

When Misha hesitated, the youth said, "Look, I heard this was all on the up and up, and I've been looking for a way out for years, but if you can't help me, I will just have to find another way."

Mama cocked an eyebrow. "Another way?"

"I know it's not supposed to be possible, but I'd find a way to off myself; can't keep doing this crap." He turned to go, shoulders drooped.

The youth seemed genuine enough. Misha looked at Mama with a question. She nodded and said, "Wait."

As they escorted the young male to The Painted Lady, Mama whispered to Misha, "We'll have to get Gerry to give him a thorough going over."

Misha spoke to Gerry as Mama and the youth entered.

"Wow. It looks like a vacant block." He tried to step forward, but Gerry planted his meaty hand on the youth's chest.

After he scanned the young man, he frowned like Mama. "How did you hear about us?"

"Word on the street."

241

As Misha had never questioned a traveler before, he could only assume that was how it happened, but he had thought there might be something about the *Father* directing him. But then, over the years, he'd discovered the fallens' embarrassment at speaking of the *Lord*.

Gerry persisted. "What exactly are you seeking?"

"A way out."

Again, Misha had nothing to compare the response to, so while his expectation led him to expect words like forgiveness, redemption, or reunion, he had no real way of knowing what the travelers thought.

At the silence, the young man said, "I'd heard this was all on the QT, so what's with all the questions? I'm here. I want help. I'll do what you ask, but if you won't accept me, and if I can't find another way, I'll just end up being Lucifer's pawn screwing up people's lives for eternity."

Misha gave him credit for being candid. "Misha see truth in words. What you think?" He looked between Gerry and Mama. When they both nodded, Misha indicated to Gerry to let the young man enter.

Mama and Misha accompanied him to a room where she explained the preparation and the ceremony and what was expected of him.

When they closed the door, Misha said, "Misha think he know only part why he here."

"No, he didn't have the usual reactions to the prospect of going home. When I said, make the journey, he just looked blank, but only the *Father* knows what is in a heart."

"Misha think might be time to change way we do things."

⚭

As Mama approached me as I sat on the couches in The Painted Lady, the same strain that had been on her face for the past few days caused me concern. After she recounted her odd encounter and asked me to keep an eye out, I thought it might just have been a result of that, but then she told me how much it meant to her to have me here, how much she'd learned and grown since knowing me, and that I had a special place in her heart.

I thanked her but, at the same time, thought it a little odd. I watched her circulate among the family—a little pat on the arm here, a kiss there, a hug. It seemed to me as if she were saying her goodbyes.

I'd been indoors most of the day and needed some air, so I went out to the courtyard. Expecting to be alone, the presence of a young male surprised me. Given I hadn't seen him when I delivered dinner, this had to be the one who concerned Mama. He crouched near the ground, and I thought I saw a small animal leap from his hand. When he straightened and saw me, his posture became defensive.

He said, "I was just—"

I put my fingers to my lips. "Not supposed to talk, but while you're out here, get some meditation in before the ceremony and journey home."

"Right, sure." He plopped on the nearest garden bench and shut his eyes.

I went back to tell Mama.

Lucifer picked up the gerbil that scurried around his feet in the park. "Well, hello. I've been waiting for you. What message have you brought?"

He unclipped the small harness and retrieved the note. It read:

Hidden building

Preparation

Ceremony

Journey

Midnight

He tapped the paper on his lip. It appeared the rumors were correct, and it explained the disappearance of a few demons. But how exactly are they sending the traitorous bastards back to Heaven? He promised himself he'd find out tonight and put a stop to it. And he'd enjoy it.

Chapter 33

Eternal Struggle

The pure joy of inhaling the holy oil's perfume as the travelers made their way down the stairs ignited memories of the Heavenly Realm within me. The subtle fragrance of rose from *Shekinah Mother,* as *she* the family, relieved me.

At the sight of Naamah dressed in the simple, pure white linen shift, with her hair framing her face as it had in the past, I wanted to sing praises to the *Father* for having given me the gift of one last encounter. My love for *Him* and Naamah exceeded the Earthly Realm.

As Naamah stepped off the stairs in front of the family, Dai cried out her name. Naamah turned her head and nearly dropped the slim candle. Both sets of eyes sparkled with tears and happiness. Naamah faltered, and she stepped out of line, but Mama moved to her and directed her back. As Naamah moved forward, she glanced over her shoulder; regret etched her features.

When all the travelers entered the Holy Place, Mama and I revealed our angelic selves. My heart bounced like a kangaroo at the recognition on Naamah's face. A surge of love so deep that it left me giddy emanated from her. We must have looked like star-crossed lovers because Mama nudged me.

I indicated that the travelers should prostrate themselves. The grace with which Naamah knelt distracted me, and Mama had to nudge me again.

I moved to the north corner and lit the black candle asking the *Father* to banish negativity, and then I recited the selected verses from Psalms 25, 28, and 40. The flame danced and swayed while I spoke the Angelic tongue and seemed more vigorous when I finished. I moved to the east and lit the blue candle and prayed for forgiveness. The selection from Psalms 49, 50, and 73 followed. To the west, I lit the purple candle, praying for spiritual healing, followed by Psalm 32 and, finally, the southern yellow candle and prayed for the joy and manifestation of the *Holy Spirit*. At each point, I also sent up a silent prayer for Naamah.

In the candlelight, she glowed. I remembered that aura, and my soul yearned to embrace it. I shook my head. Knowing she had reunited with the *Father* would have to be enough.

I asked the travelers to rise and moved among them, lighting their candles and praying for each other that they might find purity, peace, truth, and hope.

I returned to the front and held the star rose quartz crystal in my palm, focusing my angelic spirit on it. As the initial soft glow bloomed into a radiance that filled the room with my aura matching it for intensity and color, I stole a glance at Naamah. The wonder on her face gratified me.

I spoke the incantation with an excitement countered by a solemnity I had not experienced in the trials.

My attention fixated on Naamah as the last clock chime struck and crystal blazed on my final words. The look of wonder when she witnessed the portal open, flooding the space with a light so pure and holy that only the righteous could be in its presence was all I needed to be at peace with Naamah's departure.

I asked the first traveler to make his confession.

"Most *Holy* of *Holies*, I sinned against you when I followed Lucifer. I sinned against you when I rejected your call. I sinned against you when

I inflicted suffering on the humans you love. I am unworthy of forgiveness as I have committed atrocities, but I confess to you and ask for your mercy."

As she crossed the threshold, a blue flash of Holy Fire of *Elohim* marked her return to the *Father*, a detonation so loud, so powerful that the gust of wind it created extinguished the candles, shattered the peace of The Painted Lady.

Mama rushed out of the Holy Place.

Over the sound of debris crashing to the floor, I heard Lucifer barking orders. My instinct said, 'confront him,' but my first duty had to be to the travelers to get them home safely and then to protect the doors until they closed.

I relit the traveler's candles, reenergized the crystal, and then shepherded them through the portal. When I came to Naamah, I took her hand, kissed her on the cheek, and said, "Go. Go quickly."

She shook her head. "I'm staying. Lucifer must be stopped."

Before I could prevent her, she dashed out the entrance.

The young man still stood there. At a strange look that passed over his face, I lunged at him and pushed him into the portal. I didn't know why I did it, but I understood why Drake found the story of the human spy so funny. My face and white robe that had taken so long to clean after the last episode now looked like a child had finger-painted me with blood and globules of what was once a body.

Misha and Mama had been right to be suspicious. We needed to take more care in the future.

When the portal flashed with Holy Fire of *Elohim* one last time and the doors ascended to Heaven, I tucked the crystal in my pocket and exited the room.

Naamah, now as her succubus self, stood toe to toe with the giant fly, Beelzebub, her tail, with its heart-shaped tip, stiffened as a weapon. He towered over her, head touching the ceiling.

was various shades of startling blues and aquamarines, flecked with gold as it flashed and pulsated around him.

In contrast, his twin, Omael, has an aura of plasma, fire with tangerine, ruby, and yellow also flecked with shimmering gold. When they worked and fought together as one, their auras blended into the pulsating royal purple color used in the holy veil, which separated the Holy of Holies in the Temple of *God*.

Caliel was our colossal Nephilim of Illumination; he was as an archangel over the lands and peoples of Great Britain and Ireland. He was one of only a few Nephilim of Illumination allowed in Heaven. He was awe-inspiring, twelve feet tall, and weighed over six hundred pounds.

Being of Scottish descent, he wore his full battle tartans and wielded devastating twin eight-foot long claymore broadswords that weighed over thirty pounds each. Caliel was an imposing archangel whom *Father* chose as our 'blunt instrument' of destruction if we needed to call upon one. Cally, as he was lovingly called, has the disposition of a charging rhinoceros. He also knows only one direction when the call for battle sounds; that direction is full speed ahead and through anything having the great misfortune to be in his path.

His head is clean-shaven with his beard kept in long braids of striking blond hair, with blond eyebrows that narrowed over snow-white eyes. Caliel's mere physical presence is enough to send scores of demons running away, screaming in stark fear for their miserable lives.

I was glad those five were with us that day as they quickly dispatched several legions in the forward forces, on point within the advancing demonic hoard along with their demonic commanders. Lucifer was trying to finish us all right then and there, in one massive strike.

As I drew in my power, I threaded my way through the restaurant tables and yelled, "Hey, chicken legs, over here."

Asmodeus pivoted his mount, his dragon-like tail sending a shower of sparks over Ashtoreth as it hit the protective barrier. The eyes in his goblin-like central face narrowed, and his hand moved as his mouth recited a spell.

I summoned a ball of Holy Fire of *Elohim*. The spell and the ball crashed together with a display of energy that a rock concert lighting team would have been proud of.

I got my next ball off before he finished the spell. The rupture of the unfinished spell backfired on him, sending an energy spike through his three brains that knocked him unconscious. I strode to where he lay, fully intending to dispatch him permanently, but Lucifer's voice called out across the room. "I don't think so, little brother."

He opened a portal under the unconscious form, which fell through to Hell.

Ashtoreth's gravelly voice sandpapered my ears as he said, "Don't think I will be so easy."

Salvia drooled from the fangs of his mount as it twitched its batwing-like ears. He urged his mount forward, its snarling jaws snapping. I attempted to drive my sword into the beast's chest, but its armored hide prevented me.

I yanked my arm back just before it locked its jaws onto it. Distracted by his mount, I almost missed Astaroth turning his snake into a poisoned spear and striking at me. I twisted my body sideways, the spear point ripping my robe. I struck the spear, but my sword shattered.

My mind stuttered as I scrambled to think about what to do. I dodged another strike. An image of a sword formed in my head. Of course, I reached into the air and drew a holy sword out of the Heavenly Realm.

This time, when the blade connected with the spear, the spear splintered into shards.

Ashtoreth sat too high on his beast for me to do much other than aim at his legs. I needed him off the creature. The next time the wolf-like thing lunged at me, I plunged the sword into its eye. Aqueous humor and vitreous gel splattered over me, adding to my collection of demon bodily fluids. The beast howled, and as the tip of the blade met the brain, it crashed to the floor, hurling its owner off its back.

Before Astaroth disentangled himself from his mount and gained his feet, I sprang toward him, but he, like Beelzebub, called his portal and escaped.

I turned to face the rest of the room. I could see *Shekinah Mother's* protective shield surrounding Misha, Gerry, Alexi, and others. It was the only thing preventing the demons from killing them.

Mama had engaged Belial in the center of the room between the restaurant tables and the couches. Being a lower angel, she had no Holy Fire of *Elohim*, and he outclassed her in strength, experience, and skill. He seemed amused by her. He preened his dark feathers with one hand while languidly deflecting her blows with the other. Even if she could get through his defenses, the likelihood of her penetrating his armor remained slim.

Toward the end of the room on what was once the stage before the wall blew out, Behemoth and Gerry slugged it out. More evenly matched in stature and strength, both being bovine in nature, Gerry held his own, but Gerry had a limit to his stamina where Behemoth did not. Behemoth would wear him down if Gerry didn't get a killing strike.

Misha pranced like a colt in front of Lilith on the dance floor. He ducked and weaved around her fireballs, firing arrows at a rapid pace, his quiver replenished continuously by the *Father's* hand.

I glanced back toward Naamah. My pride at her loyalty in defending the Holy Place welled as I watched her parry Abaddon's blows.

Lucifer, of course, loafed on a couch out of harm's way, it being beneath him to actually fight.

Torn between helping Misha or Mama, I hesitated.

Lucifer said something in the demonic tongue, and the demons ceased fighting long enough to direct a coordinated blast of fireballs at *Shekinah Mother's* shield. *Her* shield wavered and blinked out for a second, all the time needed for the demons to strike.

My wail of pain drowned out all other sounds as Belial drove his sword through Mama, its point protruding between her shoulder blades. Red welled over her white angelic robe. Her arms fell to her sides, and her head slumped. Belial raised his cloven foot to Mama's stomach and pushed to remove his sword. Her graceful slide to the ground brought hot tears to my eyes.

If only I'd decided sooner, I could have saved her. At that thought, I pivoted toward Misha. *Shekinah Mother's* shield had begun to flicker back into life. Time stopped as Lilith unleashed a fireball. My eyes tracked the course of the two in slow motion. The fireball crept toward Misha as the shield inched up. An alarm in my mind sounded, and I flung myself at Misha. Time reverted to normal as I collided with the centaur, and we crashed on the floor. I rolled over and crawled toward him. Had I made it in time? His ragged breath told me he lived, but the extent of the burn on his chest suggested not for long.

Sera and Drake screamed. I heard running.

Lilith grinned; "Ooo, goodie . . . children."

I scrambled to my feet. The holy fireball I generated contained all of my anger over the deaths of my grandfather, Mama, and Misha. My hand slammed the ball at her. Fear registered in her eyes, but she had just enough time to conjure her portal and disappear. I cursed, but I had the satisfaction of seeing the ball explode the door to the portal. She wouldn't be back anytime soon.

With Lilith gone, Sera and Drake angled toward Belial, Sera throwing holy fire. Her shots went wide as she lacked training.

Belial's sickening grin expressed the depravity of his being. He stepped forward as Sera approached, his manner indicating he expected an easy kill. Once she entered his range, he lunged.

I launched Holy Fire of *Elohim* at him as I ran to intercept Sera, but it was not I who saved her. My mind balked at what my eyes beheld. No Nephilim of Illumination I had ever known could do it. Drake unveiled into the most spectacular dragon I had ever seen. A kaleidoscope of iridescent colors slid over his scales. His muzzle spewed fire between six-inch ivory canines. His nine-inch claws ripped up the floor as he sped toward Sera. I wanted to see his wings, but he needed a bigger space.

He planted himself between Belial and Sera, Belial's blade not even scratching Drake's scales. Then he turned the full force of his dragon fire on Belial. Belial screamed. His feathers turned to ash. His armor melted into his skin. He beat at the flames, but they continued to burn. The skin on his face and hands peeled off.

At that point, Lucifer clicked his fingers, and a deluge of water extinguished the flames. He clicked his fingers a second time, and Belial disappeared. He gestured to Abaddon and Behemoth to go.

For a moment, I thought we won, but then Lucifer said, "Release the horde."

I'd faced them millennia ago, but the words still instilled fear combined with the sound of thousands of tramping feet. I had to stop them before they killed the family. As I raced for the breached wall, the weight of the crystal thumped on my leg, sparking an idea. It might work, but I only had one chance to stop the horde before it overran The Painted Lady.

It took me a moment to comprehend that the darkness I perceived didn't come from the night. The blackness of the damned had sucked all light from the immediate world. But I didn't need to be able to see for this. I just needed faith.

I retrieved the crystal from my pocket and concentrated my angelic spirit on it. At the same time, I conjured a wall of Holy Fire of *Elohim* directed at the swelling ranks of demons.

The crystal began to light up the street, and I could see its reflection in the eyes of the enemy. Gone were the buildings between Misha's and the park. Gone was the park. In their place, thousands upon thousands of glittering eyes in the blackness marched toward me.

As I waited for my aura to synchronize with the stone and the star in the rose quartz to shine, the massing horde pressed forward. The few demons that streaked past me didn't concern me, but would the crystal fully activate before the throng charged?

The mass grew denser while I waited until the star peaked so I could time its blast to the release of the Holy Fire of *Elohim*.

The horde charged.

It was now or never. I unleashed the blast of Holy Fire of *Elohim* as the star in the rose quartz blazed. The pink and blue wave of energy that pulsed from my center caused my knees to buckle, but even as I knelt, I kept my focus on the wave as it ripped through the horde. Thousands of eyes extinguished as the screams of the exterminated filled the night air.

The night returned, and with it, the buildings and the park.

I had expended so much of my angelic energy, I struggled to stand. Once upright, I swayed for a moment as the blood drained from my head. Using my sword like a staff, I staggered into The Painted Lady.

Chapter 34

The Torch Passes

he few skirmishes remaining were in hand, so my attention turned to Sera and Drake, sitting by the bodies of their adopted parents.

I knelt beside Sera, who cradled Mama's head in her lap. Her heartbroken sobs shook her lithe frame. I laid my hand on her shoulder. "I know from experience, rejoicing that she is at home with the *Father* does provide comfort. It may not take away the pain, but it balances the hurt with rejoicing."

Sera sniffled. "If I hadn't been such a coward hiding behind the barrier, I might have saved her."

"You might also have died trying. As it was, Drake only just managed to save you from Belial in time."

Sera lifted her head to look at Drake. "Did you know about Drake?"

"I had no idea. I thought I was seeing things. I've never known a Nephilim of Illumination to do that."

"I knew Drake was special. I just didn't know how much."

Drake called to Sera, "Papa's still alive. Come say goodbye."

I called those family members who weren't still engaged in putting down demons to speak with Misha before he passed and knelt down beside him.

Misha asked for Anna to help bring Mama's body so he could say goodbye as she was the closest to her. "Misha, look out behind you; that is not, Anna!" Sera yelled as she had recovered from the initial battle

They had possessed Anna and escaped, all but one.

"You're mine, old woman, and I'm hungry." The stench of the demon possessing Anna's vessel filled the air as it waddled closer and closer to Mama's body from behind.

"Wait, young Sera, I know this kind!" Gerry rushed in and grabbing the possessed Anna, held her, as he invoked a powerful casting-off spell against the demon.

"Release me, you Geryon colossus, or I'll be feeding off you for weeks, just like I did to that stupid girl's mother!" Pointing and grunting in Sera's direction.

"What are you talking about you fat ghoul!" Gerry tightened his grip around the disgusting creature's flabby jowls, threatening to crush her like some disposable paper cup.

"Wait, stop Gerry. I heard that." Sera stopped Gerry from finishing it.

Bravely approaching it, she demanded, "Tell me, you foul beast . . . now!

"It was you wasn't it, you loathsome cow. You killed my mother, Abigail, didn't you!"

"Stupid human. We don't kill; we gorge ourselves upon the dead!" When I rode that old hag witch, I watched. I've been watching for years! I saw your pathetic mother killed. I saw them take her carcass away and put her in the basement . . . in the cooler. Then I waited. That was the best meal I had in a long time!" The danella chortled wickedly, mocking Sera's pain.

"It's a danella!" Gerry roared. "Stay clear of this thing, Sera; get ready. You'll only have a few seconds; your aim has got to be spot on! I can save Anna!"

"I'm ready big guy, do it!"

Gerry invoked an ancient Enochian casting-off invocation against the demon, in the power of *Yeshua HaMeshiach,* finally commanding: "In the sovereign power of your *Creator Yahweh,* in the mighty name of *El Shaddai,* I command you, Danella, to come out of our friend, Anna."

The demon screamed in agony as it evacuated Anna. "Now, Sera, now! Nail the ugly sucker!"

Sera called forth the power of her Holy Fire of *Elohim* and hit the danella point-blank with a powerful energy ball, vaporizing it instantly.

"Eeeewww, what is that smell, is that . . ."

"The danella are a putrid and foul race of morbidly obese demons, not unlike a wraith but far viler. They are carrion eaters, slow-witted, and quick-tempered—a very dangerous combination. The females are especially odious and loathsome creatures."

"They feed by defecating highly corrosive digestives onto the body, and then . . . and this is the really gross part . . . they feed by using their forked-tongue proboscis to suck up the mixture, of partially digested carrion and their own . . ."

"Um . . . boo-boo?" Sera cautiously asked.

"Yes . . . that!" Gerry confirmed.

"Ohmygosh . . . I think I'm going to be sick." Sera wretched as she ran away, over to where Mama's body was with Misha.

He stroked Mama's dark hair and ran his finger over the curve of her jaw. He mustered the little strength he had left to speak to his family. "Misha and Mama's time is over. Misha and Mama go to *Father* now. Misha want you to know, Misha and Mama loved each of you like our own. Misha and Mama proud and grateful to know you, but a new time has come and need a new leader.

"Chamuel. Misha pass mantle to you in name of *Father;* Misha ask you promise take care of Sera and Drake; raise to be leaders, too.

"Misha have secret. Misha's Mish Mash only one of many. Misha tell where—"

At a screech behind me, I leaped up and spun to be confronted by a rakshasa. It sprang at Naamah's back, yelling, "You traitorous whore. I'll see you in Hell!"

As it slashed at Naamah with its fingernails, Dia screamed, "Naamah, look out!" She pushed Naamah out of the way.

At first, it seemed Dia had escaped unscathed, but then she mopped up the trails of blood on her forearm. The family faced the rakshasa, which seemed less keen to attack. But then it grinned. It wiggled its fingers. "Give it a minute."

It pained me to see the realization dawn on Naamah's face. She grabbed Dia's arm. Even from where I stood, the angry black lines corkscrewing out from the wound, winding their way up Dia's arm, stood out against her honey-colored skin. Naamah embraced her. I couldn't hear what they said, but the love that passed between them flowed through the room.

Naamah launched herself into the air, running her hand down her tail to transform it into a spear. The grace of her aerial display as she dove at the rakshasa thrilled me. It turned to run, but the dive's momentum impaled the creature on Naamah's barbed tail. Naamah lifted the rakshasa off the ground and laughed as it writhed on the spear. Then she flung it across the room like a child throwing a rag doll. It smashed into the wall, cracking the plaster, before flopping on the floor in a broken heap.

For the second time tonight, my mind refused to accept what my eyes told it. Naamah formed a cobalt blue ball of Holy Fire of *Elohim* and, using her dexterous tail, thumped it at the rakshasa corpse, incinerating it instantly. My heart rejoiced that the *Father* had given her this great gift. The daughter of Lilith and Lucifer had been redeemed.

I knelt again by Misha so he could finish what he had to tell me, but when I took his hand, it lay limply in mine. I prayed for his safe journey home and went back to Dia.

The poison had taken hold fast. Gerry held Dia like a babe in arms on the floor. The huge brown eyes in his minotaur face glistened. "Ms. Dia, don't go. My life will be miserable without you. I've never told you, but I think you are more beautiful than the Blue Diamond. You have way more sparkle."

Dia reached her good hand to his face and ran her fingers through the rough coat. "I think you're pretty special too, Gerry."

Naamah squatted down beside them. She reached out her hand to her sister.

Gerry jerked Dia back. "Don't you touch her; it's your fault. If she hadn't tried to save you, she wouldn't be dying."

I patted the bump between his horns. "Gerry, you know whose fault it is, and it's not Naamah's."

Dia's voice rasped as she fought to get the words out. "Gerry, I want you to promise to do something for me."

Gerry nodded.

"I want you to promise to take care of Naamah like you have taken care of me."

Gerry's shaggy head shook. "If that's what you want, I promise."

Naamah took Dia's hand. "Thank you, my sister. You laid down your life for me. May the *Father* bless you."

Dia's smile faded as she drew her last breath. Gerry closed her eyes and kissed her on the forehead.

Shekinah Mother spoke to me, and I relayed her words to the family.

"Do not grieve for the fallen. The *Father* has a place in Heaven for them where they will be honored for their deeds. Mama and Misha have served Him faithfully, and they will be rewarded. Dia's great sacrifice will not go unnoticed. Neither will it be in vain.

"Naamah is marked by Lucifer, and he will hunt her to the end of time, but I give her this gift—an alias.

"Gerry, please lay Dia on the floor."

Gerry hesitated, but I encouraged him to relinquish Dia.

"Naamah, lie on top of your sister."

Naamah looked at me, her face questioning. I nodded to reassure her. She lay down, face to face with her sister.

"Naamah, receive your sister."

At the sight of Dia's body being absorbed into Naamah, several family members gasped. I had to admit, it was pretty creepy.

"Rise, Nadia."

Nadia's body twitched and convulsed; it jerked into a sitting position, its expression unresolved. It extended an arm and then brought the hand to its face. Light came into its eyes, and a human countenance took hold. A voice croaked, "Is it possible?"

I bent down and put my arm under Nadia's and helped her to stand. She wobbled for a moment and then righted herself. "Welcome to the family, Nadia."

Everyone would need time to adjust to this, including me. When I drew my gaze away from Dia-come-Naamah, Dia's spirit came into focus, smiling at her sister.

A voice sounded behind me.

"Behold!"

For the third time in one evening, I blinked at what stood before me. Misha noble and strong in his prime, his mane rippled as if in a soft summer breeze on the plains of his beloved Russia. On his back sat Princess Anastasia, glowing with the vitality of youth; beside them, Sylviel.

I stepped forward and held my hands out to her, grinning like a fool.

"You have four wings. You're Cherubim. *Mother* said the *Father* would reward you."

"I know. I can't believe it, but the best bit . . . I get to accompany Misha and Anastasia."

A hum rose in the Holy Place, and cedar doors opened of their own accord. The *Father's* brilliance flooded The Painted Lady, but this time, no one was in danger.

The hubbub in the room echoed with laughter, tears, and rejoicing as the family clustered around the four spirits.

Misha, Anastasia, and Sylviel beamed with delight as they crossed the threshold into that far, green country with never-ending sunshine that was their version of Heaven.

Dia hung back as if reluctant to leave. Then Satan stepped out of the portal and extended his hand to her. She said, "I am honored."

"The honor is mine, dear lady."

As he escorted her spirit into the vortex, he turned to me. "I'll be back," he said in a perfect impersonation. He laughed as the doors closed behind them.

Typical Satan.

As I turned to address the family as its new guide and protector, the kernel that had been steadily growing blossomed into an overwhelming love for them. What we had endured together this past month had forged a bond where I could finally say I understood the *Father's* love for His Creation. "I want to thank you for accepting this stranger into your hearts. I want to thank you for teaching me the meaning of family. Sure, I had a family who loved me, but I was too young to appreciate what they meant before I blew them off. And yes, there was 'The Family,' but the creeds between that and ours are so desperate that I can't comprehend ever being part of that world.

"At this moment, our hearts sorrow for our losses but, at the same time, rejoice at the return of our loved ones to the *Father*. We will miss them, particularly Misha and Mama's leadership.

"As Misha bequeathed me the responsibility of leading us into this new phase, I pledge my angelic soul to the cause the *Father* has given us.

"The stakes have risen. Now, I have the crystal, and Drake can track the vortex events; the *Father* has enabled us to hold more ceremonies. But with it comes the knowledge that Lucifer will escalate his efforts to stop us. We need new protocols and procedures to keep us safe.

"Misha spoke of other families like ours. He died before telling us more. It is our duty to find these families and aid them.

"But first, let us take time to rejoice in Drake and his newfound gift." I applauded, and the family joined in.

Drake gave the gathering a sheepish look. "I didn't mean to burn the furniture."

Gerry slapped him on the back. "Furniture's replaceable. Sera, is not."

I held up the angelic sword. "Sera, I gift this to you. It is of the Heavenly Realm."

Sera reached out her hand and grasped the hilt. I watched as the forged metal bonded with her hand and arm.

Sera shook her arm, yelling, "It's alive. Get it off me!"

"It's OK, Sera. The sword recognized your angelic lineage and is giving itself to you."

Sera relaxed a little and waved the sword in front of her.

"It is bound to you and will never forsake you. It is a reminder of the *Father's* infinite protection. Through it, you will learn to focus your Holy Fire of *Elohim*. Listen to it. Learn from it."

She ran her finger down the engraved pattern, and it glowed blue. "I can feel its power. It's kinda cool."

"It will take hard work, discipline, and constant practice to learn how to wield it effectively."

I held my hand out to Nadia. "I have a favor to ask. I want you to train Sera to become a swordmaster. Show her everything."

"I'd be delighted, as long as we can have some girl time, too." She winked at Sera.

"It's been a long night and a long month; time to get some rest. Tomorrow, we begin rebuilding here and start our quest to find our brethren."

Chapter 35

The Last Chapter . . .

Mama would have been delighted with the Christmas tree dominating the corner of the recently finished rebuild of The Painted Lady. Sera and Drake squabbled over who got to put the star on top. Ever since his unveiling, Drake had shot up like a beanstalk after rain. Sera could no longer call him "little" brother. Mama would be so proud of the way the two of them had handled her and Misha's passing. Yes, they had their moments of grief, but on the whole, their faith in the *Father* had deepened, if anything. Comparing theirs' to my behavior put me to shame.

Nadia wrapped her arms around me from behind and rested her chin on my shoulder. "So, what does my husband want for Christmas?"

Even though I'd been "husband" to her before, the newness of our vows still delighted me. We were not the only newlyweds. Word of our success spread through the networks, and an old flame of Alexi's knocked on the pawnshop door. She asked me to tell Alexi his little curried goddess was home. The look on Alexi's face and his race to the bathroom to brush his hair and check his attire still makes me smile. Dr. Arisha Ahuja is the newest member of the family, and she and Alexi were away on a working honeymoon.

Before I could get a word out, Nadia said, "And don't say something altruistic."

I raised an eyebrow.

"Not that either."

"In truth, I'd like a night off, just you, me, a bottle of wine, and a fancy cheese platter."

"That I think I can arrange."

"How is Sera's training progressing?" I inquired, changing the subject.

"Early days yet, and Drake's 3D computer simulation course is really testing her out. He's working on an enhancement for it for her Christmas present."

"She'll be delighted. I get so little time with them. I don't even know how he is managing his dragon temper."

"Arisha's meditation techniques and the alarm on the monitor he wears are helping, but he's a teenage boy—hormonal."

"Have we heard from Alexi today?"

"Mm-hm. Alexi said they were making progress on finding the family, but his bigger news was running into an old student of his—Serge some-one. He couldn't believe the coincidence of Serge and he being in the same remote village, particularly given how busy Serge's restaurant is over the festive season."

I didn't hear the rest. It seemed like too much of a coincidence to me.

Chapter 36

Spring Forward

ꓵꙅꓦꓘ ꓘ꒦ꓮꙅꙅꓘ

"How goes the training, guys?" I asked, walking back to the space that Nadia had designed to give Sera a realistic and arduous course to develop her close hand-to-hand street-fighting skills. With Drake's vaunted, technical wizardry and coding prowess, the holographic course could be programmed to millions of various scenarios.

Drake designed the holographic "adversaries" to ping with the precise strike point from Sera's blade itself or to use it to direct and focus her Holy Fire of *Elohim*. This would help Sera learn the most lethal and effective strike points on any corporeal human form or non-corporeal, non-human created being, whether fallen angel, demon, or other supernatural creature.

Nadia was also instructing Sera on how to use whatever was around her at the moment as either an offensive weapon or defensive buckler.

"Take a knee, pretty girl; you've earned it," Nadia reassured her young protégé with a sweaty hug and a kiss on the forehead. "Hmm, sweet and salty, my favorite combination," Nadia said playfully, giving Sera a resounding *whack* on her backside before turning, giving me a wink, and coming over to report.

"Hey! That hurt . . . but I liked it!" Sera giggled.

"How's she doing, my love?" I was laughing at their burgeoning fondness for each other. "I'm glad I suggested this; she has developed quite an admiration for you. I certainly understand why," I said as I gave Nadia a playful *whack* on her own well-proportioned posterior.

"Ah, I remember—beautifully prodigious, bodacious, and taunt as ever . . . gorgeous!" I reminisced fondly.

"Oh, watch it, angel-boy, or I must arrange our own private, 'training session' to teach you some manners!" Nadia teased.

"Is that a promise? I always loved your private umm, tutoring, and now that you're back in my life, I don't want to ever lose you again. I need you every day; I missed you so much. It has been so long without you Nemea . . . I'm sorry, *Nadia*." I couldn't hold it in anymore and openly wept deep, cathartic tears.

"Okay, what did I miss?" Drake came in holding his laptop.

The two were inseparable.

"Shh," Sera admonished. "Dear Camie has taken on so much here lately, I'm worried about him. I think he blames himself for us losing . . . for losing . . ." Sera was now the one crying.

"Okay, young dragon, what did you do now? I leave for one week on a business trip to take care of our final IPO investments and when I return . . . this?" Gerry teased his young charge.

"Why is everything my fault?" Drake protested, his dragon nature rising. The monitor he was wearing on his belt sounded an alarm followed by Dr. Arisha connecting with him via a secure VPN on the same laptop.

"Drake, what is going on over there?" Chef Alexi's friend and the family's new private doctor checked in. "Drake, we talked about this didn't we, have you been taking your meditation and doing the yoga routines I taught you to help control your emotions? Remember the last time you lost control? You almost set fire to the entire Painted Lady, son. You must take this seriously—understand?"

"Yes, ma'am. I have been and they are helping, but sometimes, I get so busy I forget."

"Alright, well . . . just don't. They must become a habit for you, Drake. Not just to help you but to protect the family as well, understand?"

"I will ma'am. I'm sorry to bother you and Chef over there. Gotta run, I just came up with a significant improvement to Sera's training, and I want to get it installed. It is very cool if I do say so myself!"

Dr. Arish laughed. "Humble as ever . . . good, that's a wonderful sign, Alexi, and I will see you all when we get back. Give my love to everyone there. Goodbye."

"Bye, Dr. A. Have fun; see 'ya when you get back!"

"Hey everybody, this should cheer everybody up. Check this out!" Drake proudly unveiled his latest marvel on his laptop simulation.

"I've now programmed the hologram to Sera's enhanced audio abilities."

"Please, Drake . . . in English?" Nadia implored.

"Oh, sorry, sis. I've isolated and analyzed all available fallen angels, demons, and other supernaturally created beings' natural frequencies that they emit. I have now added those frequencies to the hologram.

"What that means, Sera, is that, over time, you can train yourself to listen for and learn each of the different frequencies and commit them to memory. You will then be able to react more quickly, even sometimes before they even appear. It will give you precious extra seconds for a frontal attack or to defend yourself if they come at you from the side or worse, from behind. What do you all think? Isn't that an outstanding thing?"

Sera just came over and gave her younger brother an enormous hug.

"I'm so glad that you're on our side Drake, developing this ability could very well save my life, brother. I love you. Thank you for this!"

Drake blushed and looked up at his great guardian, Gerry.

It hadn't really dawned on anybody that he had returned from Europe. He was completing the investments he had put into place that would eventually bear incredible fruit, securing the family's future and the global redemption mission, for generations to come.

"Gerry, you're back. Welcome home, big guy! How did it all go? Well, I hope." Walking over to my friend and recovered from my momentary loss of composure, I held out my hand to the love of, not just one lifetime, but my entire one-thousand-year exile.

"It's a beautiful day outside, Nadia, a touch of early spring. I'm starving since Chef is on vacation. Want to take a walk and get some fresh air, my love . . . maybe grab some pralines from River Street Sweets?"

"Yes, baby, that sounds great. I think everybody needs a break right about now. But not sugar; I need meat. Ruth's Chris. I made reservations for us five for eighteen hundred tonight. We still have a few hours to get cleaned up. We can always hit River Street Sweets afterward. How does that sound to everybody?"

Nadia always had perfect timing and control, which made her such a formidable adversary.

"Oh, yeah—my forty-ounce, Tomahawk Ribeye with those Cremini mushrooms sounds perfect right now! Airline food just doesn't do it for me." Gerry exuberantly rubbed his huge hands together, anticipating the coming buttery extravagance of a massive slab of USDA Prime, Midwestern corn-fed goodness, seared perfectly medium-rare. We all couldn't help but laugh at our enormous guardian's starry-eyed admiration of all things beef. Considering he was related to it, it was a rather disturbingly comedic, moment of bonding.

※

"Is everything alright back there in Savannah? Do we need to get back, darling?" Alexi inquired of Dr. A. "Drake's alarm went off again, didn't it . . . is he okay?"

"He will be alright as long as he follows my instructions. I'm a little more concerned about Chamuel right now. I thought I heard him crying in the background. I'm worried that he blames himself for losing Mama and Misha last Halloween. He is putting so much pressure on himself right now."

"I'm sensing that he is still angry at *Father* for all of this and being denied Naamah—I mean Nadia—for all these centuries," Alexi added.

Dr. Arisha consoled her beloved Alexi.

"Well, if you're sure they are all okay then can we please try to enjoy the rest of our vacation here in Lyon; there is still so much I want to show you that you haven't seen yet, but for right now, I'm so glad we're back here at Bocuse where it all began for us. Do you remember my love?"

Chef Alexi caressed Arisha's hand as the enveloping glow of candlelight cast a soft and comforting shield of detached contentment around them. For now, at this moment, the rest of the world was out there somewhere.

"Oh, Alexi. This is all so beautiful, even more than I remember restaurant Bocuse to be so many years ago now.

"I've never seen Lyon at Christmas. Do you remember? It was the summer after I had just graduated from Harvard Medical, and my father wanted to celebrate. Alexi, thank you so very much for inviting me back here to spend our Christmas holidays together. I know everybody at the Painted Lady was sad that you would not be there with them, but in their saddened hearts—and to their credit—they all agreed it would do you a great deal of good to get away," Arisha cooed in support.

"I remember, Arisha, I remember," Alexi sighed a bit with a heaviness that seemed out of place amongst all the surrounding joy and celebration of Christmas in Lyon.

"Alexi, my love, I can't imagine the pain that is still so fresh in your heart and mind after all that . . . well, after all that horror just two months ago, but now we're here in this happy place. Maybe healing can begin, yes?"

Arisha did her best to assuage the deep, raw, and sorrowful emotions that were still lingering and tearing at Alexi's spirit. Alexi just smiled a polite smile at his love. He stared off into the quickly fading twilight as it darkened into night.

Thousands of strands of festive Christmas lights twinkled inside of Restaurant Bocuse, all around, up and down streets, neighboring shops, and businesses, lacing through surrounding trees.

Try as he might, Chef Alexi just couldn't throw off the remnants of his murderous retribution. He wanted to unleash his rage on the nearest demon of any ilk that would have the misfortune to cross his path at that precise moment.

All he could do, however, was stare blankly off into the chilly, early winter's night there in Lyon, France, the place that had put his feet firmly on the path of his destiny in *Father's* will. Alexi was lost in the panoramic scene before him—a postcard-vista that was still enjoyed by tens of thousands of people from all around the world.

Memories became flesh.

"Chef, chef, is that you after so many years?"

A familiar but disembodied voice tried to break through Alexi's subconscious mind, bringing him back to the moment. Chef Alexi Romanov was caught in a plethora of deep-seated and very mixed emotions in his spirit, which had caused his subconscious mind to take control.

He relished memories of that summer day, so many long years ago. He remembered those feelings of his heart racing, wanting to leap in rapturous beats of wonder, at his first breathless sight of a striking, young Indian girl named Arisha Ahuja.

Alexi would later call her his "little curried goddess" in glowing infatuations that would never cease to give rise to one of Dr. A's patented and very infectious little girl giggles and a big Russian, belly laugh from her new *amoré*—Alexi.

Alexi was also still dealing with wave after stinging wave of nauseating rage at the demonic forces that stormed The Painted Lady, causing the losses of so many of his family: Mama, Misha, Dia, and all the others. In stark contrast, he was also here now in Lyon to celebrate his thirtieth Christmas holiday season.

Alexi was fortunate enough to do so in his destined chosen career, his calling that was also his great passion. For thirty years, he had loved being a chef. Those years seemed to pass so quickly, and now, they were but a vapor. Not gone, just stored away as great and priceless treasures.

Savoring another taste of one of a host of sips of a glorious ten-year-old St Joseph—a deep garnet red from the nearby Côtes Du Rhone, Alexi contemplated the tumultuous events of these last two months leading up to the passing of his beloved Mama and Papa Misha. The present moment in time would not be denied. Alexi's subconscious mind finally relented.

"*Excusez-moi, je,suis, desole avez-vous dit quelque chose?*" ("Excuse me, I'm sorry, did you say something"), Chef wondered, as he glanced up at the owner of the voice, who now had come into focus. Suddenly Alexi's entire demeanor lightened.

"Serge, is that really you?" Alexi abruptly stood up, knocking over the antique chair, and gave the very best apprentice chef he had ever trained a huge Russian bear hug, lifting the substantially smaller Frenchman completely off his feet. The dining room patrons, waitstaff, and the entire kitchen took a brief pause to erupt in joyous applause at what was obviously a momentous reunion.

This was followed by great, cathartic laughter by both teacher and student—more like father and son. The catharsis was complete. Two months of built-up anger, rage, soulful mourning, tension, and stress silently but abruptly evacuated Alexi's spirit and escaped back into the abyss.

Alexi's strength abandoned him as he collapsed back onto the luxuriously upholstered, antique chair that had just been righted for him by the ever-attendant maître d'hôtel of Restaurant Bocuse. Chef Alexi Romanov, the stalwart rock of a man, ancient Nordic elf, and great culinary master broke, but these were tears not of pain and loss but of great joy and pride.

"Serge, Serge, you made it, son! I am so very proud of you; you worked for so long. You absolutely earned this, son. Well done, well done, well done, my Serge!"

Alexi kept up his praise almost as though he was trying to hide his obvious pain, patting his protégé fondly on the back, almost forgetting Arisha was sitting there, in the vacuum of the moment of reunion between cherished teacher and mentor and his prized student.

"Alexi, my darling," Arisha gently inquired.

"Oh, my goodness, my sweet Arisha, I'm so sorry!" Chef Alexi Romanov quickly rose to his feet in formal attention and made the introductions.

"Dr. Arisha Ahuja, I am very proud to introduce you to Serge Desjardins, *Le Chef Executif du* Restaurant Bocuse (The Executive Chef of Restaurant Bocuse). He was, without question, the finest apprentice and later, a young chef of extraordinary potential, that I have ever had the privilege to apprentice."

Alexi leaned in a little closer to Arisha and whispered, ". . . and Serge is also a *fees des bois*, (woodland fae)," he added, winking at Serge.

"I also believed your given surname was a perfect match, not just for your nature, but for your unparalleled skill and touch with the preparation and presentation of your brilliant vegetable creations, *Magnifique!*"

"Chef Alexi, you made it effortless for me. I don't know about anybody else in our little group of apprentices, but for my say, you are without question, the finest chef it has ever been my privilege to apprentice with, study under, and train alongside. I will be forever in your debt, and for one as myself, my elf-kind, that will be a very long time indeed. You saved my life, Alexi."

Serge praised his mentor as he wiped tears from his eyes, turning to Arisha, he said, "You understand here, *Madame*, your wonderful friend Alexi saved me from a horrible path. My papa, he was very bad man—a drunkard. He abandoned my mama and my two younger brothers.

"At age twelve, I had to leave school to help Mama earn money for family. I was always in the kitchen with her, even before I could stand tall enough to reach the counters. I was becoming involved with local gangs you see, terrible people, and I would have ended up in prison or maybe just dead.

"My mama, through a friend, learned that Chef Alexi was seeking a small group of new apprentices, so she made a momentous decision that put me standing here now with you."

Serge turned back to his mentor. "You remember my mama, Alexi?"

"Remember, son . . . how could I ever forget her? She was a force of nature!" Alexi chuckled then continued. "Arisha, my dear, Chef Serge's mother not only would not take no for an answer, but she also warned that if we didn't accept her baby as a new apprentice, she would stand in front of this restaurant with Serge's two younger brothers every day and all day!"

Alexi smiled back at his protégé, who just blushed with love for the sacrifice that his mother made to ensure he had a bright future. "Who could say no, to a woman like that!" Alexi teased his prized pupil.

Alexi and Arisha were oblivious to the ever-watching eyes all around them in this legendary Michelin three-star *tour de force* known around the world as Restaurant Bocuse.

Suddenly, all the patrons who were blessed enough to have the privilege of dining there, stopped, stood in respect to Chef Romanov, and, raising their glasses, toasted his thirty amazing years as one of the finest chef's in the world.

"Excuse me, Alexi. I believe your phone is vibrating," Dr. A. whispered, not wanting to break the moment as she pointed to it crawling toward the table's edge.

"And so it is! Thank you, darling," the chef complimented, deftly snatching it out of mid-air as it fell off the edge.

"Oh, it's Chamuel; excuse me, everybody. I must take this," Alexi excused himself and went over to the front of the restaurant's well-stocked upstairs wine pantry.

"Well then, *ma belle dame et amie de mon cher professeur, Alexi* (my beautiful lady and friend of my dear teacher, Alexi), I must excuse myself also to see to the best meal you two very dear people have ever had in your lives, no matter how many or how long!"

Chef Desjardins winked as he returned to his stellar kitchen. Alexi answered the phone.

"Hello, Camie. Can you hear me okay? How's the connection? Is everything alright; you don't have any kitchen problems do you?" Alexi asked, always concerned about the wellbeing of everyone at the Painted Lady.

Chef Alexi looked down at his watch, "You must be very busy now, prepping and getting ready for service tonight. Is Nadia doing okay there with being in charge?"

Chamuel answered on the other end. "Yes, Alexi, everything is fine, really. . . I didn't want to bother you and Arisha during your much-needed Christmas holiday break there in Lyon. I just wanted to give you some exciting news."

Chamuel continued filling Alexi in on the profound news. It would also prove to portend events that would test them as never before.

"I just wanted to let you know that we have been given our next assignment. Are you ready for this? It will be in your origins, your roots. Alexi our next mission and night of redemption will take place in Russia, specifically St. Petersburg. Isn't that wonderful news? More fallen brothers are being given a chance for forgiveness and redemption and may go back home to paradise and spend eternity with *Father!*

"I received an urgent request for help tonight while we were at Ruth's Chris from my brother Nicholas there in St. Petersburg. He said that ordinarily, he wouldn't have asked, but this time, he said it would involve two other fallen Seraphim, along with two additional lesser angels. So, four fallen angels are being redeemed together. However, he said that they also have been warned by *Father* that Lucifer is pulling out all of the stops on this one and has assigned some duke of Hell to be in charge of trying to stop us, Alexi.

"We are going up against an 'A-Team' on this one I'm afraid, but Nicholas assured me that he has an incredible family of his own to come up alongside us so we will not be facing whatever the opposition is by ourselves. Whoever, or whatever it is, I think we will all need a break afterward, preferably somewhere warm and tropical."

After a short pause, Chamuel continued: "I'm just not feeling like myself these days—frayed, like electrical wiring that has had its insulation stripped away. Oh, that reminds me, Alexi, could I bother you to bring back some of those rare Cuban cigars, if possible. I'm sure you know how hard they are to get here in America. The humidor is getting a little thin here."

Alexi wasn't sure he heard correctly amid all the festive revelry around him. With an elevated voice Alexi asked, "I'm sorry, Camie, but son, it sounded like you said our next night of redemption will take place in the city of St. Petersburg, Russia. Did I hear you correctly, son? And yes, I do my best to find some of those rare Cubans over here for The Painted Lady's humidor. I know just the man to ask to help us here. I will talk to you later, Chamuel. Goodbye."

"Okay, thank you, Chef. Have a good evening in Lyon, and I'll see you guys when you get back. Have a safe trip!"

"You're right, Arisha, something is not right with Chamuel. He sounded exhausted and unsure about himself. I'm worried about him, especially now after what he just told me. This could be too much for him. We need to pray for him, my love."

Alexi put on a brave front for Arisha, then turned away and gazed blankly through a random window and out into the chilly night of Lyon. He pondered what the challenge of the coming days, weeks, and months of the new mission would bring. Unaffected by strangers, passing through his gaze, he was totally unaware that they were not as alone as they believed.

Epilogue

A Premonition of Evil

⸱ ⁊ℓ⅂⁊ⅼⱽ⁊ℓ⅂ ⅃ℰ ⱥ⁊ⱪℓ

Chef Alexi did hear that news correctly, but unfortunately, so did an unwelcomed eavesdropper: the sommelier of Restaurant Bocuse who was a plant—an agent of evil.

The real sommelier had been murdered several years ago and was replaced with a spy. A demonic undercover agent, provocateur of a grand duke of Hell who, over the centuries, had placed literally hundreds of such replacement spies all around the world to ensure a steady flow of vital intelligence. There would be secrets and information that would be used to maintain control of people in power in all of the world's dictatorial, legislative, judicial, and executive branches of government. That information would be used to contaminate the hearts and minds of men. The purpose? To plunge the world into total, spiritual darkness and condemn men's very souls to an eternity in Hell and separation from the *Father*.

The faux-sommelier quickly finished his prep for the evening service and excused himself, directing the other wine service staff to take over.

"Finish here, then report to Chef Desjardins, I need to make a very important phone call."

As he slithered out the front door to a secluded spot, out of the view of Christmas holiday tourists, he hissed: "C'mon, c'mon, pick up the bloody phone."

Someone answered.

"Yeah, yeah, you heard me right the first time, now shut up and let me finish. I don't have a lot of time here. I told you there's some American here with some Indian woman. They are not what they appear to be . . ."

(The connection on the other end tried to interrupt but is cut short.)

"I already told you, I . . ."

(The phone played acoustic music.)

"Hold . . . you put me on hold? Bollocks! Are you bloody kidding me here, son of a b—!"

A deep, malevolent growl. Someone picked up the phone and spout one word: "Speak."

"Oh, good; it's you, sir. I'm sorry to disturb you at this very late hour there but . . . yes, sir, to the point, yes, sir!"

"I've been watching these people all night, and they are not people. Him, I don't know what he is, but whatever he is, he is ancient, like thousands of years old, so he must be quite powerful."

"Now, the beautiful woman, I am sure of it, she is Yakshini and quite old herself. How am I sure, sir?"

"Because I am like she is. I'm Yakshini also. We know our own spiritual nature for *Ch**st's* sake . . . oh, sorry. I didn't mean to use that name, sir. I overheard the American use these exact words: redemption, Chamuel, and St. Petersburg—in the same bloody sentence on the phone to somebody in America. What else could it mean?

"Sir, the duke must be told immediately. I believe I have found the enemy's next move, we must warn him!"

The sommelier spy protested, paused, became out of breath, and then listened. "Yes, sir. Thank you, sir. I am honored, but I just want to serve the duke, that's all. I'm honored to help with anything he asks; thank you, sir. I will . . . have a good evening yourself in . . . whatever it is you're doing there right now . . .

"No, really, thank you, sir. That's oka—. I really don't want to know . . ."

He hears tortured groaning and blood-chilling screams in the background as the phone goes silent.

The Sabazios reptilian demon commander, that had just received the sommelier spy's intelligence, was in charge of Lyon, France and its surrounding provinces.

He was an overseer of a company of three hundred demons there. On this night, however, he had been summoned by his general to appear in the court of the duke of Hell to give on-the-ground reports of all of the demonic activity there.

"You there, come here and finish this; make him suffer," The Sabazios reptilian demon commander ordered, pointing down to a disloyal minion who had failed to keep the duke's pantry freshly stocked with human blood. The minion was being tortured excruciatingly slowly to maximize the impact of the lesson.

"Failure will not be excused or tolerated!" The lizard commander hissed.

"I must report this excellent news to the duke immediately! He roared with sanguineous revelry as he laid a bloodied cell phone down on the table alongside the instruments of torture. He then finished cleaning himself of the remaining disemboweled minion.

"The duke will surely reward me for this. We will slaughter those fools like sheep, and we will bake them into the duke's favorite meat pies!"

He laughed maniacally, disappearing into the cold, dank darkness of the duke's castle.

And that was the end of the beginning . . .

"I am merely the quill in my Father's hand."

It is my sincere prayer and hope that you have been moved by this story, enough to seek your own redemption and come home to the light. To accept the precious and incalculable free gift of salvation, please just simply ask *Him* for forgiveness.

It is not about the words, it is about true repentance, the intention of all your heart, all your mind, and all your spirit. So if you believe in the precious *Lord Jesus Christ* and are ready to come home to the family of *God*, please, I implore you, today is the day, my dear friend, and soon to be my dear brother and sister in *Christ Jesus*.

Right where you are, right now, don't delay any longer—just humble yourself in surrender, and if you are able go to your knees or simply bow your head in reverence to the One who made you and who loves you more than you could ever comprehend. Pray with me this simple prayer of repentance.

Lord Jesus, for too long I've kept you out of my life. I know that I am a sinner and that I cannot save myself. No longer will I close the door when I hear you knocking. By faith, I gratefully receive your gift of salvation. I am ready to trust you as my Lord and Savior. Thank you, Lord Jesus, for coming to Earth. I believe you are the Son of God who died on the cross for my sins and rose from the dead on the third day. Thank you for bearing my sins and giving me the gift of eternal life. I believe your words are true. Come into my heart, Lord Jesus, and be my Savior. Amen.

The Bible promises that if you believe with all your heart what you just confessed and that you truly accept *His* gift of salvation, trusting completely in the power of *Jesus Christ* to forgive you of your sins, then my new brother or sister, you have been forgiven, saved, and will be with *Him* in paradise for all eternity. Welcome home, precious child of *God!*

I truly want to hear from you. It would greatly bless me here if you took just a brief moment to let me know of your glorious decision today. Please drop me a quick note—or longer if you wish. I promise each one of them will be read.

"May *God* richly bless you and your families, as you live, for *Him!*"

Thank you for staying with me. I have been given a singular message by *Father* throughout my Redemption series novels. It is the eternal message of hope that we all have in the power of the redemption in *Christ Jesus.*

I hope in some small measure, you have received that message here today as you grace me with a few more moments of your precious time. *Father* spoke to me this morning as I write this:

Tell them my message is contained within the words of my Son's apostle, Matthew.

We are called to be sowers in this world, to plant the seeds of the hope of mankind that can only be found in your *Lord and Savior, Jesus Christ, God's* only *Son.*

As you go about the business and the 'business' of your lives, you sow by the love you show to one another, in the blessed name of *Jesus Christ.*

In the workplace, in your schools and colleges, visiting the sick and those who have been incarcerated, at the merchant and the banker, at your customer's place of business, on public social media, and in private business networks we have been called to sow the seeds of the love, grace, and mercy that was so freely given to us

We are called to take that good seed and not hide it, nor hoard it, but to freely share with the rest of our brothers and sisters in *Christ Jesus.* This is what mankind is and that is our singularly paramount reason for being.

It is the family of man. Do this one thing, each day, and you can change the world for *Him* one heart at a time.

Choose to be a sower today; for today is enough.

May the love of *Christ Jesus,* our *Lord and Savior,* be with you and yours, today and forevermore.

B.D. Vannoy

About the Author

[This was not only a sacred project for me it, is also my divinely-inspired purpose and mission. This incredible journey for me took over twelve years from its initial conceptualization and through the sometimes not too subtle urgings of my *Shekinah Mothe, the Holy Spirit.*]

Mr. Vannoy is originally from the Philadelphia area. He has worked in a diverse array of fields, including as a design draftsman for five years in the Philadelphia area before the era of CAD.

A professional and classically-trained chef for fourteen years in various food service venues, from a Fortune 500 company, four-star hotel, premier caterer, and hospitals, spanning from Texas to Massachusettes. He has a formal AOS in Culinary Arts from Johnson and Wales University in Providence, Rhode Island.

Mr. Vannoy worked in the auto manufacturing industry with Ford for eleven years in Norfolk, Virginia as a work group leader over the largest work zone in Norfolk, making the F150 truck, and as an over-the-road trucker for the last ten years with over 1,000,000 safe miles to his credit. Mr. Vannoy has a daughter from his first marriage. He is also "Daddy" to Bella, his scary-smart and crazy, yet lovable, eighty-pound sable German Shepherd.

When he is not writing fiction novels, Mr. Vannoy still loves to cook when time permits. He has an insatiable appetite for new discoveries. He believes that the *Father of all Creation* is too large to fit into any one religious dogmatic box, so while he accepts the label of Christianity, he his gifted and devoutly spiritual beyond normal Christian beliefs.

Mr. Vannoy has deep angelic and demonic connections through over twelve years of intense study and personal (and real) encounters within those realms. He also has a profound and abiding love for the nation of Israel and the Jewish people.

He has been personally involved, through the power of *Jesus Christ*, in leading the freeing of several people from demonic possessions. He has had several real-life encounters with both angelic and demonic forces that served as inspiration for this book and the entire and fully conceptualized eight to ten fiction novel Redemption series and more fiction novels outside of the series that are sure to follow.

A free ebook edition is available with the purchase of this book.

To claim your free ebook edition:

1. Visit MorganJamesBOGO.com
2. Sign your name CLEARLY in the space
3. Complete the form and submit a photo of the entire copyright page
4. You or your friend can download the ebook to your preferred device

A **FREE** ebook edition is available for you or a friend with the purchase of this print book.

CLEARLY SIGN YOUR NAME ABOVE

Instructions to claim your free ebook edition:
1. Visit MorganJamesBOGO.com
2. Sign your name CLEARLY in the space above
3. Complete the form and submit a photo of this entire page
4. You or your friend can download the ebook to your preferred device

Print & Digital Together Forever.

Snap a photo

Free ebook

Read anywhere

CPSIA information can be obtained
at www.ICGtesting.com
Printed in the USA
JSHW051309140322
23860JS00001B/2

9 781631 953248